Memories of Sorcery and Sand

Joanna Maciejewska

Contents

Lightning Source France, 1 Av. Johannes Gutenberg, 78310 Maurepas, France. compliance@lightningsource.fr

Also by the author

Pacts Arcane and Otherwise

By the Pact

Scars of Stone

Shadows over Kaighal

Demon Siege

Shadows of Eireland

Humanborn

Myth-Touched

Snakebitten

Collections

Scourges, Spells, and Serenades

To the girl who kept dreaming

Chapter 1

The fleeting memory within the desert sand

The sands were calling to me, and I didn't know why.

I leaned on the limestone-carved railing at the edges of the elevated dining terrace, the pride of the most luxurious hotel in Quathan, with a view of its splendid gardens. Yet instead of enjoying the sight of lush greens stretching out below me, my eyes kept escaping to the horizon marked by golden dunes.

The simple reason was that I chose the exotic over the mundane. I'd never been to the southern continent before, so endless sands were new to me, while I'd seen enough gardens back in my homeland and in the neighboring countries when I accompanied my father during his scholarly travels.

But those dunes... There was something so familiar about them, like a dream almost forgotten with the first morning light. Except that it didn't feel like a dream, more akin to a long-lost memory.

A memory.

My breathing became shallow and rapid, as always

whenever something reminded me of what I'd lost, and my fingers were tight on the stone railing as if my imbalance was physical in nature. I fought to steady my thoughts and kept reminding myself that I'd never been to Quathan—or anywhere else in the southern continent—so I couldn't have lost that particular memory.

Slowly, the feelings of panic and confusion passed, and I gently breathed out with relief. My father was right when he said the recovery of the mind would take longer than that of the body. Three years in a coma was long enough for any wounds to heal, but it seemed that I'd need even more to regain my inner peace.

The family trip to Quathan was meant to ease the process of recovery. Away from places in which every detail, scent, and sound seemed to set off an anxious reaction like I'd forgotten something important, I could strengthen my mind before facing the gaps in my memory once more.

And the sands... The sands were crippling my efforts—calling, teasing, and shaking my composure with their grains' subtle movements in the breeze.

They brought foreign thoughts to the back of my mind, images of my bare feet sinking into the warm golden desert. Flashes of their presence were like glimmer-scaled fish in a stream: enough to know they were there, but not enough to catch any detail that would prove their existence.

Perhaps my own imagination, fed with too many stories of Quathan's vibrant history or shaken by three years of stagnant blackness, was playing tricks on me, telling me of things that didn't happen... That couldn't have happened. It seemed my mind was desperate to fill the holes in my memories with any images that could put my world back together.

"Sae, come sit with us!"

My mother's voice urged me to return to the table. If I did, I could enjoy the richness of boldly spiced meals and the sweetness of exotic fruit in the hope of chasing my anxiety away, but doing so meant unwanted conversation.

I glanced at her over my shoulder. Brown-haired, in her expensive evening dress following the latest fashion that demanded a low waist and revealing cleavage, adorned with matching jewelry to frame her tall and gaunt body, she looked every bit the blue blood she was. She also looked nothing like her daughter, since I got my black hair and rounder face from my father's side.

Beside her sat Philidert, and as always when he had my attention, he gave me a dashing smile of a confident, rich man. I had to turn away to conceal my grimace. I might have fallen for his charms when I was younger, making my mother hope for a beneficial marriage, but spending more time with that annoying braggart had cured me of any romantic affections. Other young ladies could fawn over his regular features framed by locks of carefully groomed golden hair... I knew better.

Unfortunately, no matter how much I expressed disinterest, my mother still nurtured plans for our future, having gone as far as informing Philidert about our family trip so that he could join us in Quathan. His loud and imposing presence was hardly what I would prescribe to a patient recovering from a prolonged illness, but complaining about it would achieve nothing except for increased attention under the guise of concern for my wellbeing.

So instead, I sought solace in making my own plans for the future that wouldn't be dictated by my mother. No matter how much understanding I might have for her overbearing behavior, and no matter how compassionate I was about her three-year-long ordeal, I was a grown woman, and the accident hadn't ruined my reasoning faculties… only some of my memories.

Yes, as soon as we were back home, I would have all the doctors proclaim me healthy and recovered, so I could take an extended trip around the continent or enroll in a university far enough away to keep Philidert at a distance. My father would surely support such plans.

I chanced one more look back at the table, but he still hadn't shown up, which meant that instead of having an engaging conversation about Quathan's history and culture, I'd be stuck making small talk about food and pretending to laugh at Philidert's lousy jokes. Keeping away was a better choice, and I intended to stay in my self-imposed solitude for as long as it was appropriate, or even longer if needed. With most guests dining at their own tables, and no one seeking company beyond their immediate friends and family, there was little risk of anybody else bothering me.

I could watch the sands on the horizon and search for answers within them.

A man leaned on the railing right beside me, and I shifted to move away to a more acceptable distance. Judging from a glance I sneaked while in motion, he didn't come from Kvesa or any other northern lands, so it seemed pointless to remark on how a gentleman should act.

"It's an interesting world, isn't it?" he asked.

His accent was heavy, though he didn't speak in the way the local people spoke. Most of them knew my native tongue only well enough to sell wares and offer services. Yet his mistaking "world" for "country" or "land" suggested he didn't have a perfect command of the language either, and he definitely didn't know of proper forms to address a lady.

His tone of voice was casual too, as if we were familiar with one another.

Engaging in a conversation justified a longer look at him, and I took in his features while sifting through my memories. He was tall and well built, though not muscular like the labor workers in the area, and as far as I could tell by the subtle wrinkles in his skin, he was similar in age to my father. His complexion was of that warm shade common of the local people, but his sharp features didn't match their rectangular faces. Come to think of it, they bore no resemblance to any nation I knew of, civilized or not. Perhaps his parents were of two different cultures—an origin uncommon but possible.

His outfit mimicked what Quathani nomads wore, but its fine make and quality fabrics suggested he was both wealthy and confident enough to choose clothing according to his needs and taste rather than submit to the fashion that currently favored narrow-cut lounge suits. If one of my dear friends was around, they would likely describe him as having an aura of mystery or excitement, but I'd seen enough rich travelers and explorers to recognize the stranger as one.

"I don't believe we've met," I offered the usual courtesy, even though my own heart kept insisting that I'd seen him before.

Alas, my mind did not support such a claim, even if the way he spoke and looked at me with his emerald eyes carried that genuine notion of acquaintance or even more— of shared experiences.

He arched his eyebrow as if unsure whether I was serious, but then his expression changed, his eyes narrow and inquisitive. "You don't remember me, do you?"

I didn't remember many things, and for all I knew, he could indeed be one of them, but such a personal confession was hardly suitable in the presence of a stranger. With his age and outfit, he could be a nobleman looking to charm a future wife, young and innocent enough to sweeten those autumnal years of life when travels and adventure had to be replaced with some other kind of excitement. Or he could be trying to swindle me out of my money, because luxurious hotels full of guests from the northern continent lured those kinds of charlatans.

Yet his posture and expression had nothing in common with the poorly concealed slyness I'd seen so often on the faces of lowly swindlers.

"I apologize." When there were doubts, courtesy was always the best choice. "Was it one of my father's seminars?"

Kithandar, my father, was a renowned historian, and I often accompanied him to guest lectures back home and abroad. Even if it was our first visit to Quathan, the stranger might be a scholar too, traveling for knowledge or leisure, and we'd crossed paths during some academic event. He could have spotted me in the hotel and decided to approach a familiar person, perhaps hoping I'd introduce him to my father.

He shook his head, and the way the corner of his mouth curled downward gave me a shiver. A piece of me recognized his reaction as if it were as familiar as my mother's smile, and his disappointment resonated within me, bringing an unexpected feeling of guilt... and fear. My instincts demanded that I did anything in my power to shift his grimace into an expression of approval, and the strength of that urge pushed me to the brink of panic. My mind was reacting in alarming ways, but my memories remained as blank as they were before.

"What happened to you, Saeryn?"

Eyes wide, I took a step back. No common thief would know my name, and the way he spoke it, softly, like my father when he worried about me, sounded genuine and was hardly fit for a passing scholarly acquaintance.

All of a sudden, retreating to the table, to my mother and Philidert, felt more enticing than I'd have ever thought it would. The man in front of me might seem familiar, but it didn't mean I was safe in his presence. He could pose threats I couldn't even begin to imagine.

"What are you doing here?" My father's voice came like a last-minute rescue. He always had a way of appearing at exactly the right moment.

I turned to him with a smile of gratitude, but his full attention was on the stranger. An aura of hostility, unlike his usual composed demeanor, thickened around him, offering an unvoiced confirmation of my concerns about the encounter.

"I'm collecting the payment for my assistance," the man replied in a casual manner, ignoring my father's imposing stance.

"That has nothing to do with my daughter."

My heart swelled at my father's confident and protective manner. I could leave this situation in his capable hands and never think of it again, but the way they both spoke made it clear that they knew each other. There had to be more to the story than some swindle, and my curiosity forced me to stay.

"Of course it does." The stranger's posture didn't change. Yet the longer I looked at him, the more convinced I became that he could match my father's anger if he chose so. "She was the one who asked me to... visit her."

Bewilderment wasn't a ladylike expression, but it would be impossible to chase it off my face after such a claim. He might know a thing or two about me, but to be so bold as to claim that I had a part in whatever deception he was weaving... I had to put a stop to it. "Father, I—"

His gesture might have been one of calming, but when he spoke, concern rang in his voice. "Everything's fine, my dear. Why don't you join your mother? This isn't something you should bother yourself with."

I could tell a dismissal from a suggestion, and this once, arguing never crossed my mind. Courtesy demanding, I offered my rushed excuses and farewells, and turned away with a wave of relief that would drown me if I allowed it. My father would take care of everything, and I could indeed let myself forget about the incident. That one memory was probably better gone forever.

"She doesn't remember me. Does she remember anything?" the man asked as I walked away.

At his words, I spun on my heels, inspecting him once more. The question alone mattered little, but the language... the language was everything. One of the forgotten dialects my father had studied so meticulously, passing this knowledge onto me. When I was a child, I thought vizari was a secret language I shared with him, especially since he also made me practice it when my mother was around. Even nowadays, as petty as it might be, we used it to keep things secret from her.

And now, a stranger met by chance in Quathan destroyed that childhood memory, though the more I thought about it, the more I wondered whether the meeting was indeed as accidental as I first assumed.

"Remember what?" I demanded in vizari, abandoning all pretense of proper behavior.

"So you *do* remember the language." The stranger inspected me with renewed curiosity.

His command of words and grammatic structures in vizari left nothing to be desired, and his accent sounded perfect as much I could tell, considering it was a dead language.

My father stepped in front of me, his body like a shield. "Leave," he said in a cold and unyielding tone. "Take your payment and use it as you see fit, but leave us alone. You've caused her enough harm."

If my father thought I would let that last remark slip, he was mistaken, but it had to wait until we were alone.

"Perhaps I did." The man smirked, his tone of voice dismissive and suggesting such harm, whatever it was, mattered little to him. "But she did ask me to come." He lifted his finger before I could deny his claim. "Apparently, though, she doesn't remember doing so, so I'll take my leave." He walked past us both, the slow and nonchalant stride of a man who left when he chose and not when he was told to. "Just one more thing..."

The way he turned toward me had something predatory about it, and the intensity of his emerald gaze, vibrant and timeless in his otherwise aged features, locked breath in my lungs. The smile that crept up his lips had nothing to do with warmth or friendliness. Only satisfaction lurked on his face, as if he'd found a way to get whatever he was after.

"Kneel before your master like a slave should."

His words struck like a ram hitting the gates of my mind. I shivered. I could swear my body fought to act against my will, ready to drop to my knees. Only a firm grasp on the railing prevented me from making a scene by fulfilling his demand.

The stranger was already walking away and didn't even look over his shoulder to check my reaction, but I had no doubt he knew what it was.

"Sae, are you all right?" My father's hands supported my balance.

Any reassurance would be pointless, so I asked, "Who is he?"

As peculiar as it was, the stranger's last remark conjured an image in my mind. I desperately clung to it, hoping that at some point I could make sense of it. Even without a clue of where or when, I had no doubt he'd spoken those very words before, and back then I was on my knees within a heartbeat.

"He's... a rival from a long time ago," my father replied, "but one who apparently still wishes us both ill. He'll use mind games to unsettle you, so you shouldn't trust anything he says." He glanced back at the table. "Come. Your mother is looking suspiciously at us, so we should join her and that pompous youngster. If she asks any questions, just tell her you had a spell of weakness from the heat. We can talk later."

He put on a smile and headed for the table, so I had to follow him. I'd rather barrage him with questions, but at least I had the promise that he'd tell me more after my mother retired for the evening. Approaching her and Philid-ert, I made the best impression of a carefree woman, even if my thoughts couldn't have been further from.

～

I wouldn't be surprised if my mother and Philidert conspired to put me in their conversational crossfire with the way they chose their seats at the table. Opposite each other, they left me no choice that would allow me to sit beside my father.

Throughout the whole meal, I suffered their trivial exchanges while looking at the furrowed brow of the one person I wished to have a conversation with. My father didn't meet my eyes, instead searching the terrace with a wary expression while I was bursting with questions.

Everything about the encounter with the stranger seemed eerie, but at the same time, I couldn't shake the feeling of familiarity, as if it was only my lack of memories that made it so peculiar. And what sparked my curiosity even more was that as unsettling as the conversation was, it didn't lead to the familiar reactions my body resorted to when facing my never-present memories. No hastened breathing, no panic... Nothing.

That alone made me believe the stranger could be what would bring them back, but I couldn't help wondering whether I was desperate and thus falling for a charlatan's manipulation.

My mother chatted away with Philidert, both of them glancing at me every now and then as if they expected me to join in the discussion of whatever trivial topic they chose to fill the silence with. I focused on my food instead. The sooner we got through the meal, the sooner I'd have a chance to talk to my father.

"Sae, is everything fine?" my mother asked. "You seem so quiet."

I forced a smile. "Just enjoying listening to the two of you talking," I lied smoothly. Usually, I'd claim weariness and excuse myself from the company, but I couldn't risk that she'd ask Philidert to accompany me back to my room. I didn't want to wait until the morning to speak to my father. "It's so soothingly familiar, and I don't want to disturb that feeling."

Her expression softened as always when I mentioned, even indirectly, my condition. As she returned to her conversation with Philidert, now convinced it contributed to my wellbeing, guilt stabbed at me. She cared for me, even deeply so, but her misguided efforts made me deceive her more often than not. I couldn't remember exactly when or why, but I'd lied to her like that before—my untruths so terrifyingly familiar, I had to question whether I'd ever told her any truth at all, and worse yet, what kind of person had I been before my accident to deceive my mother so frequently?

Over the table, I caught my father watching me, and he gave me an almost imperceptible nod, as if he approved of my lying to her.

That, too, felt familiar, and before I realized, my breath was hastening in a foretelling of the approaching anxiety attack that always came when I couldn't recall any specific memory. I focused my eyes on the plate in front of me, food less appealing than it was moments ago. Unexpectedly, instead of spiraling into panic, my thoughts escaped to the stranger, and the fresh memory of his green eyes forced my mind to think straight again. And though I knew this image might bring more questions than answers, something told me that those questions were the right ones to ask.

The rest of the meal dragged, and as dusk set in, I'd had enough of waiting.

"Father, would you mind escorting me back to my room?" I asked. "I think I could use an early night. Mother, Philidert, please excuse my departure."

"Of course, my dear." He rose from his chair immediately, and I could only hope he was as tired of the family dinner as I was. "I'll be back soon," he added for my mother's sake, though I caught no warmth in his voice.

For as long as we were within eyesight, we walked without a rush and in silence, me holding my father's arm as if I needed this kind of support. He let go as soon as we left the terrace and looked at me, a clear sign that he'd seen through my deception.

I knew he would appreciate a straightforward conversation, so I bluntly asked, "Who was that man?" Since other guests, waiters, and hotel workers passed us by, I spoke in vizari.

"A rival from long time ago." His words rang with the weariness of someone who had hoped the matter had already been resolved. "You were very young back then. I think you saw him once or twice, but I doubt you'd have remembered it. We had a fallout over research. Nothing worth your attention, really, just some clerical disagreements that caused a bigger rift than they should have, but ever since then..." He shook his head. "I didn't think he's still bitter enough to disturb your peace with lies."

After all the stranger's peculiar claims, it was a relief to hear my father's reasonable explanation. Yet that comfort faded away, because no matter how much I wanted to believe him, his words didn't ring true. With no memories of my own, I had to rely on vague flashes and feelings, and for some reason, they didn't align with what my father was saying.

In the turmoil of emotions that demanded I call out his lie but offered no substance to support such a claim, I searched for any way to get more information. We were already in the corridor leading to my room, and once we made it to the door, the conversation would be over.

"And those words he said before he left?" I asked the first question that came to mind. Anything to get my father to share more.

"Oh, that." He huffed, as if amused by a memory. "He had an assistant he treated quite poorly. One day, after the assistant—I think her name was Herrela—had failed at some task, they had quite a fight. At the end of it, he told her that she had no say in any of his work, and she was to obey him without question. He ended the argument saying that she should fall to her knees like a proper slave should. You've heard it, and for the next few days you walked around repeating his words and trying to mimic his tone and expression." He rubbed his chin. "I suppose he found it amusing enough to bring it up, or perhaps it was the only thing he remembered about you."

If this was such a lighthearted story—save poor Herrela's plight as an abused assistant—why did I feel the strong echo of fear and desperation whenever I recalled the stranger's words? Right at that moment, I was almost convinced that my very life depended on meeting his demand, and even after his voice faded from my ears, becoming but a memory, it still elicited such a strong reaction.

I forced a smile. If this was the story my father chose to tell, he had his reasons, and he'd not reveal anything else.

"Thank you for telling me," was all I said as we stopped at the door to my room.

I wanted to ask what he'd meant when he said that the stranger had already caused me enough harm, but I suspected he wouldn't offer the truth on that matter either.

My father hesitated. "He's a dangerous man, Sae. Given

an opportunity, he'll fill your head with lies, and nothing he says can be trusted, no matter how convincing it sounds. I fear that his presence here is not accidental, and that he approached you with vicious intentions in mind."

I swallowed and nodded. No matter how much I doubted other things my father had told me, this one rang true, echoing my own emotions. Though nothing in the stranger's behavior during our brief conversation stood out as malicious, save maybe for his last words, my instincts screamed of danger.

My father looked at me. "It's best if you never speak to him again."

I said nothing to that. To argue with him would be foolish, but I wasn't ready to make any promises, because lies, no matter how improbable, often carried a grain of truth within so that they would root easier in reality, and those grains could be the key to my fractured memory.

"Have a good night, Father," I said before the lingering silence made him force a promise out of me.

Thankfully, he allowed me to retreat into my room.

It was decorated in Quathani style, with soft carpets and muslin curtains. A hollowed shell of some local nut served as a vase and was filled with blooms of a tree I didn't recognize. Its sweet scent carried throughout the room but didn't overwhelm me. There was a continental-style vanity and wardrobe, but they were hand-carved in the local style of intricate floral patterns, and a small door led to the bathing area. The bed, though, was the highlight—so wide, three people could easily get a good night's rest in it, and it had a plethora of pillows and a selection of light and heavier covers.

Yet the sight of it reminded me that I was, in fact, not tired at all.

The hotel boasted modern amenities, so I was able to prepare a bath for myself without having to rely on their staff. I didn't linger in the water. Once in my nightgown, I pulled the heavier curtains open and laid on the bed, looking at the stars and thinking about all that had happened.

The accident I suffered had not only put me in a three-year coma, it also took parts of my memory, some in bigger chunks, some smaller. Back at home, wherever I turned or looked, everything forced the same reaction, because it felt like someone had ripped random holes in my mind. Those memories weren't blurry, and they weren't vague notions of events. It was like they were never there. Yet I was still painfully aware of their absence. I knew I should be remembering *something*. I just didn't know what.

Meeting the stranger had—for the first time since I'd woken from the coma—stirred something deep within me that seemed like it could fill those uneven, random gaps.

I had to figure out how to bring those flashes to the surface.

IN THE PRIVACY of my hotel room, I could allow myself a yawn and gentle eye rubbing, both too unladylike for my mother to witness any other time. The sun shone straight onto my face. Of course, preoccupied with my thoughts and speculations the previous night, I'd forgotten to pull the heavy curtains closed before I drifted off to sleep.

Even upon my waking up, my mind still circled the stranger. Before succumbing to slumber, I'd kept replaying the meeting with him through my head as if it were a favorite song on a gramophone... as if it contained a secret key able to unlock whatever my memory kept hidden.

In the past, such attempts had proven futile. No matter how hard I tried, I was left with days of fractured existence and nights of restless sleep. I never found any answers.

Yet last night was different, and the very thought of it made my blood rush.

From the scattered visions that had been haunting my dreams so frequently formed a scene staggering in its coherence, even if the meaning of its particular details escaped me. I dreamed about the stranger, but in a different place and time... I was there too—a part of the story, not a mere observer.

Throwing on a robe, I walked onto the balcony. The nighttime vision was already fleeting, as if the morning had scared it off. I clung to its pieces, once more feeding my vain hope that they would reveal what my conscious mind denied me, even though I knew that so far trying too hard had never gotten me anywhere.

I needed a distraction that could help my thoughts wander in the right direction, piecing together the story hidden within the dream's images.

It was still early, so I had an hour or even two before my parents would expect me to join them for breakfast. Enough time to enjoy a short walk along the palm-tree-guarded alleyways at the back of the hotel. Philidert wasn't an early riser, so I didn't have to worry about him imposing his company on me.

Yet I stood at the balcony undecided, as if still in the dream's grip, and my eyes wandered across the landscape before me. Early in the morning, the hotel grounds were empty, so a lone figure leaning against the railing of the sun-soaked terrace drew my attention like honey lures flies—

even more so the moment I recognized the man I'd met the previous evening.

Of course, seeking him out would mean going against my father's wishes, but if I was to piece the past together, I needed the stranger's knowledge. Even if some—or most—of what he'd tell me were lies and deception, I had to risk it for the grains of truth he might offer. Besides, prepared for his games, I could play one myself, and no matter what the stranger said, I could always ask my father about it later.

I quickly changed into an appropriate outfit, a mid-calf skirt and beige jacket, and rushed past the vanity, since promptness was in order if I wanted to talk to him. Besides, he didn't come across as someone who'd be bothered with my hardly done hair or less-than-perfect clothes.

My soft shoes made no sound on the corridors' thick carpets, so every now and then my hurried passing startled a maid or another guest. My heart raced to the rhythm of those steps, and I scolded myself for hoping the stranger would still be at the terrace when I reached it.

When I got there, he stood at the same spot, watching the desert dunes above the gardens' green line. Relieved, I slowed down, both to catch my breath and to search for words. I had to ensure he wouldn't be able to deceive me with any weaselly claims, and well-shaped questions would help me to pin the truth.

"Kithandar wouldn't be happy that you came to talk to me," he said in vizari, even though he'd never turned his head to acknowledge my approach.

Such a remark earned him only a dismissive huff. Had my father not been so evasive the previous evening, I wouldn't have to seek knowledge elsewhere.

"You said I asked you to come," I replied in the same

language. Not only did it offer privacy, but I could also test his proficiency. "Where? When?"

Instead of a reply, he first granted me a long, unnerving stare. "How much has your father told you?" he asked finally. "About what you both are?"

It must be the second or third time when he'd mistaken one word for another—this time it was "what" instead of "who," and those words didn't even sound similar in vizari. With his perfect accent, such slips stood out, and perhaps his command of the language had more space for improvement than I'd initially believed, but it mattered little, as it didn't offer any clues how he'd became familiar with it in the first place.

Besides, correct grammar or not, his question made little sense, so I kept my response simple: "I don't know what you mean." I wanted *him* to talk instead of forcing me to provide answers that would reveal too much about myself.

"Nothing, then," he concluded lightly, as if he'd expected such a reply. "It makes me wonder whether he even *wants* you to remember."

The way he kept watching me, like he was observing a peculiar specimen, must be an attempt to shake my composure, but I would play none of his games.

"Trying to turn me against my father isn't going to work," I said.

Despite my frustration with his evasiveness the previous day, I trusted my father more than anyone else in the world.

Unmoved, the man looked back at the desert as if he cared little about my accusations. "It's *you* who came to see *me*."

I knew he meant today, and pointing out he'd approached me the previous day would only bring a familiar grimace of disapproval to his face. Though I couldn't tell how I knew it, his message was clear: just like I wouldn't tolerate his games, he wasn't going to tolerate mine. If I wanted to learn anything, I had to take the first step.

The step that, I had no doubt, would be my undoing.

"I..." A deep breath did little to steady my thoughts, and I leaped into the abyss of lies and deception that might be awaiting me. "The words you spoke yesterday... I had a dream about you speaking them." Revealing even that much meant that I was already inviting a strike I couldn't foresee. "But it wasn't here. It was—"

"In a castle in the mountains," he finished. "One of my warriors brought you to Kithandar's study."

"How...?" was all I could say.

I expected him to use my confession to manipulate me, skillfully collecting pieces of information to create an impression that he knew it all. Instead, it seemed that he actually *did* know it all. Such a precise detail couldn't have been a lucky guess.

"Tell me of your dream. Tell me of that *memory*, and I'll give you answers."

A memory... At first, I was ready to dismiss such a notion. But if my father had told me the truth, then I'd seen this man back in my early childhood, and parts of the dream were real. The other parts, all the impossible imagery, were likely nothing more than embellishments my mind had conjured. With so many years having passed, I wouldn't even have remembered his face, but he could still have appeared as familiar as he did the previous day.

I flexed my fingers, on the verge of walking away. Nothing good would come from giving the stranger more information. I should have consulted my father instead of foolishly rushing into another distressing encounter, driven by a dream and my father's lack of candor.

The man in front of me stood motionless and silent, as if he intended to wait out my doubts rather than disperse them.

He might be a charlatan. He might be my father's enemy. He might be a threat to both of us. But the calm gaze of his emerald eyes and the ageless wisdom within them drew me in. No matter what it might be, I wanted to hear his part of the story.

So I recalled the dream-memory for him.

Chapter 2

The Sorcerer from the Desert

The armor-clad man who dragged her through the stone hallway wasn't gentle. His rough fingers crushed her forearm, and Saeryn fought him only enough to give the impression she was trying to free herself. With her life at stake, she couldn't risk being cut down in an attempt to escape, but she had to resist, since he likely expected her to.

It wasn't long before they reached her father's study, and the confidence with which her captor pushed on the heavy wooden door told her what to expect as they entered.

Kithandar stood by the window, his plain gray robe so unfitting for the master of the castle, though at the same time matching the bare stone walls of most of its interiors. He looked so different without his usual outfits: stylish jackets and trousers in dark but vibrant colors, contrasted by snow-white shirts and discreet jewelry. Even though she'd been a frequent visitor to the castle throughout the years, she still couldn't get used to that change. Yet the local people expected him to wear scholarly robes, so wear them he did. Even her own outfit matched the local fashion—a simple long skirt and a plain tunic that back at home no lady would allow herself to be seen wearing publicly.

Saeryn's attention shifted to the others in the chamber. Accompanied by two more warriors in iron-plated armors was a tall man. She had never met him before, but she knew his name. Malatrius—the Sorcerer from the Desert, as many called him—had arrived to reclaim his property like she and her father expected.

She drew a cautious breath. The game that could cost her life began.

"I told you we'd find her." The sorcerer's intense green eyes locked on Saeryn, but he spoke to her father. "Maybe now you'll be willing to talk."

Kithandar sighed and nodded, much like a man ready to surrender. "I'll make a trade. My daughter's life for the scroll... and my library."

The concern in his voice reminded her that they were treading a thin line, but she refused to give in to doubts. The time to change her mind had long since passed. Either she succeeded, or she died.

Malatrius shook his head. "What use would I have for a library so far from my lands? And why would I leave an enemy's daughter alive? But if you give me back my property immediately, you'll both die a painless death, and I'll spare your servants."

Saeryn shivered in the guard's grip. Malatrius's detached voice suggested he didn't cherish cruelty but simply sought the best solutions. In a way, she couldn't argue with his reasoning. To let her live, to risk that she'd wait for an opportunity to strike back, was a fool's choice, and the sorcerer was not a fool.

She'd hoped her father would manage to change Malatrius's mind, but now that she'd met the sorcerer in person, it seemed much less likely than back when she first considered the possible outcomes of their confrontation, and cold sweat ran down her spine.

"You can tear the castle down stone by stone, and you won't find the scroll," Kithandar said with confidence. "The library is hidden in the prism cube, and only my daughter and I know where it is. You spare her life, and she'll take you to it. She'll also carry it wherever you want to nest it again."

The mention of the powerful artifact made no impression on Malatrius, or he concealed his thoughts well. Without a rush, he walked over to Saeryn, and the warrior beside her took a step back, releasing her.

"I could make one of you talk." Malatrius cupped her chin with his hand as he looked into her eyes. "I wonder if your daughter is as determined to keep your secrets as you are."

She jerked her head free, responding with a defiant stare. The prospect of torture and pain was a paralyzing one, but so was the prospect of death if she submitted.

The sorcerer burst out laughing, but she caught no cruelty in his voice, as if he was sincerely amused by her response.

"Saeryn, isn't it?" he asked. "Your father stole something from me, and now he's ready to beg me not to take something from him in return. At least what he offers in exchange has some value... Though I'm still not certain it's worth the risks." He smiled knowingly. "If I spare your life, proud daughter of a proud father, how long will your gratitude last? How long will it take before you attempt to kill me in revenge?"

Silence and clenched fists were her only response. No matter what she said, he wouldn't believe her, and rightly so. After all, what kind of daughter wouldn't dream of avenging her father? She knew the answer: the one who not only wanted to live, but also *had* to live, and the one to whom her father's death meant little. Yet she kept her mouth shut. Such a reply would encourage questions and even more distrust, and she had to convince the sorcerer that she wasn't hiding anything.

"You're wise for your age." Malatrius gave a nod to her silence. "I'm curious how much pain you can endure before you or your father breaks... With your own life at stake, and if you are as resilient as you seem wise, it would take some time—time I'm not willing to waste." He sighed, looking her up and down. "Very well. I'll generously accept your father's bargain."

Relief washed over her, but she couldn't help being suspicious. Malatrius had agreed too quickly.

"Swear it," Kithandar said. He must have arrived at a similar conclusion. "Swear on your powers and the gods you worship that you won't kill her or have her killed, and that you'll keep her from harm."

"Gods?" Malatrius snorted, and that reaction made him almost approachable, almost humanlike. He reached for the ritual knife in the jeweled sheath on his belt. "Do you know the binding oath, girl?"

His words left her gaping, and even the subtle insult of calling her a "girl" went unnoticed. When broken, a binding oath would bring much more dire consequences than calling higher powers for witness. After all, gods could ignore or absolve an oath breaker if they chose to, but blood never forgave.

Mustering a nod in response was all she managed.

The confident and—dare she say—slightly smug smile that Malatrius offered made it clear he knew the weight of the oath. Without hesitation, he cut his palm, just by the wrist, and droplets of blood bloomed on his brown skin.

He held the red-stained knife between them as the ritual demanded. His voice softened when he began the oath, reciting melodic words in a language of ancient sorcerers. Saeryn joined in, matching the pace of his incantation, but her mind raced in search for an answer. Choosing an unfavorable ritual that left him no way out seemed like a madman's choice, and Malatrius was far too cunning. There had to be more to it.

They finished the incantation, and she looked at him, waiting. Before she sealed it with blood, he had to set the terms, and the words he chose could be a trap leading to her death.

"I swear to neither bring you harm nor ask others to do so in my stead as long as you stay loyal. Any disobedience, disloyalty, or betrayal I see or suspect will set me free from this oath."

He opened his hand, offering the knife to her, and Saeryn hesitated.

He might be the one who'd be bound by the oath, but he was also the one to decide what dissolved it. Accepting it meant he could find her disloyal on a whim, even as soon as she'd led him to the prism cube library.

Kithandar stirred. "Saeryn, my daughter, no."

He understood the risks too, and he was right to advise against entering such a binding, but they had gone too far already to consider alternatives. Her father might claim to be a match for Malatrius, but open battle always posed risks. Besides, if she wanted the plan to succeed, she had to trust that the preparations she'd made and her own wits would suffice to keep her alive.

She gave her father an apologetic glance and then took

the knife. It was her life, and the decision was hers as well, even if it turned out to be her death.

She cut her skin and held the blade between them. Malatrius placed his hand on the hilt, over hers. They spoke the last part of the oath together, and magic flowed between them like a gust of a summer wind, dry and warm.

Malatrius smiled with satisfaction, and she loosened her grip on the knife, letting him take it. Behind the sorcerer, she glimpsed her father and his tormented expression by the window, and this once, she couldn't help her frustration. No matter how dangerous this oath might be, she could make it all work. The lack of Kithandar's trust in her skill and cunning, which he displayed by behaving as if she were already dead, grated on her composure. She'd spent months preparing for this moment and for what could come after. She was ready. Kithandar had to know she was.

"You'll fetch the prism cube now." Malatrius gestured at one of the warriors, and the man moved to Saeryn's side without a word. "There's no need for you to watch what happens next."

Saeryn shot one last glance at her father. They both knew that stealing the scroll, one of only three in existence, from a sorcerer like Malatrius would bring consequences, and they said their goodbyes before they even set their plan in motion. Yet she wouldn't mind one last hug, one last reassurance that everything was going to be fine... that she was capable of seeing things through.

But Kithandar made no move and said no word. He stood motionless by the window, and she'd remember him like that forever, however short that "forever" might be. Then she headed for the door.

"Just one more thing..." Malatrius's voice held her midstep. "Kneel before your master like a slave should."

His name was indeed Malatrius, just like my dream suggested. While I recounted what I saw in my slumber, he filled in many details he couldn't have known if he wasn't there and if it wasn't a memory—one we shared. Such a notion affected my calm more than any mind game could. If all of it were true, how much more had I forgotten?

"That's all there was in the dream," I said.

I didn't bother mentioning magic and peculiar outfits. As a child, I likely perceived a casual event as more fairy-tale-like, or perhaps the dream warped my memories, adding its own surreal flavor.

I kept other things to myself as well. He didn't have to know that his arrival at the castle was part of my father's plan. The dream suggested I'd partaken in it as well, but likely I would have been too young for any elaborate schemes.

Whether it was true or just part of the dream setting, this wasn't something I would share with Malatrius. No matter how helpful he might seem, he offered me little information, save some details that only confirmed we'd met before. And if my father told me the truth, this man held a grudge against him... perhaps even against us both.

"I don't know what happened next," I offered when Malatrius remained silent. "I don't even know how old I was back then, or the place where it happened. I can't recall ever visiting such a castle..." Until I shared that memory with him, I had been convinced that the scenery was part of a dreamscape, but his words suggested that it was as real as it felt.

He looked me in the eye. "You know what happened next. You know what I did even if you never saw it."

I did know what he was talking about. In my dream, I was certain that my father was about to die, and that there was no way to avoid such a fate. But if it was a memory, my father should be dead, and I struggled with reconciling those two notions. For a moment, I let ridiculous theories swarm my mind, even questioning whether my parents were truly my blood relatives, but the way Malatrius was watching me made me rein in my wild thoughts.

This wasn't the time to indulge in speculation. If, instead, I played along, I could learn what *he* thought was true, so I asked, "How is it possible?"

He glanced at me with curiosity and perhaps even suspicion, as if something in my voice or behavior warned him that I wasn't being sincere, but he didn't bring it up.

"Since your father didn't tell you anything, I'll give you a simple explanation," he replied. "We first met in another world, in your father's castle there. What you believe to be a dream was quite a detailed memory of those events. Then, after you died, you were reborn, or I should say reshaped, in this world, just like your father was after I killed him."

It wasn't what I'd expected, but for the first time since the beginning of this conversation, concerns abandoned me, and I burst out laughing. I'd heard about the concept of rebirth, popular deep in the uncivilized south and among one or two Quathani sects. It couldn't explain how Malatrius knew so many details of my dream, but I wasn't aware of all possible ways to set up such elaborate traps. Hypnotists, hallucinogenic substances... They must be common enough in a land that didn't condemn any quackery and resisted the reason of the modern world. Curiosity demanded I learn how he achieved his deception, but with a claim so absurd, I could do so from a position of confidence.

I stifled the chuckle that still refused to die and looked

at him. "So you say it was all in another life? That we were... How do they call it around here?" I didn't know if there was a vizari word for the concept, so I used a sanedian one. "*Reincarnated?* And maybe you're also going to tell me that back then we were in love, and that's why you sought me out through time and death?" A little mockery could goad him into a reaction that would reveal more than he intended to share. "I commend your skill, but your games end now."

His posture remained one of confidence and calm, but his slight grimace suggested he didn't like what he heard. "You were my slave, not my lover." His voice was cold, so when he smirked all of a sudden, it caught me off guard. "Though I did kiss you once... Now, *that* would be an inter-esting memory to restore, but I don't think you're ready."

I let out an unladylike snort at the clear bait, a surpris-ingly comfortable reaction around the man, as if I knew he didn't bother with what society considered proper. As if... we'd interacted like that before.

I didn't give into that feeling of familiarity. "So, a slave, not a lover. And you promised that slave you'd come and find her once you were both reborn? A strange thing to do. Not to mention that you're the only one to have a clear memory of everything that happened."

He huffed, amused, in response to my veiled accusation, but his reply carried seriousness and honesty—both of which I found unsettling given the circumstances.

"I don't know why you forgot it all, but your father did recognize me. That means he remembers. As for me... I wasn't reborn. I traveled to this world shortly after you died. Three months ago."

His tone, filled with genuine regret, made my blood freeze. Even if his claims were pure fantasy, he clearly believed them true. With delusions driving him, he might be more dangerous than my father thought.

"This can't be true," I said before considering playing along with his madness. After the mockery I'd dished out, my denial could push him into rage.

Less confident, I looked around. It was so early in the morning that the terrace was empty, but in the distance, waiters began setting breakfast tables. If the conversation went horribly wrong, I could seek help from them.

Malatrius shrugged. "I have no answer for you. But humor me... Where were you, let's say, four months ago? Or for the last three years, for that matter?"

If blood draining from my face could have a sound, I would have been deafened by its rush. I took a step back. My father had claimed they kept the accident private, but it didn't mean Malatrius couldn't have found out about it —via servants, friends of the family, even the hospital staff.

No matter how he'd obtained that information, he was quite skillful to use it the way he did. Three months earlier, I was waking up from a coma, and he'd woven that event into his own story of my supposed death and rebirth.

To my surprise, he didn't take the opening my silence gave him. Instead of a barrage of questions to throw me even more off balance, he held out his hand, palm up. By his wrist, a silver scar stood out against the warm brown of his skin.

"With your death, I'm free of the oath, but this scar will never fade, and I believe you have a matching one. Possibly others as well. Three wide ones across your back. Scars you likely can't explain if you don't remember me."

The thought of how he might have come to know this about me was already terrifying, but what made my blood turn cold again was his guess that I, indeed, had no idea of how my scars came to be.

My father had told me they were related to the accident, but this explanation confused me even before I met Malatrius. I couldn't imagine how I could have gotten them during hiking, and, of course, I was unable to recall any details of what happened. My father refused to tell me, unwilling to bring up such a traumatizing event, even though I insisted it could help me regain my memories.

There were more oddities too, from before we'd arrived in Quathan. Ever since I woke up, my body had seemed perfectly healthy. No matter what the doctors said about taking good care of me when I was in a coma, I'd expected that such a drastic event, followed by years-long immobility, would result in pains or weakness lingering in my bones and muscles.

Yet I felt no ill effects at all. I was missing only some of my memories, perhaps even more of them than I'd thought, and until I met Malatrius, their absence had sent my mind in endless spirals of sudden panic whenever I struggled to recover them.

"But you could explain them." I hid my unease. Asking Malatrius for help meant that instead of staying lost in the black hole of forgotten events, I could be stuck in a maze of lies and half-truths forever.

"I could try to help you remember," he corrected me. "But your father was right when he said I caused you harm. Those might not be memories you'd like back. It might be better if you take whatever explanations Kithandar has for you and live your life peacefully... with that man by your side, if I'm guessing his intentions correctly?" He gestured over my shoulder.

I looked around and almost grimaced at the sight of

Philidert approaching. The conversation with Malatrius was difficult enough without my unwanted suitor's overbearing presence.

"There you are!" Philidert's loud voice only confirmed what I expected of his behavior, and the stunning smile that followed must have been an attempt to dim the other man's presence, as if he didn't notice that Malatrius was at least twice my age and unlikely to be a romantic rival. "I knocked on your door, and when you didn't answer, I thought you were still sleeping."

"The sun woke me up," I offered the first excuse that came to mind, "so I decided to go for a walk before it gets too hot."

"I guess I should thank the sun, then," Malatrius chimed in smoothly. "Otherwise I wouldn't have had the pleasure of such an interesting conversation." He stretched his hand out toward Philidert. "Professor Mal Atrius, pleased to meet you. I'm here for a series of guest lectures on ancient languages, and it was delightful to have an opportunity to talk to a fellow linguistics enthusiast." He sent me a smile.

I couldn't help arching an eyebrow at that. A believable lie like that stemmed from extensive knowledge... No matter who he really was, Malatrius must have taken his time to learn as much as he could about me and my father. At the same time, no one could become fluent in vizari over a few weeks, so that wasn't a part of his deception.

"I'm sure the conversation must have been *fascinating*." Philidert's expression made it clear he thought otherwise. "I'm Philidert Asnu-Thigai. Pleasure to make your acquaintance." He shook Malatrius's hand. "Now, if you'll excuse us, we need to get ready for breakfast."

As soon as he reached for my hand, I moved away,

glaring at him with ire. He might have my mother's favor, but if he thought it gave him any right to make decisions for me, he was mistaken. One thing he had right though—if I wanted to avoid uncomfortable questions, I couldn't go to breakfast underdressed. Not that it meant he didn't deserve a bit of harsh treatment to put him back in his place.

So, ignoring Philidert, I turned to Malatrius and asked in vizari, "And what if I want to remember?"

Philidert, of course, pouted. It might have been a bit too blunt of me to exclude him from the conversation like that, but I wasn't about to let him hear even the tiniest piece of it.

"You'll need your father's permission, then. I won't start a war with him," Malatrius replied. Then he smiled to Philidert and switched back to sanedian. "You have to forgive me. The sheer excitement of being able to have a conversation in the very subject of my studies makes me forget my manners."

"Then you should speak to Kithandar Alrothi-Mara instead." Philidert's tone was verging on impolite. Usually, he was subtler when he looked down at others, so being excluded from the conversation must have hurt his pride— and since he couldn't take it out on me, he'd chosen Malatrius as the target for his spoiled mood. "I'm sure he'll be delighted to oblige when it comes to conversations in ancient tongues."

"Oh, yes, Kithandar." The corner of Malatrius's mouth curled ever so slightly, showing that Philidert's crudeness, though not unnoticed, had no effect. "We've met before, but we don't seem to share the same connection as the one I've found with Miss Saeryn." He rubbed the edge of his palm in a casual manner, and I could swear my own scar responded with a slight burning sensation. "But I have no doubt I'll get a chance to talk to him as well. Now, if you'll excuse me, I won't be taking more of your time. I'd hate to stand in the way of your... social obligations." He looked at me. "Should you have any questions on the topics we've discussed, I'm certain the hotel's receptionist can direct you to me."

Without waiting for any farewells, he walked away.

"I thought he'd never leave," Philidert said as soon as we were alone. "I hope he didn't bore you to death with some linguistic details nobody really wants to hear about. No wonder he doesn't feel like talking to your father. They probably can't show off their knowledge to each other."

Not that Philidert would ever know, but my chuckle wasn't at his joke. It was at the thought that the animosity between my father and Malatrius was much more personal. If I were to believe the supposed sorcerer, death marked their mutual past, and that was something my father would hold a grudge for, no matter who provoked the situation or what had really happened.

I furrowed my brow. The dream revealed no reason for the plan we'd supposedly conceived together. I only caught glimpses of what must have been my own thoughts from the past, and such broken strands told me nothing. As far as I could tell, Malatrius was unaware that he'd been played in some way, and it seemed better to keep it from him. While I had no idea what he was truly capable of, his confidence and mysterious aura suggested he was a dangerous man who wouldn't take being someone else's pawn lightly.

Either way, I had to speak with my father, but this time I was armed with the right questions to ask. He'd have to tell me the truth.

He and my mother would be up soon, which meant I had little time to prepare for the conversation, and Philidert's company was the last thing I needed.

"I need to get ready for breakfast."

Not waiting for his response, I headed inside the hotel.

THE MEAL DRAGGED PAINFULLY. My mother kept going on about sunsets at riverbanks being unforgettable and romantic, suggesting in so many ways that Philidert should take me for a walk in the afternoon. Of course, the only person delighted by the idea was Philidert himself. My father seemed as absent-minded as usual, and I hardly paid attention to her blabber as well, busy with my own thoughts.

I couldn't stop thinking about the conversation with Malatrius. I tortured myself with endless speculation of what bits could be true in his rather implausible claims.

"I'd ask your father to take me as well," my mother said to me, "but I think that over the years he's lost that last bit of romanticism he was saving up for our thirtieth anniversary."

I nodded without paying much attention to her, but my father tensed. His face became a mask that hardly concealed anger, and it couldn't have been in reaction to my mother's remark. Her vitriol never bothered him, no matter how directly she applied it. I followed his gaze, and the source of his aggravation became clear.

Malatrius was just sitting down at a nearby table. As the server brought him coffee and listened to his order, he seemed to pay no attention to us, but he was undoubtedly aware of our presence. I held my breath when I realized that if my father confronted him, and Malatrius left the hotel, I'd have a hard time finding him on my own.

I hoped the conversation with my father would play out

in a different way, but the circumstances sealed the decision for me.

My mother was still talking, and Philidert encouraged her with eager nods and exclamations, but since I wasn't an actual participant in that exchange, I didn't wait for her to finish. As bad as such a habit was, I'd picked it up from my father who tended to ignore her in my favor whenever he saw fit.

With little remorse and with a daring idea, I said in vizari, "It must be difficult to be in the presence of a man who killed you."

Even if I didn't exactly believe Malatrius's claims, the remark made excellent bait to get my father talking. A bold statement could yield better results than any questions, as he would have to correct my claim and, at the same time, reveal what actually happened.

Both parents glanced at me with disapproval, though each for different reasons, and I paid no attention to my mother's discontent, my focus fully on my father.

"You talked to him against my advice," he said coldly, "and let him fill your head with lies."

I should have expected he would avoid giving me any answers, but I was far from giving up.

"Is this a lie too?" I stretched out my hand, demonstrating the scar, but I needed something more to win. "His odd words yesterday... They made me remember. I dreamed about the events in the castle."

His eyes wide, he leaned forward, hopeful and ignoring my mother's and Philidert's curious glances. "What did you remember?"

"Not much. Only what happened in your castle study, that's all. The bargain we were making for the scroll." His reaction reassured me that at least parts of my dream were real. "Why didn't you tell me?"

He gave me a smile lined with sadness. "Would you have believed me? The last thing I wanted was for you to treat me like some madman. I hoped that in time you would remember on your own."

I took a deep breath, taking the opening he gave me instead of allowing myself to ponder how much of last night's dream might be true. "Malatrius said he could help me remember more."

My father tensed. "He's not our friend, Sae. If he's offering help, he must have his own reasons. I tried everything to restore your memory and failed. If he can do it with such ease, it makes me wonder if *he* made you forget in the first place."

I didn't reply immediately. Whatever the reason my father disliked Malatrius so much, their squabbles meant little when compared with the prospect of regaining pieces of what could be the life I wasn't aware I had, but I couldn't argue that Malatrius was trustworthy.

I chose another approach.

"He claims he doesn't want to start a war with you, and he won't do anything unless you agree to it." That earned me an arched eyebrow, so I pressed on. "I think we should at least talk to him. If you're with me, you can help me uncover what's true and what's deception." I tried to make it sound more like a plea than a threat that I would go behind his back if he refused. "And if he has some hidden reasons, making him help me could reveal something of what his real scheme is."

His hesitation made me hold my breath. His next words could smother the hope glimmering in my heart.

"Are you talking about that linguist?" As usual,

Philidert didn't like being left out, and having caught our glances toward the other table, he butted into the conversation at the first moment of silence. "Professor Mal something-or-other? I forgot his name," he added with the shameless smile of someone who didn't bother burdening his mind with anything related to commoners.

To me, it sounded like an attempt to win my father's favor by belittling another scholar, and I grimaced, but my father would have none of it anyway.

"Indeed, we are." He gave Philidert a cold glare he reserved for people who'd violated the privacy of others. "But it's hardly courteous to talk about him while he's sitting a table or two away. Since we're done with the breakfast, why don't you do me a favor and invite him over to have coffee with us?"

I almost chuckled. He didn't share my mother's fondness for the young aristocrat and wasn't beyond letting it show. Sadly, it had little effect on Philidert. Taking offense for such treatment and leaving for good would be granting a huge favor to my whole family—save maybe for my mother.

"Maybe it would be more reasonable if you joined him instead," Philidert replied. "The ladies wouldn't get bored with all the academic talk. I'm sure that I can entertain them with more lighthearted stories."

He threw my mother a dashing smile, undoubtedly seeking her support in the matter.

"I'll do it." I stood up before anyone could protest. "Professor Mal Atrius seems to be a knowledgeable scholar, and I'd love to learn his insights on ancient linguistics." With that, I walked away from the table.

When I approached Malatrius, he arched his eyebrow in a mix of polite interest and slight amusement, and that expression felt so familiar... like the beginning of yet another game between us.

"My father is wondering whether you'd join us for coffee." I didn't bother with empty pleasantries.

He rose from his chair, amusement now clear in his expression and his breakfast left unfinished. "I'd never pass on such an opportunity."

As we made it back to our table, I couldn't help but feel that I'd indeed delved into a game I didn't understand, and found myself desperate to hope—contrary to what my memories suggested—that it wasn't the game in which my life was at stake.

Chapter 3

Between the mundane and the unknown

The ship cruised through the river bends, and I eyed the shore with growing frustration. Stuck onboard with my mother and an unwanted suitor, I threw silent curses at my father, who had cheated me out of the conversation with Malatrius. Despite my quite blunt protests, he'd sent me away with the others. How could he?! It was my life and my memories. I should have been present.

Philidert, of course, had been delighted and undoubtedly took it as my father's permission to get closer to me, and that brought a tiny smile to my face. What my father wanted had nothing to do with him, and if Philidert thought he'd finally received both my parents' blessings, he was in for a nasty surprise. I might not relish cruelty, but seeing his disappointed face when he realized my father still disliked him all the same would be the brightest moment of my day.

I moved away when Philidert brushed his shoulder against mine.

"Are you all right?" he asked. "Is the sun hurting your

eyes?" He moved closer, his cologne lingering like a cloud of poison around him.

I didn't hide my displeasure when I looked at him. If anything was about to hurt my eyes, it was his choice of perfumed water—or rather, an excessive use of it. I also didn't appreciate that he was still using my accident as an excuse to be overbearing.

"I'm *fine*." I hadn't intended to put that much ire into my voice, but it slipped in nonetheless, fueled by my other frustrations. "Maybe we should check on my mother."

As much as I'd hate to once again become an object of the lousy matchmaking my mother seemed to enjoy, at least Philidert would feel obligated to keep the conversation going. With the two of them exchanging empty remarks, my thoughts would be free to wander.

"You don't look fine," he replied. "You haven't been yourself lately. Maybe this whole trip is too much of a strain for you. After all, you've only been out of the hospital for mere months."

Hospital... I never mentioned to my mother or Philidert that I remembered none of it, not even flashes nor disjointed images. The first clear memory was a doctor's office, where an older woman explained to me in broken sanedian that I had been in a coma after an accident. Her words were a bit of a blur—a side effect of the medicines they'd been giving me—and all I could remember clearly was my father's hand holding mine.

Both he and the doctoress reassured me that temporary memory loss wasn't anything to worry about, but the more time that passed and the clearer my mind became, the more I wondered whether it I'd *ever* piece myself together. I could believe that the shock of the accident pushed any memory of it from my mind, and the coma would leave no mark in my mind either, but at least I should have remembered the moment of waking up. I kept asking my father about the extent of my injuries, but he evaded answering in so many ways that, in desperation, I turned to my mother.

Unfortunately, she knew nothing except that my father had found an expensive and highly private facility in another country that promised him my full recovery, but they had harsh conditions: no family visits at all, and only he would receive information about the progress of my recovery.

With no other possible answer, I'd believed that my awakening from a three-year coma was indeed as miraculous as it seemed, but Malatrius's claims made me question what I knew. For three years no one had seen me, awake or not. The accident, my coma, and the medical facility might have been all deception, and my father must have been party to it.

And to think that he was now alone with Malatrius, perhaps devising another mystification, affected my mood, already spoiled by Philidert's presence, which was as annoying as a tenacious fly.

True or not, at least I could use the accident to my advantage. "Maybe you're right." I sent him a sweet smile. "I probably overdid it, and all the excitement of an exotic place isn't helping. I should go to bed early tonight." An early night would make any sunset walks impossible, and I would have more time to catch another dream or think over all that Malatrius had told me.

"Of course!" Philidert eagerly agreed. "I hope you'll feel better, and we can fully enjoy this exotic vacation." He brushed my bare arm. "I was delighted when Lady Zefinia invited me to join your family here."

I bit my tongue before remarking that he was the only

one. If my father could, he would've undoubtedly ensured that not only Philidert but also my mother stayed home. I indulged myself in a daydream of spending this vacation with him alone. All the interesting ruins to explore and museums to visit would keep us busy and entertained. We'd fill our time with learning and researching instead of empty conversations and dull walks on the hotel grounds. Come to think of it, it seemed like a miracle that my mother had agreed to the cruise along the river, with all the inconveniences of such a tour.

"Speaking of my mother, would you mind going to the upper deck to check if she needs anything?" I asked innocently. "I'll take a moment to rest in the shade and join you at the exit after we moor." I walked over to an empty bench and sat down, giving my best impression of being exhausted.

He beamed at me. "Not at all. You get some rest, and I'll be right back."

I was hoping my mother would take a bit longer to come down from the upper deck, where she'd retreated at the beginning of the cruise under the pretense of enjoying the sun: a clear ploy to leave Philidert alone with me.

"Take your time. I'm not going anywhere."

But I actually was. As soon as he disappeared, I headed to the emptied prow. The riverbank wasn't much to look at, with its red, hard soil and scarce shrubs. The greenest parts were the small islets in the river itself, lush with grass and dwarf bushes. Once or twice, I'd seen local men ferry cows to them—an amusing and somewhat disconcerting sight as they navigated their tiny reed boats through the busy waters, with animals too big for the size of their vessels. Yet I imagined such rich feed was worth the effort and the risk, when one considered the price of livestock feed in a country that didn't have much farmland.

In the distance, the limestone houses of the town appeared, and my thoughts immediately returned to the morning's events.

Both my father and Malatrius had played the roles of scholars engrossed in research as they bade us farewell, but I had no doubt that they'd abandoned those masks once everyone else was gone. Countless speculations ran through my head, feeding my anxiety. For all I knew, my father had simply insisted that Malatrius left for good before we returned.

The cruise ship rounded the last river bend, and the buildings became more frequent. The cheap houses were made of reed and clay, with wood so scarce in Quathan. Out of the roofs sported jutting beams from the forever-unfinished parts of the building—a common practice to avoid taxation in a country where people paid dues only on finished homesteads.

In front of those houses, men sat smoking pipes and women in their long robes went about daily chores. Children ran screaming and reenacting battles from Quathan's rich history, pretending to be warriors of legends, and I chuckled at their serious faces.

Then, at the pier, I spotted my father's tall frame. He was looking toward the ship, and he was alone. My heart sank, but I fought to keep my smile on and waved to him. No matter what I had hoped for, he knew Malatrius better than me, and it was right he'd be the one to make the decision. Since I had already regained a piece of my memories, my father would likely be more willing to reveal things he might have kept from me. Perhaps I didn't need Malatrius's help after all.

As the ship anchored, sailors readied the walkways, and my father smiled back at me. His expression, caring and loving, eased my sour mood. Regardless of what had happened between him and the so-called Sorcerer from the Desert, it wouldn't affect our relationship. As long as I had my father and his love, I was whole—no matter how incomplete I might feel.

"There you are!" Philidert approached with my mother holding his arm. "Weren't you supposed to be resting?"

"I thought one last breath of the river breeze would be a good idea before we head back deeper inland," I lied smoothly.

"Dear Phil told me you're feeling unwell." My mother scrutinized me with the meticulousness of a detective. "I told Kith he shouldn't have trusted some unknown hospital and their shady treatment methods." She added a dramatic roll of her eyes and a grimace.

"Mother, I'll be fine. I just need a bit of rest. I keep forgetting that I'm still recovering, that's all." I pointed toward the pier in a blatant attempt to change the topic. "Father is waiting for us."

Thankfully, she fell for it.

"Is he? I'd have thought that he'd still be conversing with that professor... He never knows when to stop when it comes to his work."

The disappointment in her voice surprised me a little. Whatever the feelings that made my parents marry, they had died a long time ago, possibly not long after my birth. Both my father and my mother seemed content enough living together, and neither spoke of divorce, so even though I'd never witnessed the signs of affection I'd seen other long-time partners express, I didn't think my mother was missing something in her marriage. In my youth, I'd believed that this was what marriage always looked like, and the prospect of being betrothed to someone like Philidert, who showered me with attention, seemed like fate's gift. It took some growing up to understand how wrong I was about it, and I was lucky to have learned it before I chained myself to him with any vows.

The three of us waited for other tourists to disembark first. I stood silent, letting my mother and Philidert discuss trivialities, mainly the cruise. Trying to push through the people crowding around the boardwalk would not make our departure any swifter, but I was anxious to talk to my father, even if we were allowed only a brief conversation with the others present.

As we finally made it to shore, he approached, his inscrutable expression shaking my composure. Surely, even if he wanted Malatrius gone, he wouldn't do anything unsavory—a thought that wouldn't have entered my mind a few days ago, but with the unsettling memory I'd regained, I had to revisit that, which up until now, I'd considered unshakable truths.

"We thought we'd find you at the hotel's terrace, still deep in conversation with that professor," my mother said, amused. "Was he not knowledgeable enough?"

"Quite the contrary. I found our exchange very interesting," my father replied. "Sadly, Professor Atrius didn't have much time. He's going back to his lands soon."

My heart sank as I read between the lines, and some of that feeling must have shown on my face, because my father gave me a warm smile.

"He did make an enticing offer, though," he added like a magician preparing his audience for the final trick. "There is an ancient site near his lands with lots of interesting writings carved in the stones. He invited me to visit him, and it's a rare opportunity. He doesn't often have guests."

I stared at him, unable to put things together. It must have been an interesting conversation if Malatrius made such an offer. I couldn't conjure any reason for him to do so, either.

"Obviously, you declined." My mother did not make it a question.

"Yes, I have other obligations," he replied with regret, but I had no doubt it was an act for the two onlookers. "Saeryn, on the other hand, has no plans, and she could go if she wishes to."

The surprise on my face was genuine. To think that my father would let me go anywhere alone with Malatrius after expressing so many times that we couldn't trust him... They must have struck a bargain of sorts, perhaps similar to the one made in the castle from my dream. I glanced at both his wrists but saw no wounds.

"Don't be ridiculous," my mother said. "It's enough that you're head-deep in your studies. You don't have to drag our daughter into it. She has her own life!"

My father shot her a glare that could kill. "And that's why she'll be the one to decide. The professor has agreed to be her host and to ensure she's as comfortable as possible, given he lives in a rather uncivilized country." He looked at me. "If you're considering an academic future, I'd take this opportunity. You'll gain insights no one else might be able to help you find."

I nodded, once more reading between the lines. Malatrius had promised to help me restore my memories.

"Sae, dear, you should consider your health," my mother pleaded. "Such a taxing journey and lack of commodities, skilled doctors, and other necessities... There will be other opportunities, closer to home."

She didn't know that regardless of whether I went with Malatrius or not, I wouldn't be staying close to home. I'd had enough of Philidert's constant company. Besides, no opportunity like this would ever present itself again, but I couldn't tell her it was about my memories and not academics.

"I'll go," I said.

"It's decided, then." My father shot her a triumphant glare. As much as I hated being used as a weapon in their wars, at least it meant I had him on my side.

"For how long?" Her high-pitched voice suggested imminent hysteria.

"The professor generously agreed to host her for as long as she wishes," my father replied. "I've been told his lands are a tranquil area, perfect for the convalescence our daughter needs."

She pouted at that. "But we could send her somewhere civilized instead! It's not like we can't afford a resort with all the conveniences. I don't see why you'd send her to a barbaric country with a stranger you've just met."

"Professor Malatrius is hardly a stranger to me, and his academic record is more than a recommendation," he said. "I do not wish for my daughter to become a lazy, empty-headed cow stuck in an endless string of social events that don't offer any intellectual challenge. Do you?"

She stared at him, visibly hurt. Though she would never admit it, and she was far from lazy or empty-headed, my father had managed to describe her life in a single sentence. He must have been tired of the argument if he'd resorted to such a cruel gibe.

Philidert, who had so far silently watched the exchange,

stepped closer. "Sir, if I may... Maybe there's compromise to be found."

He was a fool if he thought that witnessing our private argument gave him the right to partake in it.

"You may not." My father's reply could freeze the river behind us all the way to its source. "Saeryn wants to go, and I see no reason to keep her from pursuing what her heart desires."

For a heartbeat, Philidert looked like he was going to argue with him, but in the end, he swallowed and nodded, taking a step back.

"Now, since that's settled, let's get back to the hotel," my father said with authority. "Sae, walk with me. While it would be of benefit to ask the professor for details of this journey later, there are things I can already tell you."

With no other choice, Philidert offered his arm to my mother, his dashing smile slightly wavering and his face carrying traces of negative feelings, but I paid no attention to his hurt pride. Being around my family for so long, he should have learned that going against my father was always a fool's endeavor.

We fell behind them, keeping a slight distance, and I switched to vizari.

"Thank you, Father."

"I don't trust him, but I trusted you before when it came to him, so I will do so again. Whatever you did impressed him enough to offer help, but remember that he's a powerful and vengeful man, and we both played him."

"I understand. I'll be careful."

He nodded. "I don't know what his true motive is, but you were right—it's all the more reason we can't afford to stay in the dark. I'm hoping that while you're restoring your memories, you'll discover something that will allow us to deal with whatever he might be plotting."

"So where will I truly be going?" I asked.

"To another world," he replied casually, as if he were telling me of a nearby city, "and back to his lands. I won't be able to help you there, but fear not. While you can still be killed and suffer pain, if the worst comes to pass, you'll be back in this world, alive and safe." He rubbed his chin. "Though I doubt Malatrius would resort to something so crude. It's more likely that while he's helping you find your memories, he'll attempt to manipulate you, turn you against me, or try to make you reveal anything that he could use against me."

I nodded solemnly, but I had to ask: "This is all true, isn't it? Another world, magic... You can do magic too, can't you?"

His smile was warm and caring. "So can you. I missed talking to you about it, teaching you... Now that you'll know it's real, I hope that once you return, we will resume your schooling."

Magic. Part of me still questioned whether it could be true, but the rest was shivering with excitement of what could be possible, because even though my rational mind tried to reject it, something within me was responding to the concept being real and, more importantly, familiar.

Most important, though, was that magic was something I shared with my father. I always knew we had a special bond, much stronger than the one I had with my mother, but now I understood how it came to be—through the secret of magic. I didn't even have to ask to be sure that my mother knew nothing of it.

Even if Malatrius lied to us or simply failed to help me find my lost memories, I had the magic itself to look forward to. And since I supposedly already knew some of it, perhaps it would be another key to unlocking the missing pieces of my past.

"Once we return to the hotel, go talk to him, but be sure to come to dinner on time. It'll be the last one we're going to have together for quite a while."

I looked at my mother. Her posture and confident stride were impeccable, as always, but I knew her well enough to pick up the subtle cues of distress. I'd been gone for three years, and for her, it was likely a time filled with despair. And now I was going away again.

"She's not going to take it well," I whispered.

"Leave your mother to me," he replied. "I'll make sure she has plenty of company and things to do to ease her worries."

I doubted there was anything he could do to truly take her mind off her concerns, but unless I decided to stay, I couldn't do anything either. At least she'd have Philidert to keep her distracted, because he'd likely keep close to my family in hopes of getting any news.

My father, though, wouldn't find even such meager comfort. While my mother thought Malatrius was an eccentric scholar, he knew the truth and the danger that man could pose. No distraction could remedy his concerns.

Hesitantly, I touched his arm, unsure what kind of comfort I could offer. He wasn't prone to expressions of feelings, but I knew he cared for me deeply.

"You needn't worry about me," he said. "I know you'll return to me, and I know whatever Malatrius is planning, he's never going to succeed in turning you against me."

I smiled. Instead of me comforting him, he'd found a way to comfort me, and reassure me of his trust once more.

With him by my side, I could face whatever the future—and my own past—could throw at me.

When I entered the hotel room, Malatrius was sitting at the table by the open balcony door, and the muslin curtain danced in the gentle breeze. I stood in the middle of the hand-woven carpet with intricate florals creating a maze for the eyes, undecided which questions to ask.

He wore the same desert outfit, and with the dream's images at my disposal, I knew it mimicked the clothes he'd worn in the other world. Yet he spoke sanedian fluently enough, and a room in a luxurious hotel suggested he had considerable resources here.

Malatrius invited me to take the chair on the opposite side of the table. The crystal carafe contained only water, and the plate had a selection of local fruit. As he nibbled on a date in a leisurely manner that suggested he was savoring the taste rather than sating hunger, he gestured for me to help myself.

"I'll do my best to help you restore the memories you've lost," he said. "Your dream proves that they could be recovered with specific keys... like words or places. I had enough luck to evoke a strong one, but for the others to be effective, you'll have to come back with me. You'll have to live the life you've had."

I nodded. "In the other world." Saying it still held the peculiar taste of absurdity, but my instincts whispered that truth rang within.

"There are rules you will have to follow," he continued, "and if you decide to depart with me, it means you accept them. Tomorrow at dawn, we'll leave the hotel and travel into the desert deep enough to ensure no one can disturb our crossing to Hyrinea. Once we're there, you'll assume the role you had before you died. You'll act accordingly and do everything you can to avoid any suspicion. No one in my household knows what happened to you, and I want to keep it that way. Of course, I'll provide guidance, especially in the beginning, before you regain enough memories to be fine on your own."

"My role..." The images from the dream flashed before my eyes. "You want me to act as your slave."

He shook his head. "It's not that simple. Yes, you were a slave, but things changed over the three years you spent serving me. I could explain it to you, but I'd rather keep your mind as blank, as it is, so my words don't stand in the way of your memories."

I furrowed my brow at that but said nothing. Despite his insistence that he wanted to give me my memories back, he was offering very little information.

"There is a difference between remembering something for yourself and being told what happened," he said as if he guessed what was on my mind. "Your father already believes that I intend to alter your knowledge of the events and likely warned you to not trust anything I say."

I pressed my lips together and stared him down. "Prove him wrong."

Malatrius burst out laughing and shook his head. "Regardless of lost memories, you're still mostly yourself. I'm looking forward to spending more time with you. I'm sure it will be as... *insightful* as it was the first time around."

A cold shiver ran down my spine at the strange note in his voice, but I didn't allow myself any doubts. I'd decided to take the risk, and to invite concerns into my thoughts would be losing the game before it even started. The dream suggested that in the past I'd played with my life at stake and survived long enough to have Malatrius make me a promise.

So this time, I would also succeed and regain what I'd lost.

"Is there anything I need to take with me?" I asked, steering the conversation toward practical matters. As much as I craved more knowledge, Malatrius was right. It was better if I discovered it myself.

"The less you can take without raising suspicion, the better," he replied. "Pack like you normally would for a trip, but don't concern yourself with inessential things. You won't be using anything you take to Hyrinea."

Curiosity and excitement hushed my concerns. No matter what happened, Malatrius was offering me the adventure of a lifetime, and my father wouldn't have agreed to it if there were any real danger.

"There's one more thing left to discuss." He moved his forearm in such a way that his scar caught the sun, glimmering slightly. "The oath that bound us is gone, but you will still have to behave as if I could kill you for your slightest disobedience. You never showed fear, but if you want to argue with me, you better be sure no one can see or hear us... The prism cube library would be the safest. If you show disobedience in the presence of others, not only will I punish you accordingly, but I'll also send you back. Do you think you can control yourself?"

The way he asked suggested it was meant as a reminder to me... to the woman I supposedly was. Yet, without my memories, I couldn't be sure how I'd acted and why, and the dream showed that the Sae from the past had been more determined and disciplined. I had to live up to her, but until then, I gave Malatrius the only answer I could: "I'll do my best."

The long glare from his emerald eyes suggested he shared my doubts, but he nodded. "Very well. I'm leaving at dawn. Don't be late."

I hesitated at the dismissal, but he'd already made it clear that all the memories were mine to recover, not his to tell.

"I'll be there," I promised.

THE SUN HADN'T RISEN YET, and most of the hotel's corridors were drowned in darkness disturbed only by the nighttime lanterns that guided guests to their rooms. I carried my suitcase, dragging my feet across the lush carpets and fighting tiredness. With the excitement and anxiety of the upcoming journey into the unknown and witnessing magic—and also, of course, the prospect of recovering lost memories—my mind refused to fall asleep, defying the weariness of my body. Even the temptation of discovering more memories within my dreams hadn't helped, since, if everything went well, I'd have them all back soon enough.

I also couldn't stop thinking about my host-to-be. Without any doubt, his relationship with my father verged on hostile, and I still mused on how they'd managed to come to *any* agreement, yet he didn't seem to have the same attitude toward me. The friendliness and—I chanced believing it—honesty he offered didn't match the kind of behavior one would display toward his enemy's daughter.

Of course, it might be but a ploy to gain my trust, but Malatrius didn't seem to care whether I actually trusted him, as if he had confidence that whatever I was to remember would prove him right.

The hotel's foyer came into view, quiet and empty. Malatrius wasn't in sight, but I doubted he would leave before the set time. Not seeing my parents waiting was quite a relief, because the family dinner I'd had with them the previous evening was enough of a dramatic and tearful farewell, and I felt no need for another one.

I cringed at the memory of the ridiculous show in which I'd had to participate.

While my father might have been his usual self, save for a few too many reminders that I was not to trust any claims Malatrius would make, my mother made enough fuss for the both of them. From nearly hysterical remarks that I couldn't go on such a wild trip, which carried as much authority as one would expect from a child in a tantrum, to emotional expressions of sentiment that her little girl had grown up too fast and was going out into the world on her own, as if I had never traveled without them before.

I tried to be nice to her. I could understand her feelings, especially after three years of my supposed coma, but her overbearing behavior was weighing heavily on my mood.

As for Philidert, I didn't give him any thought, though I was thankful that he had enough wits to stay quiet throughout dinner. If he made any inconsiderate remarks, it could've sent either of my parents over the edge, each in their own way.

At least it was the last time in a while that I would have to deal with such problems.

The porter wished me a good day in the perfect sanedian accent he must have acquired with so many guests around from the main continent, and I smiled to him before stepping outside.

The first rays of the rising sun teased my eyes, and the air was still cool, with each breath making my body feel refreshed and my mind clearer. In the driveway in front of the hotel stood a vehicle. Quite a sight for Quathan, which was years behind continental progress, and, even over there, such vehicles were still scarce. What was more, this one had thick tires and a solid frame, which suggested it was suitable for all kinds of travel, not only pleasure drives on city roads. A Quathani driver leaned against its hood, smoking a cigarette and ignoring the whole world.

"On time, as expected." Malatrius emerged from the shaded archway to the side. He had nothing with him except for a small carry bag.

Before I replied, a voice called out from the hotel's foyer, "Saeryn, wait!"

Philidert rushed toward me, dragging two enormous suitcases behind him. His face bore marks of sleep, and his clothes were hardly in order.

"I made it." Panting, he stopped in front of us and straightened himself up. "Professor, I apologize for not notifying you earlier. I'll be accompanying Saeryn during her trip."

I shot him an angry glare, as he'd failed to notify me as well. Had I known, I'd have ensured he abandoned such a notion, even if it meant convincing Malatrius to leave earlier and in greater secrecy.

Malatrius shook his head with an apologetic smile. "I'm afraid that's impossible. My invitation is exclusive to certain members of the Arlothi-Mara family. And please, do not waste my time saying that you insist, because I won't have you imposing your company on us."

"Yet, I must insist." Philidert stared him down. "You see, I asked some questions. The local university, the one you were supposedly giving guest lectures at, has never heard of you." He looked at me in triumph. "This man isn't who he claims to be."

"He's *exactly* who he claims to be," I replied with confidence. "Though true, the professor is but a persona he uses to travel incognito." It seemed the best explanation, since I wouldn't even entertain the thought of properly introducing the Sorcerer from the Desert to him. Especially not when I had yet to witness any of Malatrius's sorcery.

"Then there shouldn't be any objection to me going with you." Philidert stared at me. He must have been certain that he was but a step away from convincing me. "Surely, if the false professor has nothing to hide, he won't mind an additional guest."

I grimaced, searching for words of refusal that would leave him no more openings. I didn't care much if he revealed his discovery to my parents, because I trusted my father would deal with it, but I'd rather avoid a scene that would delay us or arouse Malatrius's ire.

"This is going nowhere." Malatrius's remark mirrored my own thoughts. "We will depart without you, Mr. Asnu-Thigai, whether you like it or not. I could warn you to not try following us, but I fear you're one of those insolent people who wouldn't listen. Therefore, I won't apologize for what happens next." He gave Philidert a friendly pat on the shoulder. "The poison isn't lethal, but it will cause a spell of weakness for an hour or two. I suggest you use whatever strength you have left to find a seat."

Philidert stood motionless, his eyes wide and breath rasping. Malatrius turned away, so I shot the foolish aristocrat a glance—pitying rather than compassionate—and rushed after the sorcerer. As he approached the vehicle, he removed a thorn from between his fingers and secured it back in the pocket of his bag. Busy arguing with Philidert, I'd missed the moment when he prepared it for the strike. I had to appreciate that he'd chosen that approach rather than resorting to magic that would likely draw too much attention—though at the same time, it made me question yet again, against even my father's word, whether magic was indeed real. Stripped of any memories of it, my reasonable mind still tried to fight against the concept.

The driver loaded our luggage and started the vehicle.

I eyed the open seat in the front. "I'll sit in the back."

The knee-length skirt and light jacket that made up my travel outfit weren't suitable for unladylike sitting at the vehicle's bed, which offered no comforts, and the rules of my world demanded Malatrius give me the seat, but going with him meant agreeing to his rules and leaving such notions behind.

He seemed pleased with the offer but said, "We both will. I'd prefer you remember everything on your own, but some things you must know before we arrive, so that you can play your role convincingly enough."

As we drove away, I looked back only once. Philidert slumped by the wall at the hotel's entrance, his two suitcases abandoned nearby. His dumbfounded expression, that of someone who was still trying to comprehend what had happened, oddly reassured me that I'd made the right choice.

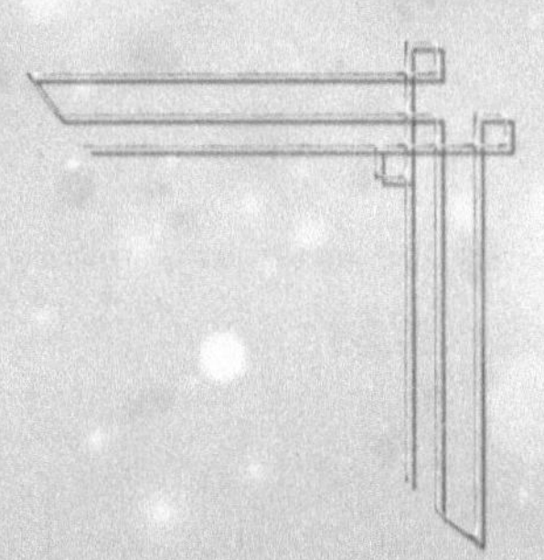

Chapter 4

Dreams become memories

The driver left us deep in the desert, and as soon as Malatrius paid him—generously, from what I glimpsed—he drove away without any apparent concern about how we would get back to civilization.

The vehicle's tires left marks in the dunes, but aside from that, nothing spoke of a human presence among the sands. My head was bursting with the information about the other world, and my body slumped in response to the night of lost sleep, yet I inspected our surroundings with curiosity and a pinch of suspicion.

"Not exactly what I expected," I said.

Ever since we left the hotel, we'd been using vizari to communicate. I thought I was fluent, and Malatrius had proven me wrong, but engaging in a conversation unlocked my linguistic memory. With every sentence, I found myself more and more at ease using it, even when discussing more complex topics.

Malatrius said nothing and led me through the sands. As we rounded a small dune, a ruined building appeared. With most of its structure crumbled, I had a hard time guessing whether it was a former trading outpost, a forgotten homestead, or something else, but it was clear that its owner must have abandoned it decades earlier. Yet its remaining walls provided some shade from the merciless sun, and this was where Malatrius led me.

"I need to open the passageway between the worlds, and you need to dream," he said, as if either of us could command my mind to conjure dreams.

The mention of a passageway revitalized my tired body with excitement. Both he and my father mentioned magic casually, but I had yet to witness any of it. To sleep through a magical occurrence was the last thing I wanted, even if I could use some rest and insightful dreams.

"I only had the one I told you about. I can't make them come, no matter how much I wish for them."

"Dreams will always be a game of chance, but we'll keep trying." He passed a hip flask to me, one unlike anything I'd seen before, shaped and hardened leather, carved with decorative swirls. "Drink this. It'll help you sleep."

Hushing the voice of caution, I took several sips. The liquid tasted bitter, likely another poison. I could only hope that I wasn't drinking my own death, because no matter what my father had said about being reborn, I felt no rush to learn how it worked or whether it was even true at all.

We sat down in the shade. I rested my back against the warm stones. Malatrius stacked our luggage beside me.

"Before the essence starts working, unbutton your shirt and bare your cleavage," he said.

A flurry of thoughts ran through my head as I stared at him. The poison was already numbing my senses and clouding my mind, and I fought it as I tried to comprehend his odd request. No gentleman would ever ask for something so unbecoming, but it must be nothing more than a test, because if he wanted to do unscrupulous things, he could simply wait until I fell asleep. I had promised that I'd obey his orders, and even though we weren't in the other world yet, he might want to see how far I was willing to go.

I forced my numb fingers to undo several buttons and pushed the shirt's fabric to the side, revealing too much of my cleavage to be considered appropriate, even if fashionable evening dresses favored deeper and wider necklines.

Malatrius didn't stare, but when he leaned toward me, I had to fight the urge to flinch or move away.

He touched my skin just below my clavicle. "Something to dream about," he said with a sly smile.

As he whispered words I didn't recognize, pain tore through my chest in an instant, forcing a hiss out of me. It faded quickly, and Malatrius moved his hand away, revealing a swirly shape on my skin, dark like a tattoo but swelling slightly. The first display of magic had turned out to be quite meager... yet I kept staring at it.

"What's that?" I slurred, already in the grip of the poison, my consciousness fading.

"You tell me when you wake up."

THE SLAVE'S mark still burned the skin below her cleavage, its magic pulsating like a reminder of what she'd agreed to, and Saeryn locked her eyes on the prism cube she was carrying. Without its inner powers awake, the cube looked like an ordinary stone pried from a wall in her father's castle. Of course, she knew better, and before Malatrius gave the order for departure, she'd activated the cube for long enough to prove she had what he'd requested.

Her shoulders ached from tension, and it was only the beginning of the journey. Maybe later, when Malatrius grew used to her presence, and she could allow herself a bit of carelessness, she'd find a way to remedy the stiffness of her muscles, but now was the time to remain focused, because one misstep could cost her life. It had taken her weeks to convince Kithandar that her plan would succeed, and she had to bear the risk if she was to reap the rewards. So until she could do more, she had to ensure she stayed alive. Tense shoulders were a small price to pay.

A long caravan of people marched down the winding path toward the valley: Malatrius, his warriors, and the people of the castle taken prisoners. She had no doubt most would end up on slave markets, which, according to her father, were prominent in Hyrinea—a plight she might have shared if not for the scab marking her wrist.

Yet her own skin was blemished with the sorcerer's mark of property, reminding her than at any time Malatrius could simply sell her as well, putting an end to the scheme he wasn't even aware of. Hopefully, the oath he'd sworn also protected her from any attempts he'd make to get rid of her. As with everything, it was up to interpretation, but most chose to be careful when it came to the binding oath—one couldn't argue their point with magic.

With her head down to conceal any emotions, she walked behind the sorcerer. She couldn't decide whether he chose to keep her close because he took his oath of keeping her safe so seriously or because he was hoping she'd turn on him, tempted by the opportunity. If she tried anything, he'd be free of his oath, and the contents of the prism cube would be but a small price to pay. Or, perhaps, someone as powerful as him didn't need her to open the library hidden within the stone she carried.

When the sun sat in the sky low enough to touch the mountain peaks, Malatrius ordered a rest. Several men set up a tent while others saw to the prisoners, offering enough water and dry rations to keep them alive.

The sorcerer gestured at Saeryn to follow, and they entered the tent. Inside, a servant had already prepared a simple meal, served on a cloth stretched over the ground. As he sat, she stood in the middle, unsure what to do.

"Sit down," he said. "Since I didn't expect to be returning with a rather unusual slave in tow, you'll eat with me during the journey."

"Yes, master."

She took a seat opposite him and rested the prism cube beside her.

"You've shown you're capable of opening it." Malatrius pointed at the cube. "And you had no trouble reciting the binding oath. It means you know the arts."

"Only the basics," she replied with caution. "I know of more complex spells and rituals, but I have never been permitted to learn one. I mostly took care of the library and copied scrolls."

At least that's what she'd been doing for the past few months, enough to get her acquainted with the library's collection and—if needed—be able to copy the contents of fading parchment. Malatrius was to never know she'd led another life as well.

He cut a piece of a cold roast, and as he dropped it on a piece of bread, he casually passed the knife to her, the same one that drank their blood. Saeryn froze staring at the blade. Malatrius was offering it with the hilt toward her, but she couldn't bring herself to touch it.

"You're testing me, master," she said.

"A bit," he admitted. "Though I wouldn't expect you to

be foolish enough to try anything so soon, when I'm still watching you closely. I think you'd rather let me become accustomed to your presence, to pay no attention to you. You seem patient enough to wait for days, if not weeks or months." He watched her intently as if he intended to evaluate how much of a threat she was.

Everything between them seemed to be a game, from eating together to the ostensible openness, and to win, she had to play. She took the knife and cut a generous piece of meat for herself. It might be one of her last opportunities for a decent meal, so she intended to make the most of it. She left the blade by the roast, leaving Malatrius to retrieve it if he wished. His scrutinizing gaze remained on her the whole time.

When they were done, he chose one of the blankets covering his bedroll and threw it to her, then pointed at an empty space by the tent's wall.

"I'm surprised you trust me enough to let me sleep here, master," she remarked.

He grimaced as if he hadn't expected her to speak. "You're an inconvenience, and I hope the prism cube's library is worth it. But if you're close, you'll have more opportunities to do something to free me from my oath. One day you won't be able to overcome the thought that I killed your father, and you'll act upon your hatred."

Saeryn smiled, as the mention of her father must have been intentional to stir her emotions and break her composure. "I think I might disappoint you, master."

"Perhaps." He nodded, though clearly remained skeptical.

She couldn't blame him for having doubts. Yet if he'd wanted her to be blinded by that hatred he expected, he should have made sure she had witnessed Kithandar's death.

"Either way, you sleep here," he continued. "This way you'll have your chance to kill me if you so choose, and I'll be making sure you come to no harm... until you make your move. I won't have you among other prisoners or within the hired henchmen's grasp and risk the oath being broken."

With the terms he'd chosen, it made sense he didn't want to risk the magic binding them to react to negligence in her protection, and it told her that Malatrius was a cautious and calculating man who didn't take risks. She headed for her sleeping spot. One blanket was hardly enough to cover herself, and she'd have to lie on the bare ground. Even with the early summer's warmth, the night would drain the heat from it... and from her.

Malatrius arched an eyebrow, as if waiting for any protest or plea, but when she remained silent, he turned away, undressing. Shamelessly, she watched his back and arms as he took his robes and tunic off. He didn't have the muscles of a warrior, and she hadn't expected him to, but his shapely body revealed that the Sorcerer from the Desert wasn't a frail man who indulged in food and drink. He was fit and healthy for his age.

His turned bare back was like an invitation to strike, and the knife was still by the roast, but she knew better than to act. No matter what he said about hatred that would consume her, Kithandar's death was something she expected and was prepared for.

Curled under her blanket, she closed her eyes in the hope that her body, after the events of the day and the long march, would succumb to slumber despite the hard, cool ground.

THE SAND under her feet was soft, and its sun-heated grains teased her skin as she walked barefoot. Sinking in it almost ankle-deep, she glanced over her shoulder. Malatrius sat in the shaded area of an open tent set between the dunes, watching her in thought.

It'd been only five of them for the past weeks. The sorcerer had parted with the henchmen at the end of the valley, and while they herded away their soon-to-be-sold prisoners, Malatrius boarded a river barge with her, a servant, and two warriors that comprised his personal guard. They sailed down to the sea, where another ship awaited them, and after a three-week journey they arrived at a town on the edge of the desert.

Its most prominent feature was the docks where ships resupplied and sailors found respite in local taverns. Saeryn longed to explore the town's narrow streets and brightly painted buildings—so different from her father's castle built of gray rock and surrounded by equally gray mountains—but Malatrius didn't venture into it. Instead, he sent off his servant to make arrangements and then set up camp on the outskirts.

He kept Saeryn close all the while, even though there was no need for it in such a small company of people loyal to him, but he didn't pay much attention to her otherwise, and she found herself bored for most of the journey. The excitement of seeing new lands had faded during the monotonous sea travel, and she'd had little hope of venturing out on her own once they made landfall.

Only at the sight of the desert did her growing apathy vanish as if soothed by the golden dunes. Not caring whether the sorcerer would laugh at her, she'd asked him for permission to take off her travel boots and enjoy the unfamiliar sensation under her feet.

Yet when he called her with a gesture, she was back at his side in an instant. From what little she'd learned to decipher from his expressions, he was pleased with her prompt reaction.

"Have you ever ridden a kampi?" he asked.

"No, master." She wouldn't admit it out loud, but she didn't even have an idea what the animal looked like—or if it was an animal at all. The world was primitive, but that didn't mean the people here couldn't have invented some unusual means of transportation. Her knowledge of Hyrinea was limited, and if needed, she was to claim her father never took her along on his travels. The notion of a sheltered and protected daughter who knew little of what lay beyond her own home should cover any of her slips.

He rubbed his chin. "It's four days' journey to the oasis. You'll ride with Tatho then."

She nodded. The servant seemed strong enough to keep her in place should she have trouble riding.

"The oasis, master?" she dared ask before he dismissed her again.

"This is where my house his. Once we arrive, you'll open the prism cube and pass the mastery of it to me."

"Yes, master." She hid her disappointment. Logic demanded that Malatrius nest the cube somewhere convenient, so he could explore the library at will, but she'd hoped he would keep her around to maintain the scrolls. Once the cube was opened and under his power, he'd not need her and she'd be unable to enter it without his permission.

Malatrius gave her a calculating look, but his expression softened. "You needn't worry about the future. I'll ensure you work for your upkeep but stay safe." He smirked. "Though I won't be personally overseeing you."

She didn't fall for the obvious bait. Malatrius was inviting her to attempt killing him during the last stretch of their journey with his veiled suggestion that she soon wouldn't have such a chance anymore.

"I didn't expect you would, master." As long as she was safe and near enough, she'd find a way to reach her goal.

"I admit, you're playing your role quite well." He leaned forward and looked her in the eye. "Or maybe I thought too highly of you... Are you a coward, Saeryn?"

"I keep my word, master. I entered the binding oath, didn't I?"

Malatrius smiled slyly. "The oath doesn't stop you from trying to kill me, because I never gave you an order that would forbid you from doing so. And if I die, the oath won't matter anymore."

"You're right, master," she replied with a hint of amusement. She'd discovered that Malatrius enjoyed when she participated in his games, even if it meant a bit of informality between them. "But aren't you concerned I could actually succeed?"

He looked content that she'd taken his bait. "I doubt you could, but I'm curious to find out." He paused and regarded her for a moment. "Something tells me, though, that I'll have to wait a little longer for it. Isn't that right?" At least he didn't call her a coward again.

She offered a bow. "I'm glad you don't expect me to murder you anytime soon, master."

He laughed. "For a moment, I doubted whether you were truly your father's daughter, but I see your mind is sharp and full of wit. It's a shame that you'll waste your life doing a slave's work."

"It's still better than not being alive at all, isn't it?" she replied. "Tides come and go. My father taught me patience."

"Did he also teach you that opportunities pass?"

With his now-mocking tone, it seemed better to cut the game short. "He did, master. Rest assured that I won't miss the opportunity I'm waiting for when it presents itself."

She had no doubt that he'd read her words as a poorly hidden desire to exact her revenge, but this seemed better than making him wonder what her true intentions were. If he was convinced she was after him, he could also give her an opportunity to act only to see if he could force her hand, and that meant he would be around every so often, despite what he'd said earlier about not overseeing her anymore. Those rare moments were all she needed for her plan to move forward.

And if he was convinced that he knew what she intended, her secrets would be safe.

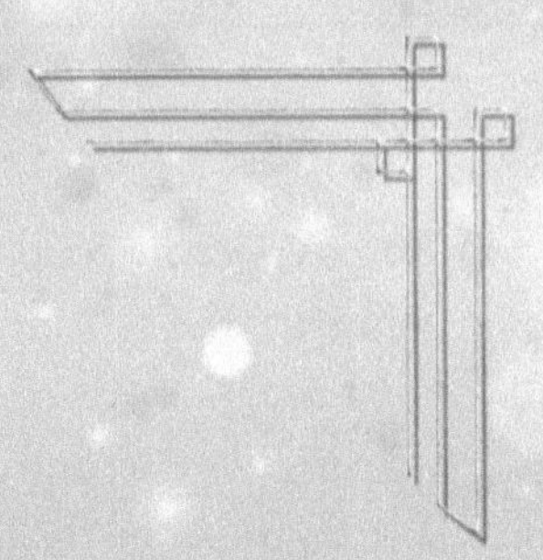

Chapter 5

Stepping through...

Malatrius's voice stirred me from my dream. I fought to stay asleep and grasp the last glimpses of memories. Only upon his insistence did I open my eyes as if I were still wrapped up in the servile attitude of my past self. At least now I understood better how enormous was the risk she... *I* had taken.

Judging by the shortened shadows, the morning had already shifted to noon, and the air over the sands rippled with the heat.

"It's time." Malatrius was sitting nearby, his expression weary and his forehead marked with beads of sweat. "If the dreams changed your mind, it's your last opportunity to turn back." He didn't even ask me if I'd dreamed at all.

I didn't hesitate. "I'm going."

The dreams had only reassured me that an important part of my memories was missing, and within them was a secret to uncover. No matter the danger, no matter the consequences, I craved those lost pieces of my life—exciting even if dangerous pieces, unlike anything I'd known.

He smiled softly as if rewarding me. "Come. I can't hold

the passageway long. We can talk on the other side." He pointed at the shifting air.

The empty space in front of us was not how I expected a passageway to appear, but I sensed energy there. It felt both familiar in the way it flowed and unfamiliar in the shape it took, and I understood that my senses were recognizing the magic itself, but not the spell and its function.

I wanted to study it more, taste the unfamiliar energies, but Malatrius was watching me expectantly, so I picked up my luggage and took several steps forward.

Sudden pressure left me breathless, and the air around swirled, hot and cold at the same time, blinding me and sending my head spinning. With nausea unsettling my stomach, I forced myself to take another step. The world darkened and disappeared, but the discomfort remained.

I kept walking, or at least it felt like I did, and soon the sensations passed.

My vision clear again, I found myself standing in a library full of shelves carved from gray stone. Countless scrolls and crude leather-bound books filled them, and symbols in the walls glimmered with mesmerizing rainbows, providing enough light to chase the darkness away even with no window in sight.

No dream was necessary. I knew this place—the prism cube library.

The air shifted with a hiss, as if filling a void, and Malatrius stepped in from nowhere.

"Welcome home."

The smile he gave me was full of warmth and—dare I say—friendliness, so different from the one the Malatrius in my memories had, but until I regained more of my past, there was no telling which of his expressions were the genuine ones.

"I prepared appropriate clothes for you, so we can go outside as soon as you change." He pointed to the nearby table.

I unfolded the fabric. My new outfit consisted of wide pants and a sleeveless tunic with an emerald scale-shaped emblem on the front, right above the heart, with the likeness of a black snake embroidered on it. Two other pieces of fabric gave me pause, but they must be what passed as lingerie in Hyrinea.

I stepped behind a shelf and changed my clothes in a rush stemming from anticipation rather than fear that Malatrius could catch a glimpse of my bare skin. For all I knew, he'd already seen all there was to see... Especially as he'd mentioned my scars that no one knew about.

When I joined him at the library's exit, he reached out and adjusted my tunic. "Keep the mark hidden. The Saeryn people know isn't my slave anymore."

That got me curious, but I doubted he'd share the details with me. "Couldn't you remove it, then?" After all, I didn't need it anymore—I had already restored the memory related to it.

"I will... when you remember why I removed it the first time." He stepped out of the library. "Do try to contain your excitement and curiosity. There will be time to see everything without raising the suspicion of people who know you well enough to expect composure."

Duly reprimanded, I exhaled slowly and forced a neutral expression onto my face. He was right. My past self had to be well acquainted with Malatrius's house, so I should act the part, no matter how many peculiar things I spotted.

We walked through the corridors of the vast three-story building. Each turn, each archway, and each room we passed screamed to me with memories. Images resurfaced, blurry and chaotic but nevertheless demanding attention, and I could hardly focus on where Malatrius was leading me.

Several servants and guards passed us by, their faces familiar even if I couldn't quite place them yet. They didn't react to me in any way when they offered a bow to Malatrius, which proved his words true: my presence by his side was something obvious and unsurprising. I had lived in this house, and I was a part of it. Of course, it could all be an elaborate ruse I was yet to discover, but with every step and every flash of an image I didn't know I remembered, I doubted Malatrius had orchestrated such deception. Within the walls of his house, there was enough truth for me to find.

Malatrius led me down to the kitchens, and the cook's voice sounded with familiar complaints at everyone's sluggishness, servants and slaves getting their share alike. I didn't have to see the woman to recall her face, pulpy and always red from the ovens' heat.

"Fas'hya," I whispered as her name resurfaced. "I carried water from the well and food from the pantry for her. And in the evening, I'd sit outside and scrub the smaller pots." Memories kept returning as I spoke, so ready and eager, like children vying for attention, as if they had never eluded me.

"Good." Malatrius gave an approving nod. "But you didn't stay in the kitchens long."

No explanation followed. Instead, he led me outside through the servants' door. I eyed the worn doorstep, fractured images telling me of countless times I had almost tripped over it, spilling some of the water I was carrying. Each time, Fas'hya scolded me, going on about useless slaves who sought to eat as much as they could and get away from the hardest tasks.

"Long enough to know she never dared hit me even though she was generous with the strikes of her wooden ladle with everyone else."

Malatrius smirked, and his old and wise expression shifted, revealing a more joyful and playful side, one I hoped was real for my own sake. "I swore to keep you safe. I didn't want my oath broken just because my cook had a bad day."

"She *only* had bad days," I murmured in response.

Every little detail was returning to me. My hands with blisters and my arms sore. Tiredness bending my back and hunger tightening my stomach. Malatrius was right when he said I might not want such memories back, but at the same time, every recollection made me feel a bit more whole. I didn't know what to expect when I crossed worlds and thought I'd be amazed by the odd, unfamiliar land or feel lost within it, but walking through Malatrius's house felt as familiar as entering my father's study.

I'd returned home, and I was starting to remember it.

As we walked into the courtyard, I caught sight of a lone wooden pole by the wall, and another memory struck unexpectedly.

ONE OF THE high-ranking servants brought news that Malatrius wanted everyone gathered in the inner yard by noon—all the servants, workers, and slaves. Fas'hya complained about it all morning, listing all the things that needed to be done for the evening meal, but she didn't dare oppose the master's order. She rushed through the food preparation, finishing what couldn't wait, and before noon arrived, Saeryn was on the brink of exhaustion.

She had never considered herself to have poor stamina, but her life until now had been easy. She wasn't prepared for such physical strain. Even after several months of serving in the kitchens, she still couldn't match the endurance of other slaves... Though how they did it was beyond her, as the food they all ate hardly helped build up body strength.

Shortly before midday, all the rooms emptied. Everyone walked outside, and the small crowd made Saeryn realize how many people lived under Malatrius's rule.

Months earlier, when she first arrived, she'd only caught a glimpse of a lush valley that had little to do with her concept of an "oasis." Malatrius's homestead was nested between tall rock formations that shielded it from the desert's expansion, and she noticed a pond and an orchard on the far side of the three-story building, which suggested that the secluded valley had plenty of water and that Malatrius made use of it and the land.

Yet to see all those people together was different than just having an idea. At least three dozen servants, even more guards, and orchard workers. There were some slaves too, from what she could tell, but it seemed Malatrius didn't rely on them. Perhaps, like her, they had made deals with the sorcerer or crossed him.

As people continued to gather, and Malatrius was nowhere in sight, she stole another glance toward the orchard, longing rising in her chest. To sit down in the trees' merciful shade and enjoy the breeze and a good book... But such thoughts belonged to her previous life, to Saeryn Arlothi-Mara, not to a sorcerer's daughter and another sorcerer's property.

Then Malatrius walked into the courtyard, and all her daydreams vanished. By the wall, a single wooden pole stood at the stone podium, and he climbed the three steps leading to it. Silence fell as he looked around at his subordinates, the dire kind of quietness laced with fear. Saeryn shivered when she realized that they knew what was coming, and it wouldn't be good.

"My enemies fear me and hate me, but those who serve me have nothing to be afraid of." In the morbid silence, his voice carried over the courtyard. "I take care of you all, providing food and shelter. You repay me with your work and loyalty. Yet, every now and then, a fool falls for the allure of my adversaries' gold and tries to take advantage of my generosity and trust."

He gave a signal, and his guards dragged out a middle-aged man. He wore a servant's tunic and fought with his captors every step of the way. His bewildered eyes seemed to be pleading, but he didn't try to say anything, and the way his lips moved made it clear they had been sealed with a spell.

Saeryn cringed. Once, Kithandar had used such a spell on her. She was only six or seven back then, but she should have known better than to argue with her father. Kithandar had kept the spell on her only for an hour, but she still remembered the torture of being unable to open her mouth, as if her lips were sewn together.

"This man forgot who his master is," Malatrius continued. His cold and detached voice contradicted his dramatic words, and together they seemed like a sinister prophecy. "He betrayed me, and he'll pay for it." He looked around at the crowd. "His punishment will also be a reminder to all of you that while loyalty is rewarded, betrayal will never go unpunished."

Saeryn fought to stand still when Malatrius's gaze stopped at her. Somehow, he'd picked her out of the crowd and made the message personal, even though so far she'd given him no reason to suspect her of deception or disobedience.

The guards tied the man to the pole and removed his tunic. With a small gesture, Malatrius removed the silencing spell, his control of magic nothing but masterful.

The man took in air as if barely reaching the water's surface before drowning. "Master, pl—"

The rest of his words shifted into a scream when the sorcerer cast another spell. This one placed a glowing symbol on the man's chest, the mark of a traitor, and even from this distance Saeryn couldn't miss the fiery worms slithering under the man's skin. Magic entered his bloodstream, burning his veins and spreading pain, but he lived on, as if the same magic kept him alive for the torture.

The people in the courtyard fidgeted. Their faces revealed poorly hidden fear, and Saeryn couldn't blame them. Such a punishment was beyond any cruelty they could have imagined, yet Malatrius stood unmoved, as if it were but a slap on a hand. Instead of watching his victim, he kept his eyes on the other servants. That gaze alone could ensure the loyalty of his subjects, replacing any doubts with fear and obedience.

Then, with the snap of Malatrius's finger, the man behind him became silent again, though his jerking body made it clear the torture hadn't ended.

"There's no need for anyone to listen to it any longer, but the traitor will remain here until his death," the sorcerer said. "Let this be a warning for anyone who carries treachery in their heart." His expression lost its cold edge. "On to brighter things, then. As a sign of my appreciation for your hard work and loyalty, all of you can enjoy an afternoon of rest. Those who still have work that must be done will be able to rest in the morning instead."

Saeryn almost snorted at the clear carrot-and-stick approach, but people around her seemed excited by the prospect of rest. And nobody pitied a man who was foolish enough to betray Malatrius.

"I'm also in need of another scribe now, so before I search for one elsewhere, I'm willing to give a chance to any of the slaves or lower servants who can read and write in vizari," Malatrius added.

To Saeryn's surprise, the crowd stirred, and a young slave pushed through to stand in front of Malatrius.

"Very well. Anyone else?"

Saeryn hesitated. Even though the sorcerer never looked at her, she had no doubt he expected her to step forward as well. It would be better to keep away, avoiding the obvious bait, but at the same time, volunteering could mean the opportunity she needed. Staying in the kitchens was staying safe from Malatrius's games, but also meant throwing away her life doing simple labor... Much like the sorcerer had told her before they arrived at his homestead.

She stepped out of the crowd and stood beside the man, who threw a jealous glare at her. His worn clothes and thin, wiry body suggested he worked harder than she did, or had simply been in Malatrius's service much longer, so he was more desperate for the chance. Yet his attitude wiped away all of her compassion, and the voice of reason reminded her that in her position, she couldn't afford to be charitable.

"Follow him"—Malatrius pointed at a man standing nearby—"and do what he says."

The man wore the robes of a high-ranking servant. He led them both through the building to its east wing. Saeryn held her breath when they entered a vast hall. There were seven rows of bookshelves that seemed to stretch endlessly. The amount of knowledge gathered there...! Until now, she'd thought her father's library in the prism cube was an endless treasury of secrets and magic, but it paled in comparison with Malatrius's collection. She couldn't help wondering whether the sorcerer would have made the trade back in Kithandar's castle if he'd known how little he'd be gaining in exchange for the binding oath.

In front of the shelves, by the large windows, was a small area with five tables, four arranged in opposing pairs, and one facing the others.

"Sit down there and there." The man pointed at two opposite tables. He handed out two scrolls each, one filled with text and one blank. "You are to copy those scripts to the best of your abilities. I'll judge both your speed and precision."

Saeryn took the quill in her hand. The text was a tricky one. It contained a spell in vizari using several similar symbols, but she should be able to copy it. Of course, the other candidate might be more skilled. His dark, curly hair suggested he'd been born in the local lands, so he probably knew the language better. Yet the way he furrowed his brow inspecting the scroll gave her hope.

"I'll be in the back." Their supervisor flipped an hour-glass. As soon as the oily liquid started dripping, he headed for the bookshelves.

She focused on her work, not bothered if he was spying on their progress. Time was too precious to waste on anything but the task. Engrossed in her work, she paid no attention to her surroundings, but when a shadow fell over her scroll, she reacted instinctively—she picked it up, keeping it close to her chest, like an artisan protecting her trade secrets.

The adrenaline in her veins made her worry less about possible smudges and more about the young slave who stood over her with an ink pot in his hand and a malicious smile on his face.

"Don't you even *try*," she spat, putting all the hostility she could muster into her voice. To be beaten in a fair test of skill was one thing, but to fall for subterfuge another. If her opponent tried to use force, she would make enough of a ruckus to draw their supervisor back to them.

The slave grinned at her but took a step back. She kept watching him until he put the ink pot away. To her surprise, he didn't sit back at his table. Instead, he headed toward the shelves.

She focused back on her work. Soon enough, the sounds of carnal pleasure distracted her, and she grimaced. It seemed that the young slave had found another way to secure his victory.

Disheartened, Saeryn put the quill away, but a heartbeat later, she resumed her work. Just because she was better than her rival, that didn't mean she was good enough, and she needed the transcription finished in time.

She was done shortly before the last drips in the hourglass announced the end of the allotted time. The grunts and moans coming from behind the shelves died out, and the slave returned to his desk, his smug stare like a challenge for her.

Their supervisor emerged as well. He said nothing, though his flushed face suggested he had enjoyed the intercourse, and Saeryn gave up on checking her scroll for anything she might have missed. Either he'd already made up his mind, or her work would be better than an empty scroll, even if she let a few mistakes slip by.

She froze when he collected the scrolls. She hadn't thought of signing hers, so she had no way of proving she'd done all the work. The man inspected her copy briefly, in a manner that suggested he was looking for specific parts and mistakes.

"Are they done?" Malatrius walked in, accompanied by a guard.

The man bowed. "Yes, master."

"And is either of them skilled enough?"

Saeryn held her breath when the supervisor handed her scroll to Malatrius.

"The woman, master. She'll need some schooling and practice, but she can copy scrolls well and quickly enough," he said. "The man should be a whore, not a scribe."

"Very well." Malatrius looked at Saeryn, but his expression offered no clues as to what his thoughts were. "You're the new scribe, then. Listen to Gallo as obediently as you listened to Fas'hya. And as for him..." He pointed at the young slave as he turned to the guard. "I have no place for deceivers here. Take him to the pens and tell the slave master I want him sold as soon as traders pass by. I don't care what kind of coin I get for him."

Malatrius looked back at Saeryn, his expression inscrutable, and then left.

As she watched the guard drag the other slave away, the disbelief on the young man's face brought a strange satisfaction. He must have been so certain that he'd secured his new position, and Gallo had played him. But that realization made her confidence fade. Around a man like that, she'd have to be on her guard all the time.

Gallo approached, his expression serious but devoid of

the slyness she'd have expected from such a duplicitous man.

"Let this be a lesson to you," he said. "You're free to take advantage of what's offered, but never at the price of deceiving your master."

She understood. "You didn't promise him anything."

"Good. You're smart." He nodded with satisfaction as if she'd passed another test. "Come, I'll show you everything. Scribes sleep in the room next to the library and eat their meals in the servants' hall. We wake up at dawn and work all day, but if you become weary, you come and tell me. There are other tasks you can perform while your mind and eyes rest."

She arched an eyebrow at that, though she doubted anyone was fool enough to abuse Gallo's generosity. In the end, work had to be finished one way or another, so if one dawdled too much, they likely had to work long into the night. Still, copying scrolls was something she was accustomed to and much less strenuous than carrying heavy things around. She could already see the benefits of the advancement.

And, most important, her new role meant she would likely see Malatrius more often.

ARMED WITH MY NEW MEMORIES, I found the library with ease.

On our way there, I tried not to stare, but Malatrius's house was stunning. As far as I knew, Hyrinea was not as developed as my own world, but everything was of the best quality and craftsmanship, and well kept as well. Floors of polished wood and stone had no spots nor dust, and walls covered with some kind of gypsum were adorned with subtle reliefs and occasional tapestries. Everything around me made it clear I was in the house of a rich man—one who had taste and didn't flaunt his wealth with tacky decorations.

Still, as I walked through the impressive corridors with the surprising confidence of someone who knew their way, the memory of the tortured man still lingered, reminding me that Malatrius wasn't exactly a benevolent nobleman, and the echo of fear I'd felt back then reverberated in my bones.

To suppress this too-vivid image, I focused on the prospect of finding another piece of my past. I had no doubt it would reveal itself if I sat at the scribe's desk. Yet when we reached the door leading to the library, Malatrius barred my entry with a quick gesture.

"Not now," he whispered, even though there wasn't anyone within earshot. "If you feel it could restore some minor memories, you can visit later. I'll find a suitable excuse for you. But until you remember enough of what you forgot to become a true part of this household again, you'll eat and sleep in the prism cube." He smiled. "You can have your room back—when you remember where it is."

"*My* room?"

His words were the ultimate tease. Not a slave anymore, but a part of his household. I guessed I'd held a position of significance, though undoubtedly this would be something he expected me to discover on my own.

Perhaps it was for the best. Past Saeryn, whom I still couldn't bring myself to call "me," was intent on getting into Malatrius's good graces, but I had no idea to what end. If there were memories I feared to recover, they had to do with lies she might have told and plots she might have spun.

I might be naïve for thinking so, but Malatrius seemed to trust me. If in the past I'd repaid him with dishonesty or treachery, I'd rather not know... But perhaps I *should* know. The words of the oath that had bound the sorcerer with Past Saeryn made it clear how any disobedience or deception would have ended. She might have died paying for what she did, and if I wasn't careful, I could pay for her transgressions too.

He resumed his stroll, so I had no choice but to follow him. "All in good time," he said.

"When I remember." I couldn't prevent my complaining tone. No matter what he claimed about how it was better if I restored my memories on my own, he did have control over them, deciding which ones he would help me find.

His sudden turn made me plant my feet firmly on the floor to avoid bumping into him.

"You remembered a lot already, and hardly any of it was pleasant, was it?" His green gaze was intense. "Those memories won't get any easier."

Soundlessly, I ground my teeth. "Sooner or later, I'll have to remember." I hadn't come to another world to settle for half-truths and vague answers.

He regarded me in thought. "You used to be... more careful."

The note of regret in his voice grated on my calm, because it felt as if he was telling me I was inferior to my former self, not good enough to be called Saeryn.

A servant passed by, and his bewildered glance at me suggested I was letting too much emotion show. I reined in as much as I could and met Malatrius's eyes.

"If I don't remember soon enough..." I nodded to indicate the servant's back. "Mistakes are bound to happen, and the less I know, the more likely I'll do something I shouldn't. Unless there's a reason you prefer me without my memories?"

He became serious and grim, but his voice didn't carry the anger I expected after my veiled accusation. "If I were certain you could endure it, I'd try to make you remember it all. But it won't do either of us any good if you crumble under the weight of those memories." He offered a meager smile. "I have a keen interest in restoring your memory, so if you think you can handle more..."

"Yes."

I cared little whether he spoke out of genuine concern or if it was a veiled way to discourage me from wanting more. I cared even less about why he claimed to be in a rush to make me remember. All I wanted was to feel whole again.

His expression changed, as if my response had met his expectations. "Then let's see if you can remember how you stopped being a slave."

According to his own words, Past Saeryn had spent three years in his house. No matter how much cunning and deception she might have used, it seemed unlikely she would advance in the ranks so quickly, not while Malatrius still believed she was bent on revenge.

Therefore the memory he intended to bring back must be a later one and likely out of order, but I could see wisdom in his choice. As much as I wanted to restore all of it, I needed to know the most important parts first. It would give me confidence in playing my role for others, and... in dealing with him.

He led us through the house, to its central part. The limestone walls were carved with ornaments, and filigree columns supported the ceiling. The marble-like floor shone, polished so much it resembled a black mirror or a frozen lake during a moonless night.

When we walked into a large atrium, it struck a familiar chord with its low table in the middle, surrounded with cushioned benches. I'd seen it before, that much was certain, but the reason Malatrius had brought me here remained unclear. No memory returned.

"Nothing." With so many things coming back to me, the sudden lack of images brought disappointment. Perhaps whatever had happened in this place wasn't important enough for my mind to cling to. Perhaps some memories were meant to be lost forever.

"I think you'll need something more than just the room itself," Malatrius said with an amused smile.

His lack of concern was equal parts reassuring and unnerving, but if I wanted my memories back, I had to play his game, so I took the bait. "Something more?"

"This."

Without warning, he stepped forward and held my chin in a forceful manner. Before I could react, he pulled me closer and kissed me.

I pushed away, anger and fear stirring within me, many unpleasant thoughts gathering on my tongue, ready to be expressed.

Malatrius stood in front of me, unmoved and calculating, as if his assault and my meager retaliation were of no consequence to his schemes. After such a display, I didn't care about playing my role or checking if we were alone. I would not hold back in telling him what I thought of it.

"I will not tole—"

Memories flooded me like water from a breached dam.

Chapter 6

...and into the past

The scribes ate better, slept more comfortably, and enjoyed a bath once every ten days or so. They didn't carry heavy buckets and bags, so Saeryn recovered from exhaustion and came to find joy in her work. Most of it was mundane copying, but it allowed her to broaden her vizari vocabulary. Every now and then, something looked odd in a scroll, and Gallo allowed her to do her own research. Once he learned she wasn't using it to avoid work, he stopped checking on her as often, and she enjoyed some freedom.

That small privilege earned her jealous glares from other scribes, two women and one man, but none acted against her. It seemed that even though they all wanted Gallo's favor, they weren't desperate enough to try anything underhanded, and she understood why whenever she thought of the previous scribe's punishment. No one would risk such severe consequences just to damage a potential rival.

Still, Saeryn tried to be helpful and humble whenever she could, and she was careful to not to draw attention to her progress and small successes so that they would see no reason to ignore the risks and unite against her. She couldn't afford to make enemies.

The only disappointment was Malatrius's absence. It seemed that he was happy enough with Gallo overseeing the library, and he never visited to consult countless books and scrolls. Nevertheless, she had hoped that after giving her a place among the scribes, Malatrius would come around, if only to tease her or initiate one of his games. As much as she had to tread carefully amongst his verbal baiting, his presence was necessary for her plan. A more comfortable life was quite an advantage over working in the kitchens, but she needed more.

Yet she armed herself with patience. Malatrius might be testing her with his absence, waiting for her one unscrupulous move that would free him from the oath. So instead of letting anxiety rule her thoughts, she occupied her mind with countless tasks and let days pass uncounted.

That day, they were all working on part of a large transcription, copying half-faded symbols from a collection of old scrolls. As always, it was quiet work, with only the sounds of the quills on parchments disturbing the silence. Gallo was sitting at his desk, busy checking their work so far.

When Malatrius walked into the room unannounced, Gallo was first to notice and stand up, but all the scribes followed soon after, their heads bent in a bow.

"Go back to work," he said as he exchanged a jovial nod with Gallo.

Saeryn didn't get to sit back down, as the sorcerer approached her desk.

"Come with me," he ordered her and headed for the door.

Her heartbeat drumming in her ears, she rushed after him. They were alone in the corridor, but Malatrius didn't even look over his shoulder, as if he knew she wasn't going to attack him. Nevertheless, Saeryn kept two steps behind him, matching his pace.

They didn't go far. Malatrius entered one of the rooms a few corridors away.

It didn't escape her that the door was sturdy and heavy and had an iron lock. Inside, shelves stood along the walls filled with scripts and books, and in the middle of the room there was a long table made of dark wood with one comfortable chair by it. If Saeryn was to guess, she had just entered Malatrius's study.

She gave it an appraising look. No wonder he never visited his library with so much knowledge in hand's reach.

Malatrius approached the table and picked up a scroll. Then he turned to her.

"If you were to copy this and intentionally make mistakes that would cause the spell to become useless, what would the changes be?" He handed the scroll to her.

She took it, but she'd rather have let it drop to the ground as if it were a venomous snake. Malatrius's expression offered no clue, and she wouldn't put it past him to accuse her of being intentionally sloppy with her new duties.

"It's a simple question."

That made her drop her gaze to the scroll immediately. "If it's not supposed to be obvious," she said with caution, aware that she was about to reveal how much she really knew of magic, "I'd alter it here, here, and here." She held the scroll up to him so that he could see where she pointed. "That should be enough to disrupt the spell, but it wouldn't be easy to spot. The most common mistakes are always wrongly copied symbols, so this way it would look like the scribe's rushed work if someone cared to check."

He studied the parts she pointed at and nodded with satisfaction. "Very well." He eyed her, his expression calculating. "Have you ever been with a man? Do you know how to please one?"

The question left her gaping, but she had no choice but to answer. "Yes," was all she managed. She'd rather not discuss her meager, if pleasant, experiences in that regard.

Malatrius nodded once more. "You seem capable, so I'll offer you a chance to win your freedom. If you do well, I'll ensure that your future is much brighter than a slave's plight."

"What would I have to do?" she asked without hesitation. Such a chance, to win not her freedom but his trust, wouldn't repeat itself.

"You'll make a man believe he seduced you, and you'll do as he says. He'll likely ask you to steal or copy a scroll from my library. Which, I don't know."

She took a step back. The screams of the scribe whose position she'd taken sounded in her mind so clearly that she could as well be watching the poor man's torment all over again. "You're setting me up to fail, master. I either disobey you or act against you."

"Cautious, as always." Malatrius smiled. "You needn't worry. I'm not trying to find a way to dissolve the oath. Gallo is happy with you, and I see no reason to rid him of a good scribe. All I want is the man who bribed my former servant. He'll be visiting soon, believing he's here to collect some of my secrets. I'm hoping that when he learns of the double-crosser's death, he'll try to get what he needs through other means." His green eyes locked on her. "You."

"You want him to believe I'd betray you." Despite his reassurances, Saeryn couldn't help being suspicious.

"This will require us both to bend the oath some," Malatrius said, as if reading her mind. "You'll have to behave as if you are disobeying me, and I'll have to punish you for that. Nothing that will threaten your life or maim you, but painful enough to convince everyone you crossed me."

"And you're trusting *me* with such a task?"

He spread his arms. "I have no one else. Gallo is too loyal for anyone to believe he'd take a stranger's coin, and all the other scribes lack the flexible minds they'd need to carry out the task. You seem to have the skills I need and enough wits to make your own decisions as appropriate. You also won't be foolish enough to side with a man to whom you're nothing but a tool. But if I'm wrong, and I learn about it"— he smiled slyly—"*then* you'd free me from my oath."

He was right. Siding with someone who wasn't a true ally would bring her nothing.

The smile faded from Malatrius's face. "But you have to decide for yourself whether you want to play that game. What I have in mind requires your commitment, so if you're worried that I'm setting a trap for you, I'll have no use for you."

He put the ritual knife on the table, leaving her to make the choice. He didn't know that she couldn't afford to refuse.

Saeryn took the blade and whispered several words from the binding oath. Magic condensed around her, waiting, powerful, and hungry. With the knife's tip, she pierced the skin on her scar, allowing one drop of blood to gather on the wound.

"I'll do what you ask me to do, and I'll be disobedient in

the ways you ask me to be. I'll also recognize that any harm I might suffer because of that will be the consequence of my own deeds."

She finished with the ending words of the binding oath. For a heartbeat, it felt like all the magic around her focused into that one drop of blood—an intense power bringing about instinctual fear—and then it was gone without a trace.

Malatrius was watching her, his smile wide in clear amusement. "Always so very careful... I admit, I'll be sincerely saddened upon the day of your true betrayal."

THE OUTFIT she wore revealed more than she'd like, but it was a necessary part of the deception. Plain scribe clothes would hardly fit when other women wore breast scarves and revealing waist pieces, and men's outfits were even skimpier.

Thin, narrow silks flowed with her every move, letting the skin of her legs flash underneath. An outfit of a pleasure slave that made it clear what her role was—at least for a day.

Malatrius, three other men, and two women were leisurely sitting or lying on their long benches when Saeryn walked in. The sorcerer had prepared her well, so she immediately matched everyone's names to their faces but kept the knowledge to herself.

The food on the long, low table in the middle of the room proved that Fas'hya had gone above and beyond to prepare a feast worthy of kings, and five other slaves were already serving Malatrius's guests.

"I see you've finally joined us," Malatrius said in a mocking tone. "Maybe being treated like a slave for a day will teach you some obedience and humility."

She gave him a defiant stare. "You weren't supposed to put me to work."

Malatrius laughed, and she envied the ease with which he played his role... but unlike hers, his wasn't far from how he normally behaved.

"Feel free to complain to your father." He then turned his attention to his guests. "Forgive me that moment of amusement. Her father and I have an arrangement that this little bird is an assurance of. Yet we seem to have different ideas about the role she's to have in my household, and she's been forgetting herself lately." He looked back at Saeryn, giving her one of his cold and unyielding glares. "Therefore, she will be *happy* to serve all of you today."

She huffed, lifting her chin in an expression of pride and rebellion. This was behavior everyone would expect from a powerful sorcerer's daughter, yet she felt strange acting this way, because even though Kithandar showed her caring and gave her attention, he would not tolerate any rebellious or self-indulgent behavior.

Malatrius smirked maliciously. "Or maybe I should make you my concubine instead?"

He grabbed her arm, and she lost her balance, landing on him. His hands skimmed her curves, and then, holding her chin, he forced a kiss. Saeryn didn't miss the focused expression and slightly narrowed eyes that made it clear it was part of the deception, but as she pushed him away, her face flushed and heart racing, she couldn't help wondering how far the sorcerer would go to make others believe it was real.

"You're not to touch me! Ever! I can do a scribe's work for you, but that's it!" she shouted at him.

Malatrius laughed and waved dismissively as if her outburst amused him. "Do well today, and I'll let you go back to playing with scrolls. I might even remove that slave mark."

She grimaced but grabbed a jug of wine and walked over to the other guests. Most seemed entertained by her display, likely having dealt with similar rebellious servants, but one was looking at her with peculiar interest, and despite the unease that Malatrius's behavior had stirred, she cherished the triumph of their little display.

It was her suggestion to play it out that way—even if she hadn't known Malatrius would push the deception as far as he did—so that Davarn, their target, would think she was easy to sway. The hostage daughter of another sorcerer had every reason to go against her master.

She sent Davarn a teasing smile, but instead of serving him wine, she headed over to one of the women, Bassaja. Even though the sorceress was past her prime, the years had made her look wise and composed, like the kind of powerful woman Saeryn hoped to become one day. According to Malatrius, Bassaja was also cruel and calculating rather than benevolent and thoughtful—but then, so were most powerful sorcerers.

Saeryn refilled her cup, but when she leaned closer, Bassaja waved her off, expression wary, as if she didn't want to become part of the conflict between Malatrius and Saeryn—especially not on her side. Saeryn sent her a wide smile, letting the sorceress believe she saw through the game being played.

She made rounds with the guests, but to her disappointment, Davarn didn't call her over. He seemed to enjoy watching her behave in a rebellious manner and throw challenging glances at their host. Mindful of the trap she was setting, she focused on others instead, serving food and refilling their wine. It was easy to ignore their condescending smirks and amused expressions when she knew she was playing the game alongside Malatrius, not against him.

Yet whenever the sorcerer called her over, she ignored him in favor of his guests. She'd made enough displays of disobedience to break a hundred oaths already, let alone one, and even if she did so with the protection of their agreement, every defiant act still tied her stomach in knots. After so much time spent in Malatrius's homestead, obedience and fear had become parts of her very being.

She didn't pay much attention to the conversation. Important topics wouldn't be broached with slaves present, and undoubtedly each of the guests would prefer to discuss private matters with the sorcerer alone. The gathering was nothing more than a show of Malatrius's wealth and power, or perhaps some custom she wasn't aware of.

As the meal was coming to an end, Davarn gestured to her to refill his cup. Their eyes met, and as she leaned forward to pour the wine, he cupped her curves and pulled her closer. She didn't fight when he kissed her. He tasted of wine and kissed well enough to make it quite passionate.

Saeryn tried to ignore the thought that she'd likely have to sleep with him as well. His physique wasn't appalling for a man who spent his time on scrolls and mystic arts, but she would be only a toy and a tool for him, and a trace of disgust for herself lingered in her mind. Yet she let nothing show on her face. There were worse things she would do to see her plan come to fruition, and gaining Malatrius's trust was worth any price.

"If you're done with your pitiful display, clear out the dishes and go," Malatrius said all of a sudden.

He sounded like a man who was trying to hide his jealousy, and when Davarn smiled at that, so did she.

The fish had taken the bait.

Saeryn stretched out on the large bed, enjoying the soft covers and silence. For the time being, Malatrius had given her a separate room that fitted her position of a sorcerer's daughter being held hostage. It also allowed her to move freely without drawing the attention of the other scribes. Gallo was aware of the plot, as she needed more freedom in the library as well, but the sorcerer hadn't told anyone else. Malatrius had admitted that as much as he trusted most of his servants, he couldn't be sure Davarn didn't have an accomplice among them.

Beyond the curtained window, a new day was rising, but she knew it would be at least an hour before her companion woke up. On previous days she'd left early to get to work on time, but the game was coming to an end, and Malatrius had insisted she be in the room for its final part.

Davarn had turned out to be mediocre lover, and after the third night, only her goal kept her playing the role, that of a naïve girl who had fallen for the most attractive man she'd ever met. It worked well on someone as vain as Davarn, and she made him believe that his false compassion for her sad plight had swayed her to his side.

At least watching him weave a net of deception full of calculated compliments and fiery reassurances provided some amusement. Her initial concerns had faded quickly when it became clear that he had no idea he was falling into a trap instead of setting one.

On the second night, she'd let him believe he had manipulated her into helping him in exchange for his assistance in regaining her freedom. As Malatrius predicted,

Davarn had asked her to copy a spell scroll from the sorcerer's library. She complied, and the copy—altered and useless—rested hidden in Davarn's robes, now lying on the floor, as he'd undressed the previous night to seek more pleasure with her.

She'd kept nodding at his promises that he'd be back for her as soon as possible while he sated his carnal needs with her body, and she counted the hours until dawn. He didn't know that after she was done with copying and altering the scroll, she'd leave a sign for Gallo to pass to the sorcerer, so that Malatrius could end the game. Three nights with Davarn were more than enough for a lifetime.

The door to her room swung open unexpectedly, and Malatrius walked in as if he'd answered her voiceless summons.

"Get up," he demanded. "Today you will work on—"

If she didn't know better, she'd think the shock on his face was genuine. It seemed that no matter what the sorcerer did, he always excelled at it.

Davarn stirred in his sleep and sat up, looking at Malatrius half-awake and confused, but Saeryn didn't wait for him to react.

"What? Jealous that I found a man worthy of my attention?" She left the bed, standing in front of the sorcerer naked and defiant, even though both her nature and her upbringing demanded she cover herself.

"Disappointed," he corrected her in an ice-cold voice. "I thought you knew how a person in your position should behave. It seems that I've tolerated your whims for too long. Guard!" He didn't even turn to the door as he called out. A man entered a moment later, and Saeryn had to hide a smile. In his house, Malatrius never bothered with a personal guard, so the man had to have been told to wait nearby. "Get her to the yard and have the slave master give her three lashes."

"You wouldn't *dare...*" she said, unsure how real his threat was.

With so many things uncertain, they hadn't agreed on how she was to behave when discovered, but she knew that the woman she was pretending to be wouldn't submit too easily.

"Oh yes, I would." Malatrius's fury seemed so real, it forced a shiver out of her. "And if you say one more word or try to defy me again, tonight you'll be serving food to my guards, and I'll make sure they know to enjoy... your company."

The last remark reassured her that Malatrius was only acting. Were he truly angered with her, he'd have mentioned the oath in some veiled way.

To hide the unexpected relief, she hung her head in a mock bow. "Yes, master." After all, even a rebellious hostage knew the lines she shouldn't cross.

"Finally, some obedience," Malatrius commented. Then he waved at the guard to approach. "Once the slave master is done with her punishment, bring her back here. I don't want anyone else entering."

At least the guard let her put a tunic on before dragging her out of the room. It didn't cover much, but it was still better than walking through the mansion without any clothes on.

From the corridor, she heard Malatrius say, "As for you, Davarn, I think you've overstayed your welcome. No matter how seductive this little viper was, you should have known better than to abuse my hospitality."

She didn't catch the details of Davarn's rushed response, only his apologetic tone, but she had no doubt that he blamed her for what had transpired. After all, with the scroll already in his possession, she was useless to him. The thought of being a tool to be thrown away stung, but he'd been nothing more than a tool to her as well. She could only hope her sacrifice was worth the reward. Otherwise the punishment she was about to suffer would be for naught, and in the end, she'd have been a mere tool for not only Davarn but also Malatrius.

THE WOUNDS from the lashing burned and ached, and Saeryn fought tears. She wouldn't allow herself to cry, even alone in the room that wasn't truly hers. She'd shown enough weakness earlier, tied to the pole in the yard and whipped, when she could hold back neither her screams nor tears. Only three lashes, but each felt like a strike splitting her back in half, and even though Malatrius didn't come down to the yard, she couldn't help wondering whether he was watching from afar... whether he enjoyed her suffering, the very suffering she'd agreed to herself. Or perhaps he hoped that seemingly undeserved pain would ignite her anger and make her act against him. No matter how well she might have served his plans, it didn't mean he was beyond using them to achieve his other goals.

With grim thoughts crowding her mind and gathering tears blurring her vision, she dipped a cloth in a bowl. Water trickled down the wounds as she squeezed it over her shoulder, and she could only hope to wash off most of the blood this way. Later, when she mustered enough courage, she'd check the extent of her injuries in the polished metal mirror.

Malatrius walked in, holding a small container. She

flinched when he sat behind her, but let him inspect her naked back.

His finger traced the edges of the wounds, and he hissed with disapproval. "I told him to hit *light*." He took the cloth from her hand. "Lie down."

Without delay, she stretched out on the bed. Now that the game was over, she wouldn't risk the slightest disobedience, regardless of whether the wound on her wrist healed or not.

To her surprise, Malatrius rinsed the cloth and washed her back, his moves gentle, as if he didn't want to cause her more pain. The thought that the Sorcerer from the Desert himself was seeing to his slave's wellbeing was a peculiar one, but it also suggested that he wouldn't go back on his promise.

"You did well." He opened a container he'd brought with him and applied a cold paste to her back. "This will help your wounds heal. Unfortunately, scars will likely remain. I'll have a word with the slave master, and I could even punish him for disobeying me, but it won't help your skin."

"Why did you insist on doing it this way, master? As much as I'm glad to be free of Davarn's company, I could have endured a few days more, until he left on his own."

"I did it to protect you. Davarn is a vengeful man, and if he suspected he'd been played, he could come after you. But since he witnessed your punishment as he was leaving, he won't even *think* that you could have been doing my bidding."

His reply made her eyes widen. If he wanted to be free of his oath, it would have been better to leave Davarn doubtful, or even sow suspicion, yet Malatrius had wanted to ensure her safety.

"I appreciate it, master," she said.

"What you did will allow me to find out whom he is serving and who desired the knowledge I possess," Malatrius said, "and then I'll ensure that no one else even entertains such thoughts for a long time to come."

She didn't miss the hard note in his voice that contradicted the gentleness with which he treated her wounds. The Sorcerer from the Desert truly had two sides to his nature, and she had no doubt that only fools thought they could withstand his cold anger and calculating revenge, while she began to understand why many served him so loyally.

"Now, about your reward," he continued. "I cannot free you right away without raising questions, but after some time passes, I'll arrange an escort to a nearby city for you, and you'll receive coin that will allow you to live comfortably... for quite a while, if you aren't wasteful. If you wish to stay here and continue serving me, you'll no longer be a slave, and I'll allow you to hold a position and duties of your choosing. Within reason, of course."

Saeryn didn't hide her surprise. The reward far exceeded the work she'd done. If she wanted, she could leave, having only scars to remind her of what she'd endured, but such a choice would lead her away from her goals, even further than when Malatrius marched into her father's castle, his power breaking through every protection Kithandar raised.

She needed that power, and she needed his trust as well.

"I want to stay." She sat up to look at him. "I enjoy working with scrolls and studying them, but I'd prefer to choose my own work. My father's library contains many secrets, unknown even to me, so if you trust me enough to let me work there, I'm sure I'll be able to bring worthwhile findings to your attention."

Malatrius smiled as he put the small container with the healing paste to the side. "Still thinking of killing me?" he asked casually.

She shook her head. "Why would I want to go out into the world where there are threats I can't even imagine? If I stay here, the binding oath will keep me safe."

His smile became cunning, almost predatory. "And if you stay, you'll also be able to broaden your knowledge of the arts while you work through the contents of your father's library."

"I would expect that to happen, yes." To lie in a moment like that would destroy the trust she'd worked so hard to win.

He seemed pleased with her admission. "I suspected you weren't being entirely forthcoming. How much of the arts do you really know?"

"I told you the truth back when you first asked, master," she replied without hesitation, "though I admit that I wasn't eager to share details. I don't know enough to be a real threat to your life or power, but you could have considered me as such if you knew." When one tried to keep things hidden, such openness didn't come easy, especially not with the man who—oath or not—held her life in his hands.

He nodded as if her answer wasn't a surprise to him. "And how many other secrets do you keep from me?"

Saeryn swallowed. His question meant it was time to give trust, not just seek it. "Just one. Please, master, don't make me reveal it. I can't... yet."

"But you will reveal it when the time comes?" He arched his eyebrow as if this were nothing but a word game, and the secret was of no interest to him. "Or will it reveal itself when you finally make an attempt to kill me?"

She couldn't help smiling at that. As much as she wasn't ready to share the truth yet, she could give him a piece of the puzzle and perhaps put his suspicions to rest. "No, master. It's connected to my death, not yours."

Ever since Malatrius arrived at the castle, she'd seen many of his expressions and read many feelings behind them. Yet this was the first time his face revealed sincere surprise.

"Now that's something I did not expect."

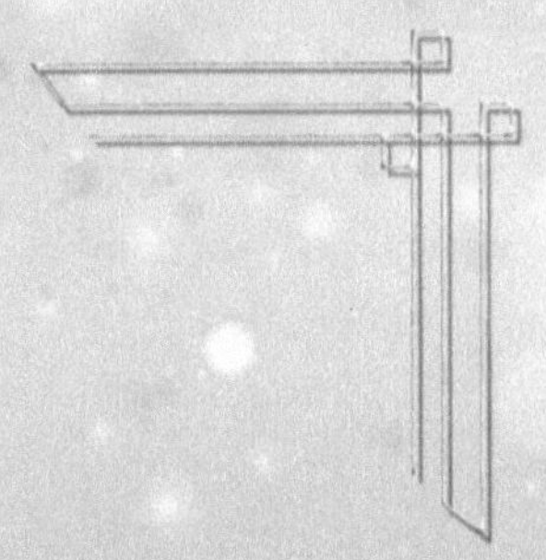

Chapter 7

The paths taken once already

I still tasted Malatrius on my lips when the wave of memories finally released me.

The sorcerer stood a few steps away, composed and calculating, proving that no matter how much that kiss shook my composure, he hadn't meant it as anything but a way to help me remember.

This wave of recollections had been so strong, I'd lost track of time, and couldn't even tell how long we'd stood like that. And even though I was back in the present, my back still burned with pain long gone but revived through a memory too vivid to be comfortable. I didn't want to dwell on it, so I looked at Malatrius in search of answers.

"You knew I was keeping things from you." Until now I'd believed that Past Saeryn had managed to keep her own plans secret, and she had succeeded at whatever goal they were leading to. On the other hand, it was likely a foolish assumption, considering she'd ended up dying. "But you didn't use it to break free from the oath."

No matter how my past self had met her demise, I was

strangely certain it hadn't happened right after that conversation.

"You said it yourself back then," Malatrius replied. "You didn't pose a real threat to me, and I was growing curious. You might have been an excellent liar, perhaps you still are, but you did seem honest when you claimed you didn't want me dead. I could understand that you were too reasonable to throw away your own life in the name of avenging a dead man, but I didn't know any reason for you to want to stay in my household when I promised you freedom and wealth as a reward."

He talked to me as if I had been the one to say those things. Yet I found it hard to even comprehend how I could have found enough resolve to sleep with a man not out of love or even lust, but as a means to an end. Something must have been so important that Past Saeryn was willing to do things I would never even consider, and it made me reel with disgust that I had supposedly already done them.

In a way, Malatrius was right. The memories weren't getting easier. When all was done, I could end up hating her... Hating the woman my memories claimed I was.

Under Malatrius's inquisitive stare, I concealed my emotions. He claimed that the previous Saeryn was cunning, so whether I liked it or not, I had to put this skill to work—assuming any of it survived my memory loss.

"So you decided to give me what I wished for and see what I'd make of it," I replied lightly.

I remembered that too. The day after the lashing, Malatrius had stormed into the library complaining about the state of my father's collection and demanded I immediately start sorting the mess my father had left. I'd still spent mornings doing work for Gallo, but afternoons were mine for long months to come. Exactly like she, like *I*, had wanted—

no matter how mismatched my own thoughts felt to those belonging to Past Saeryn, I had to start thinking of those memories as my own. Others would certainly believe them to be. It was easy enough in conversation, especially as I wanted Malatrius to believe that I was once more becoming who I had been, but in my mind we still remained separate.

And though I hated to even entertain such a thought, I had to consider that she and I might never become one.

"And in the end, you proved a loyal servant and quite a promising student," Malatrius said.

"A student? I don't remember that."

The past me had confessed to being schooled in magic, and my father had mentioned teaching me as well, but I had no recollection of it. So far, all my lost memories were connected to Hyrinea, so if I had learned any magic before that, I should have remembered it by now. The thought that it was gone forever, without me ever knowing how it truly felt, relying on vague memories to imagine what it was like to perform... It filled me with an even greater feeling of loss than the realization of how fragmented the memories of my life had been.

"In time, you will remember," Malatrius offered. "I think you've had enough for the day. Walk the grounds and see what else you might recall. Others know your position enough to leave you alone, but do try to act as you belong here rather than one of your world's... What do they call it? A *tourist*, I believe. And if you're feeling wary, go and rest. Your room is exactly how you left it."

"I can take more." I needed those memories.

"Get some rest first. Put your thoughts in order." His tone left no room for objections, and that was also something I recognized as familiar—there were times when you could voice your objections, and there were times when you didn't argue with the sorcerer. "But if in the evening you feel strong enough, we will resume," he added. "I'll be in my study."

He didn't even ask me whether I knew how to get there before leaving the room.

Alone and without anything else to do, I could take his advice, hoping that no one approached me with questions I would find difficult to answer. Taking Malatrius's advice and acting as if I belonged was a good idea. If I looked like I was busy with a task, likely given to me by the sorcerer himself, people wouldn't bother me with trivial matters. The memory of the beautiful orchard remained fresh in my mind, and it seemed like a good place to ease back into the life I'd had no idea I'd lived.

And by sundown, making good on Malatrius's promise, I'd return to chasing my past.

THE SUN WAS ABOUT to set when I made my way back from the orchard. Sitting among the trees on the green grass watered daily by Malatrius's workers made for a pleasant pastime, but it didn't bring back any memories. I must have not visited the orchard often.

Rested, I was ready to recover more of my past, no matter what dark secrets and unpleasant memories awaited me.

I walked the corridors of the main building, letting my instincts lead me where I had to go, and servants acknowledged me with respectful nods, offering their greetings and thus confirming that I held a position of importance in Malatrius's household.

With the night setting in, I hoped dreams would come,

but I still needed the sorcerer's tricks and words to ensure I got more than blurry images and scraps of conversations that would make little sense upon waking up.

I found the study quickly on the second floor of the east wing. Near the library, of course. I didn't know where Malatrius's bedchambers were, but I could easily imagine them to be nearby as well. He looked like a man who rose with the sun and welcomed its morning rays in his rooms.

The sorcerer was sitting at the table, studying a scroll, and an attractive woman stood behind him. Her marble-white hands kneaded his shoulders, and there was a familiarity and informality in her moves that made me wonder if she was his lover. My memories suggested that Malatrius had concubines, but I wasn't sure whether I'd met any of them in person. The way she glanced at me, with passing interest, suggested she knew who I was, but we were never acquainted.

I hesitated. Even though I'd entered upon Malatrius's invitation, I suspected he wouldn't be happy if I discussed the matter of my memories with another person present.

"Leave us," Malatrius told the woman with unexpected gentleness. Only then did I notice his weary expression, suggesting that opening a passage between the worlds must have been more taxing than I'd thought. Yet he still offered me attention and some more important memories before leaving me on my own.

The woman walked out without a word of protest or delay. If she was jealous, she never showed it.

"I want to remember more," I said once we were alone, "but I can't recall anything without your guidance. Nobody around here treats me like a slave, but I still don't know what happened."

The last memory I'd recovered confirmed that Past

Saeryn had succeeded in gaining Malatrius's trust, but I didn't know how he'd made her advance in his household without revealing the role she played in deceiving Davarn.

The sorcerer nodded, thoughtful and silent, as if weighing his response. "It happened here," was all he said.

"Tell me," I pleaded. Even tiniest scrap of insight could help me dream about it later.

He shook his head. "It's important that you remember on your own. I will do what I can to help you get those memories back, but... they might change how you perceive things. Think of how much you've already learned, and how it might affect your relationship with your father. Kithandar doesn't trust me, and he won't be pleased knowing that you... might."

"That's my problem, isn't it?" I wouldn't allow him to use my father as an argument, especially as my instincts were whispering that he had another reason to refuse explanations.

Before Malatrius replied, someone knocked on the door.

"Enter," the sorcerer said in a plain voice that wouldn't reveal anything about our conversation to the newcomer, and I restrained my emotions as well.

The man who walked in had sun-kissed brown skin and wore the clothes of a traveler. At his belt hung two sabers, and his smooth and balanced movements suggested he was a seasoned warrior.

"Master, I return from—"

He never finished that sentence. Instead, he stared at me. His pleasant though rough face seemed familiar, but I had no clear memory of him. I opened my mouth, ready to offer greetings vague enough to conceal my lack of knowledge, but he'd already snapped out of his motionless state.

"A demon!" he whispered, terrified. His sabers hissed as he pulled them from their sheaths.

He attacked, and I saw my own death in his determined expression. He struck with precision and speed, two blades delivering two deathblows.

For a moment, I stood frozen. Then my body moved of its own, unexpected accord, dodging the attack with more agility than I thought I'd ever had. As he turned to deliver another blow, in a flash I knew exactly how the edge of his saber would fall and how to avoid it.

But I didn't get a chance to do so, as memory resurfaced and consumed me whole.

Noises coming from the corridor woke her up. Drowsy from sleep, at first she didn't recognize the sounds of fighting, but when the alarm bells chimed through the building, she jumped out of her bed, fully awake. A night fight meant assassins—something she knew happened every now and then, when someone's grudge against a sorcerer was stronger than their common sense, and while most attempts failed, with their instigators paying a high price, there was always a chance someone would succeed.

She rushed outside with disregard for her own safety, because whoever went after the Sorcerer from the Desert was powerful and knowledgeable enough to achieve their goals. That fear dictated her steps as she made her way toward Malatrius's private chambers. He couldn't die! Not when she'd finally gained his trust and was ready to reveal her secret, the very reason she'd sacrificed so much and taken such an enormous risk.

On her way, she passed two dead strangers wearing the

outfits of desert travelers, but the echo of fighting and shouting still carried through the corridors, so there had to be more assassins. She picked up a saber from one of the fallen. Even without any fighting proficiency, having a blade could mean the difference between Malatrius's life and death. She held the weapon in a tight grip as she made her way through the dark. The sorcerer had to live, no matter the cost, even if she had to risk her own life.

She stormed into Malatrius's study without announcing herself, but the destroyed door warned that waiting for an invitation would waste precious time.

On the floor, an assassin lay in a pool of blood along with one of the sorcerer's concubines, but Malatrius himself seemed unharmed. He stood in the middle of the room, his composed posture indicating he wasn't disturbed by what had happened.

A movement in the dark warned her before another assassin lunged at her. His black eyes shone with hate, and two sabers snapped from the black faster than Saeryn could dream to match. So she lunged to position herself between the sorcerer and the stranger to give Malatrius time to dispose of the threat. She could only hope that he did so before the assassin's blade found her skin, but even if she were to die, she only had to live long enough to tell him to...

"Stop!" Malatrius shouted.

Her well-instilled urge to obey his every order overcame the need for self-preservation. She froze, waiting for the blade to fall—but to her surprise, she wasn't the only one to follow the order. The assassin stopped as well. While she still tried to make sense of what was going on, he moved again. One strike was all it took to disarm her, and with a swipe of his leg, he sent her to the floor. Before she could react, she was pinned under his weight, her arm painfully twisted behind her back.

"Do you need her alive, master?"

That one question made her blood freeze. She'd gravely misjudged the situation.

"Yes, for now," Malatrius replied as he approached, his eyes inquisitive, but his expression unforgiving. "So you finally decided to make your move." She caught an odd satisfaction in his voice, as if he cherished being right in the end.

"I didn't come here to kill you, master." Her words could change little when her actions must have been clear to him.

Barging into his study with a bare blade... How foolish of her! She should have known better than to let fear govern her, especially with her own life at stake. So many months preparing the plan with her father, followed by more months of a cautious game that was necessary for success, and she had still failed.

She deserved what was coming.

The would-be assassin smashed her body against the floor. Air escaped her lungs making speech impossible. Not that it mattered. She doubted she could talk her way out of this, and in the end, she didn't have to. She only had to live long enough for Malatrius to learn what he needed to know. Then it would be up to him whether her death was final.

He laughed. "By the oath that binds us, that's for me to judge."

She slumped, the last sparks of hope that perhaps he would understand fleeing with his cruel words. "Then before you have me killed, master," she said quietly, "I ask one thing of you. I ask you to listen to my secret and plea."

It wasn't the best time, and if Malatrius truly believed

that she had turned on him, he wouldn't be inclined to help her, but she had no other choice. Perhaps he would even understand why she'd never want him dead.

The sorcerer grimaced. "Do you really think that this secret of yours will buy your life?"

"No, master," she replied somberly. "I just ask you to listen to what I need to tell you before I die."

"Very well, let's hear it."

She moved her head, eying the man on top of her, but doubted Malatrius would tell him to leave if she asked.

"There's a secret compartment in the prism cube library," she said, weighing her words. She needed enough to convince Malatrius the secret was worth it but say nothing that would reveal anything of importance to the stranger. "In there, you'll find my father's letter and your scroll."

"My scroll was on the shelf. I've already retrieved it."

She couldn't resist a smile. "No, master. That scroll was my father's."

Undoubtedly, such a remark would capture his curiosity, and that meant she might live long enough to make him agree to her request.

"Why would your father steal my scroll if he had his own copy?"

Even though it was hardly comfortable, she twisted her head to keep looking him in the eye. The man on top of her didn't release her, as if she still posed a threat to the sorcerer.

"Because we knew you'd find out who did it and come after him," she replied. To finally reveal the truth brought relief and the feeling of accomplishment, even if she couldn't shake off the fear lurking within. "I'd let your men capture me, an arrangement would be made, and I'd end up here. It was quite a risk, and my father didn't like it, but since it was my life, I had the final say."

She read suspicion on his face, but at least he didn't dismiss her story.

"To what end?" His voice was cold. No surprise—it wasn't every day a powerful sorcerer like him learned that he'd been played.

"I won't speak more with this man around," she replied. "This secret is meant only for you. Have me bound or use a spell, but I can't say more until he leaves."

The warrior shifted, and she could swear he put more pressure on her body, as if letting her know he wasn't going anywhere. "Master, it's but a deception," he said.

"Perhaps." Malatrius showed no concern as he looked at Saeryn. "That secret compartment... I'm guessing you're the only one capable of opening it?"

She shook her head. "All you need is my blood, and I don't have to be alive for it. Just smear it over the red lizard mosaic piece."

The sorcerer looked at her with curiosity. "Is this the way you were planning to kill me?"

Frustration swelled within her. She must have been mistaken, and the sorcerer wasn't as insightful as she'd believed him to be. Or perhaps he was too intent on proving her betrayal to care about the truth.

"Then have a slave open it for you," she replied. "So far, I've never disappointed you. I served you well, and I never did anything against your will. I know you might see it differently, master, but if you read that letter, you'll understand why I would never want you dead. I need you, master, your power and your skills."

He leaned over. "That's an odd thing to say from someone who's about to die by my hand."

The corner of her lips curled in restrained amusement. "I told you months ago, master, that the secret was connected to *my* death, not yours. My father let you kill him for it, too. All I ask is that you read the letter."

To her surprise, Malatrius nodded and took a step back. "Very well, let's read it. Let her go, Rasheh."

"Master..." the man called Rasheh said, but under Malatrius's demanding stare, he moved away.

Slowly, Saeryn got back to her feet, making sure to keep her hands close to her body and avoid any sudden moves.

"Master, you didn't fall for her deception, did you? She entered your chamber with a weapon, trying to take the advantage of the outsiders stirring trouble."

She knew better than to argue the truth. Rasheh would never believe her, and Malatrius likely didn't care about it anyway.

Yet he shook his head. "She didn't come here to kill me. She was relieved to see me alive, and when you attacked, she turned her back to me to face you instead." He glanced at Saeryn. "She likely thought you were another assassin."

Her eyes widened. Malatrius knew—he'd known from the moment she entered, yet he allowed the situation to unfold the way it had. The reason instantly became clear. "You played me, master. Forced my hand."

"It seems that I was only repaying you in kind." His voice was colder than moments ago, as if he wanted to remind her that she was still at his mercy. "I hope this secret is really worth your life. Even if I know you weren't trying to kill me, you just admitted to deceiving me ever since we met."

She hung her head, saying nothing. By the rules of the binding oath, Malatrius was the one who'd decide her fate. Arguing would not win her any favor.

"Let's go." He motioned for her to lead the way.

THE FIRST THING I saw when the memory released me was Rasheh standing in front of me, his weapons bare and pointing at my throat. His posture and expression were hostile.

"Make the demon disappear, master. Otherwise I'll kill it."

The strange note in his voice resonated with me, stirring up a memory, but no clear image resurfaced, and I didn't chase it. With the newest revelations, I had enough to think about without pondering the hate Rasheh harbored toward the past me.

"She's not a demon," Malatrius said calmly. "Look at her."

Rasheh didn't. He kept his eyes on the sorcerer. "Saeryn's dead."

I froze. If he'd witnessed my past self dying, no wonder he considered the woman who stood in front of him a demon. I turned to Malatrius, words of accusation ready. Before we'd arrived in Hyrinea, he claimed no one knew what had happened.

He shook his head, his attention still on Rasheh. "It's her. She isn't dead. But surviving came with a price. Her memories are... shattered."

Rasheh huffed. "Master, please, spare me the tales you might tell others. Not even you can cure the assassin's kiss. Whatever she is, she's not Saeryn, and only your order holds my blade away. If you need this demon for anything, use her, but I want nothing to do with such sorcery."

As soon as he mentioned that, I remembered that the

"assassin's kiss" was poison, and that made me curious about him. Disjointed pieces of memories flashed in my head, and I knew that he guarded Malatrius's safety, tracking his enemies and killing those who got too close. He must have considered me a threat, and I wouldn't be surprised to discover that he was the one who'd administered said poison.

The only thing I didn't understand was a strange note in his voice, but it could have been a reaction to what he likely saw as an impossible survival. No wonder believing that I was a demon—though to my knowledge those creatures didn't look human at all—came easier than considering that I could actually be Saeryn.

But was I really?

Deep in my thoughts, fighting the creeping fear that rose whenever I felt disjointed from my past self, I almost missed the change on Malatrius's face. An authoritative glare replaced the former gentler expression.

"But you will," he said, and I knew that tone well. Refusal was unacceptable. "You'll address her as Saeryn and treat her accordingly, especially in the presence of others. You'll train her like you did before. You'll help her remember... everything."

Rasheh grimaced. "There's a line, master."

Malatrius nodded as if he'd expected such a response. There had to be more communicated that just words, something they wouldn't speak about in front of me.

"There's a long path ahead before that line comes into sight," the sorcerer said.

Rasheh didn't seem convinced, but he lowered his sabers. He graced me with a glance, and though it was hardly a friendly one, at least his expression lost its hatefulness.

"The training house is past the guards' quarters. Be there in the morning."

His words conjured another memory, of a one-story building hugging the main building's outer wall, but nothing else followed. I gave him a nod in response, uncertain how Past Saeryn had addressed him. He barely acknowledged it.

"Very well," Malatrius broke the silence that lingered. "I take it you returned because you have news?" he asked Rasheh.

"You're busy, master," came the dry reply. "I'll come back another time." Rasheh bowed and left without waiting for permission.

His furrowed brow told me Malatrius didn't like such behavior, and it made me wonder how much freedom Rasheh enjoyed as his servant.

The sorcerer sighed. "I was hoping Rasheh would be away for a while longer, and you'd remember more before he returned, but the time I spent in the other world, learning about it and searching for you, was too long."

I swallowed. "He saw... saw me die, didn't he?"

Malatrius shook his head. "He saw you struck, but we made it to the prism cube library before you died. No one witnessed it but me. Yet, as you've seen, Rasheh isn't one to be fooled easily, so at some point, he'll have to learn the truth."

I chose my next words carefully. "He seemed... disturbed seeing me alive, but there was more to it, wasn't there?"

"You died because he didn't make it in time. This was the first time when he was back home, but someone else had to protect me."

I stared him straight in the eye. "You've never lied to me before."

"Are you certain?" he said lightly. "But it wasn't a lie. I simply chose not to tell you what you should remember on your own. Before that, there are other memories you should restore. I wanted you to rest, but with Rasheh's return..." He shook his head. "You need to know more as soon as possible."

Part of me wanted to press him for some answers, but I'd learned enough to know he wasn't one to yield. No pleas nor demands would make him change his mind. Yet his avoidance was undermining the trust I had in him. If he was certain that my memories would confirm everything he'd told me so far, he could reveal some things himself. That he chose not to meant he may have other goals and motives, and my father's warning about not trusting the sorcerer rang in my ears once more.

At the same time, no matter his reasons for helping me, no matter what his schemes might be, of one thing I was certain. He did want me to remember. So until I had restored all of my past, I had to trust him.

Therefore, I nodded instead of arguing. "Prism cube library, then?" I asked. If I understood his intention to rebuild my lost memories in the right order, that was the place we had to go next.

The smile I received in response felt like a reward.

Rasheh accompanied them all the way to the prism cube, and if glares could kill, Saeryn would have dropped dead every time she took a step.

The alarm bells had already stopped ringing, and the

bodies she'd seen before were gone. Walking through the corridors, they passed several servants who, despite the late hour, were washing bloodstains off the floors. In the morning, there would be no trace of the attack, as if such trivial things simply did not disrupt the daily routines of Malatrius's household.

Saeryn had no doubt that if any news reached his opponents, all they'd see was a demonstration of confidence and power—no attempt on his life could shake the Sorcerer from the Desert's composure.

When the three of them made it to the library, she stopped. Not in a position to ask for Rasheh to wait outside, she could only hope Malatrius wouldn't insist on him accompanying them further. The prism cube library's secrets, her own included, weren't meant for common killers.

"Wait here, Rasheh," Malatrius said. "If she leaves without me, as unlikely as it is, kill her."

Rasheh bowed, but his stiff face made it clear he wasn't happy with the order. Nevertheless, he took a step to the side, and Malatrius entered the library. Ignoring the intense glare of the warrior, Saeryn followed.

As always, the colorful light and magic filled the space, and she allowed them to soothe her anxious mind. Truly, the prism cube library was a thing of marvel, and she sometimes wondered how her father had come to own one. According to him, they were artifacts from times long gone, and only a few remained in existence. Whenever she thought about it, she acknowledged the high price her father had paid to offer her a fleeting chance of gaining Malatrius's trust. She was about to learn if it had been worth it.

The sorcerer was already standing by the mosaic at the back wall, having found the red lizard made from shining, multi-edged tiles, and she rushed to him. He handed her the familiar ritual knife, and she made a shallow cut on her finger. As the drop of blood blossomed on her skin, she put it against the mosaic.

The coral used for the tiles that created the bird's likeness was unusually cold to the touch, and magic within activated as soon as the mosaic drank the first few drops of her blood. A part of the wall moved to the side, revealing a small niche. Inside lay four scrolls—not two as she'd told him to keep the explanation simple—and Saeryn picked the right one without hesitation.

Malatrius unfolded it, nothing in his moves suggesting he was concerned for his own safety, and she breathed out with relief. He would finally learn the truth. All those months of planning, of arguing with her father, and the risk of putting her life in Malatrius's hands were to finally bear fruit. And for a little while, she would be free from pretending.

Motionless, she waited for him to finish reading. He could still refuse the request made in the letter, but she hoped that the trust she'd been trying so hard to earn, the reward her father had added to that request, and the prospect that Malatrius's refusal would anger a man who'd come back over and over again to avenge his daughter's death would be enough to convince Malatrius to help.

He looked up from the scroll. "So Kithandar is alive?"

"Reborn in the other world, waiting for me to join him," she replied with confidence, though the memory of her father's demonstration of his uncanny ability still shook her slightly. To see her own father kill himself in front of her, turn to dust, and return a day later as if nothing had happened was still too much for her mind, even though her schooling had acquainted her with magic.

"And why did you choose me?"

At this question, everything froze within her, but she kept a neutral visage. With his trust so delicately balanced, she had to tell him the truth, or at least part of it. "My father insisted we reach out to Sahatiavari. I wasn't certain if she was the right choice."

Malatrius arched his eyebrow. "She's considered one of your father's few friends."

"But is she, though?" Saeryn asked. "Or is she only pretending to be one?"

No other explanations were necessary. Being a powerful sorcerer himself, Malatrius knew that many of his rivals remained amicable only out of fear or because it served their goals, Davarn being the latest among them.

Sahatiavari, the sorceress from the steppes, was on good terms with Kithandar, but Saeryn's interaction with her the one time Sahatiavari visited her father's castle suggested she wasn't the right choice for what Saeryn truly needed from her.

"Why the deception, though?" Malatrius asked.

"Because I didn't want it to be an agreement between you and my father," she said. This much was true and safe to share. "I wanted it to be *my* request. Something you chose to do for me, not for my father."

As she said it, she pushed all other thoughts away, banishing them from her mind so that the sorcerer wouldn't read on her face that she had other, more important reasons to arrange everything the way she had. Such a secret was too dangerous to reveal and would cost her life. Yet the image of a golden hairpin stashed safely in the other world resurfaced nevertheless, and Saeryn feared something, any emotion or a tic, would betray her, so she bit her lip and pretended to look away as if in shame.

"I also wanted... I wanted to be sure I could trust you, master. To learn what kind of a man you are."

To her relief, Malatrius didn't dig deeper, though she had an eerie feeling that he knew she wasn't being honest with him.

"And what happens if I decide not to perform the ritual for you?" he asked. "You have another secret or bargain for me?"

She shook her head. "That's all I have. By the oath that binds us, whether I live or die is for you to decide, master, and so is the choice of performing the ritual."

"And Kithandar is leaving that to me as well?"

"I cannot say what my father will choose to do," she replied honestly.

"But you have your guesses."

"I'm sure you do as well, master."

It wasn't hard to predict that even if her father cared little about avenging her after failing to accomplish her goals, he would still confront Malatrius, since the sorcerer now knew how Kithandar had cheated death. Accepting the request and performing the ritual was likely the only way for Malatrius to prove that he had no interest in starting a conflict that could consume them both.

She swallowed as she realized that if the sorcerer's thoughts traveled a similar path, he wouldn't like that his choice was illusory. That with her schemes and deception, she'd put him against the wall, and that wasn't a wise move.

Malatrius watched her with narrowed eyes and half a smile as if he knew what she was thinking and was pleased that she understood the implications of the choices she'd made.

"How long did your father agree to wait to see if your schemes succeeded?"

Reminding her that she was trying to manipulate him stung, but she didn't protest. She'd deserved that and more, all the way to paying with her life, and her only regret was that she couldn't tell him the whole truth.

"If I'm not reborn in five years, he'll return here."

She couldn't help thinking of her father, sitting alone in the secluded cavern he'd chosen for the place of her rebirth, day after day performing the other part of the ritual, not knowing when she would be reborn, then returning home only to do it all over again the next morning, and it sparked a hint of guilt. If not for her elaborate plan, he wouldn't have had to go through such an ordeal.

"It seems that we have about four years, then, don't we?"

Malatrius put the letter back in the niche, beside the instructions for the ritual, and a spell allowing him to traverse the worlds that was meant as a payment for performing it. To her surprise, he didn't retrieve the stolen scroll, instead guiding her hand over the mosaic. With a surge of magic, the red lizard returned to its previous place.

She didn't understand. "Master?"

The image of the scribe she'd replaced not so long ago resurfaced along with all due dread. Even though she'd never betrayed Malatrius, he had every reason to punish her.

When he smiled, she saw no cruelty in the expression.

"Despite your many flaws, I've grown quite fond of you," he said casually. "You may stay here a little longer. You'll serve me as you did, I'll teach you the arts, and when the time comes, I'll perform the ritual for you. Kithandar doesn't have to know how long it truly took you to gain my trust." He touched her cleavage, and the slave's mark faded.

"But if you'd rather reunite with your father now, I'll oblige."

Back when their game first started, they had a conversation about opportunities coming and going, and Saeryn recognized his offer as one. Undoubtedly, it came with hidden reasons Malatrius wouldn't share with her, but to have a chance to learn the arts from the Sorcerer from the Desert himself was a rare and precious opportunity. Even if it meant her father would have to suffer uncertainty even longer, and even if it meant she could become a pawn in Malatrius's game, she'd take that risk.

She bowed. "I'd be honored to stay and learn from you."

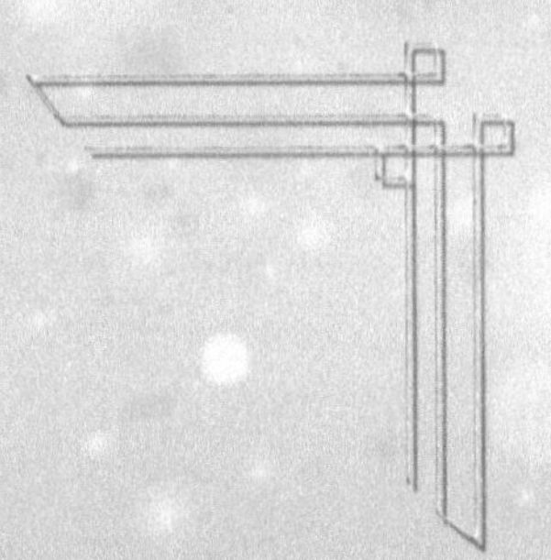

Chapter 8

In the dead woman's undying shadow

Memory-dreams filled my night, but at dawn I had more questions than answers. While I finally understood some of the reasons why past me did what she did, there were things she'd hidden so deep in her mind that I seemed unable to reach them. All I knew was that whatever she'd kept secret from Malatrius both scared her and filled her with desperation. And what filled *me* with fear was the price I might pay if I didn't discover it in time.

Since my own mind was of no help in that regard, I had to rely on Malatrius's guidance, and he wanted me to train with Rasheh. I doubted spending time with a man who clearly hated me would help my distorted memories, but I knew better than to argue with the sorcerer. Unless I wanted to be left to my own devices, I had to follow the path he'd set, even if it led to places I'd rather avoid.

Like the training area I was about to enter.

From a distance, it looked unassuming—a large tool shed or perhaps a workshop, if such things were to be found in Hyrinea—but when I stepped in, a vast space greeted me.

A plain stone floor spread from wall to wall, and in the corner stood a rack, but the weapons selection was less impressive than I would have expected. On the other hand, Rasheh seemed to favor his sabers, and Malatrius's guards likely didn't have a need for anything fancier than swords and spears.

The faint scent of sweat and dust lingered in the air. If my mother had any say, this wasn't a place a noble-born like me should ever visit. My father, on the other hand... It wouldn't surprise me if he'd like the idea of physical training, though not necessarily *violent* physical training.

Rasheh was in the middle of the room, practicing a complex routine with his sabers, and I couldn't help admiring his smooth motions and balanced steps. The longer I watched, the more familiar his moves became, and I could anticipate every single strike.

He stopped when our eyes met. To my relief, he seemed amicable enough when he asked, "So, how much do you remember?"

I took a few steps forward but kept away from him, as if the distance could prevent him from cutting me down if he so chose. Despite my father's reassurance and my own memories suggesting that upon death I would be reborn, I still felt uneasy about it, even if I had supposedly died once already. What was more important though was the prospect of losing my memories again. I couldn't risk it, not when I was finally starting to put my strange past together.

"I know that your name is Rasheh, and that when we first met, you attacked me... in the master's study, much like yesterday. This all seems familiar." I gestured around. "But I can't remember anything in particular."

He smirked in that knowing way, as if my response

proved I wasn't Saeryn. As if the true Saeryn couldn't... *wouldn't* have forgotten.

"Yesterday you didn't move like someone who'd lost her memories. Let's see how much your body remembers." The way he said made it clear he didn't believe in my memory loss and was only playing along, likely to prove me wrong.

With two quick strides he was in front of me, an elbow strike to the face, and to my own surprise, I had already ducked, swinging to hit him in the gut. He easily dodged and attack again.

We danced around a little longer. It wasn't even close to real training, but Rasheh seemed satisfied.

"Quite impressive," he said. "The master must have put in a lot of work."

I scowled. To him, I was still a demon, one given a dead woman's face and some of her thoughts. I doubted any sorcery could achieve something like that, but in the end, I knew very little of magic. If I could be reborn, someone as skilled as Malatrius or my father could have called upon a demon and shaped her into Saeryn.

A shiver ran down my spine when I considered that Rasheh could be right. Maybe the real Saeryn truly had died, and my father had created another daughter for himself.

"Are you done?" Rasheh asked.

Lost in my thoughts, I hadn't noticed that he kept watching me. I hoped my emotions didn't show on my face, because I didn't need my doubts fueling his conviction that I was a demon. Part of me wanted to give him the "yes" he was seeking, but Malatrius wouldn't have sent me here without reason—an important memory I needed to restore.

"I can practice some more," I replied.

No matter how much Rasheh's presence shook my

composure, I could endure his remarks and attitude long enough to get what I came for.

"Let's do something real, then." He threw me one of his sabers.

I caught it midair, a feat that my body claimed I'd done countless times.

Rasheh attacked, but he seemed mindful. His strikes weren't as fast, as if he wanted to ensure I didn't get hurt. Quite a surprise, considering that a training accident would be an excellent excuse to get rid of me. Perhaps he didn't want to risk Malatrius's anger.

Enthralled with the sparring, I had little time to ponder anything. He squeezed every last drop of sweat out of me. His strikes and parries flowed one after another, forcing me to move around in an increasingly familiar routine. My previous self must have trained with him a lot.

Finally, I stopped, breathless. "I think I've had enough." I saw no point in bringing myself to the brink of exhaustion if it couldn't restore my memories.

"Very well. Tomorrow, we'll repeat it." His dark eyes watched me intently, as if he were trying to uncover some hidden truth.

I lifted myself from the floor, my muscles trembling from the exertion, and handed the saber back to him.

"Thank you," I offered with a smile and headed for the bath chamber.

"So you *do* remember that."

I looked back at him, confused. "All I know, there's a bath chamber there." Exhausted from the training, I hadn't even thought about it, letting my instincts lead me. "Am I not supposed to go there?"

Rasheh's face didn't reveal anything, and he encouraged me with a gesture. "No, you've used it before. I just didn't expect you to... remember." The last word carried mocking undertones, reminding me of his disbelief I'd ever had those memories to begin with, let alone lost them.

Paying no more attention to his game, I walked into the bath chamber. The sooner I washed off the sweat and got away from him, the better. The area was small, tiled with dark stone, and the steam rising from the miniature pool carried a masculine scent. I inhaled deeper, trying to pinpoint why it was so familiar.

There was no sound, but the shifting of the air behind me put me on alert, and I turned.

Too slow.

Rasheh was already beside me, and in a move so quick I couldn't hope to counter, he pushed me against a nearby wall. His chest pressed against mine, pinning me in place, but there was no aggression in his demeanor.

"And do you remember that too?" he asked in a husky tone.

The smell of his sweat was overwhelmingly familiar, and my body responded, a wave of heat and desire drowning me. Memories flashed before my eyes in a flurry, none of them clear enough to grasp, but all of them suggesting I'd been in Rasheh's bath chamber before—and had visited his bed as well.

Another man with which I'd been intimate but had no idea about. Even if it seemed that, contrary to my time with Davarn, Rasheh and I shared passion, I'd have preferred to recall it in different circumstances. Especially as it clashed with the only other memories of Rasheh I had thus far.

My face must have betrayed me, because he smiled with satisfaction. He leaned forward, and I shivered with anticipation, my body already knowing what would happen next.

A sigh escaped my mouth when his tongue caressed my neck.

Then he released me and stepped away. "You might look like her. You might have some of her memories. But you don't smell and taste like her."

His cold words rang in my ears long after he'd left.

I LAY in bed taking deep breaths as if they could help me steady my thoughts. The sky outside was brightening as the sun rose, and soon I'd have to rise as well. The thought was followed by grimmer ones, and for the first time since arriving in Hyrinea, I was questioning whether I should stay in Malatrius's household much longer. While I was certain there were still memories to restore, it seemed that I was wasting time remembering things of no consequence.

What was worse than time wasted was that my presence here had become a form of torture, both day and night, though each differed in the suffering they offered.

During the day, following the sorcerer's request, I trained under Rasheh's guidance. Though careful not to cause any permanent injury, he didn't bother avoiding bruising, scrapes, and a general battering, and my muscles ached constantly from the strain he put me through. As if that wasn't bad enough, his cold demeanor spoiled any joy I could have found in going beyond what I thought were the limitations of my body. When we were alone, "demon" was the only name he had for me, and nothing I did nor said changed his mind.

Nights brought a different kind of torture as I relived the memories I shared with Rasheh. One would suffice to convey the nature of our past relationship, but my mind was intent on recovering them all. As a consequence, every morning I woke up sweating and longing, with the perspective of hiding my emotions from Rasheh. To him, I wasn't Saeryn, so he wouldn't be interested in rekindling anything between us, and truth be told, neither should I be.

Especially not after last night's dream.

No matter what my memories told me and what my body demanded, I would not get involved with a man who'd tried to use me.

I gritted my teeth. Last night's dream had made it clear: Rasheh had seduced me only to ensure my help in his plot against Malatrius. The cold behavior I was witnessing now must be how he really felt about me. Perhaps he was also trying to ensure I didn't get my memories back, because if I did, I'd expose his schemes.

I wagered he didn't want me to remember the question he'd asked that revealed his true intentions.

Will you help me kill the sorcerer?

If my dream was telling of real events—and so far, I had no reason to doubt it—my past self pretended to agree, but I woke up before the memory unfolded. I had to assume that the betrayal had never come to light, because Malatrius wouldn't have kept Rasheh around, let alone trust him, otherwise. It was possible that the circumstances around my death had thwarted the plot, and that meant I had to warn the sorcerer. With my return, Rasheh might feel pressured to do something before I remembered all the details, so Malatrius could be in grave danger.

Ignoring my muscles' protests, I forced myself out of bed. The life of a sorcerer's servant in Hyrinea was much less demanding when it came to socially acceptable clothing, so I didn't have to bother much with grooming, and I had to make it to Malatrius's study before Rasheh noticed my absence in the training room.

I made it through the house with due haste. The door to Malatrius's study was open, but the sound of Rasheh's voice stopped me from announcing myself and entering.

"I won't do it, master," he said.

"I won't force you," Malatrius replied, his voice composed and emotionless. "But I promised her that she'd get her memories back. If you so badly want her to leave my house, you should do everything in your power to help restore them."

It might be petty of me, but it was satisfying to hear the sorcerer put Rasheh in his place. I was quite certain that no matter what Malatrius was asking of him, neither of the choices pleased Rasheh.

"Master..."

For a heartbeat, I questioned whether it was Rasheh who spoke. With the pleading and desperation lining that one word, he sounded like a different man—a broken one.

"You've been serving me for years. You should know better than to question me. I turn a blind eye to how you treat her, and I'm giving you a choice, but you will *not* ask me to break the promise I made at her dying breath."

I almost gasped. It seemed that without discussing it with me, Malatrius had already explained to Rasheh who—or perhaps what—I was. And that mention of a promise... It made me instinctively lean forward, as if I could catch a glimpse of that secret, because I was certain Malatrius would refuse to tell me.

The silence between them lingered, and then Rasheh said, "I understand, master. I won't say a word of it again."

"Good," Malatrius replied. "How much does she remember now?"

"I can't be sure." I could swear Rasheh shrugged, so indifferent did his voice sound. "I train her, and she remembers how to move, though she's lost a bit of her agility and speed. Sometimes her expression makes me think she might have remembered something, but I don't ask."

That was a painfully accurate depiction of our training, but with the conversation's turn, eavesdropping wouldn't bring me anything more worth the risk. I took several quiet steps back, hesitant to leave. If Malatrius dismissed Rasheh anytime soon, and he walked out, he'd spot me. So instead, I forced my legs into a casual stride and headed for the doorway.

"Master?" I poked my head in, pretending to notice Rasheh as if I hadn't known he was there.

"Come in," Malatrius said. "Is something wrong?"

I stepped in, my eyes on the sorcerer. I did my best to ignore Rasheh, who watched me with sudden interest and much more attention than he'd ever paid me before.

"I need to speak with you." My clenched throat made it hard to keep my voice neutral. "Alone."

Before Malatrius could reply, Rasheh burst out laughing. "I know that pained expression. Almost the same as the one from the past. She's about to tell you that I plan to kill you, master." Amusement never leaving his face, he walked over to me. "Do you also remember when exactly I asked for your help?" His words were teasing, and the crease of his cheek almost vicious, as if he wanted to make sure I recalled his hands and lips on me back then.

With my face burning, I looked away, but my anger burned even stronger as glimpses of other memories resurfaced. Past Saeryn rushing to warn the sorcerer much like I did, and Malatrius revealing that Rasheh had wanted to test me.

I grimaced and held my chin up. I might have been a slave and a servant in my past life in Hyrinea, but I was of noble blood. I would not let him see me lose my composure.

"It seems that what I remembered was his deception," I replied coldly and turned to Malatrius. "I apologize, master, for bothering you." I took a step back, ready to retreat as soon as the sorcerer dismissed me.

"Since you're awake already, we will train," Rasheh said.

My fingers curled into balls. I was willing to do a lot to get my memories back, but some of them were hardly worth the price paid. When it came to remembering Rasheh, I'd rather lose a few memories than gain any more.

"There's no need," I said. "I don't think there's anything more you can help me remember."

Without waiting for his response or even Malatrius's permission, I walked out of the room. I made it out in time to hide my lips trembling and hands shaking.

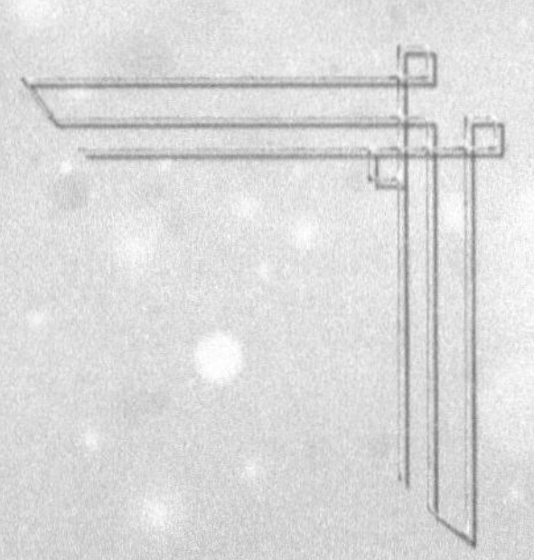

Chapter 9

The assassin's kiss

It might have been petty, but I spent the whole day nurturing my frustration with Rasheh, and that feeling alone also felt too familiar to be comfortable, breeding yet another layer of ire. Glimpses of images and pieces of conversations flashing in my memory reassured me that if I was to dream at night, it would be the truth about what I'd thought was Rasheh's betrayal. I'd been deceived back then, and though I couldn't put my finger on why, I had a feeling it wasn't *only* back then.

Of course, despite my frustration, I had no one to blame but myself, no matter how hard I tried to put in on Rasheh.

The orchard, where I spent most of the day, did little to soothe those seething emotions, but at least workers left me alone, as if sensing it unwise to approach me for any reason. Yet I couldn't stay there forever, so as the sun set, I begrudgingly made my way back. After what I'd learned, the prospect of restoring more of my memories was far less alluring, but avoidance wasn't the way. Even if I decided to spend the night in the prism cube library, reading scrolls and chasing sleep away, I had to dream again, and the sooner I was done with memories concerning Rasheh, the sooner I'd be free of his company.

The household was quiet, with most servants having retired for the night, but I still welcomed the solitude of my room, because Rasheh's presence brought turmoil to my heart that I didn't want anyone to witness.

Back when I'd taken Malatrius's offer, I expected to learn of unsettling events and painful truths, but I couldn't have prepared for discovering that Past Saeryn not only had a lover, but she also fell for a man who cared nothing for her. I'd followed her step by step down the same path, and Malatrius did nothing to warn me.

Once again I questioned the value of the memories I was chasing. I couldn't deny that I'd learned a lot and discovered things that had changed my mindset forever, but perhaps soon it was time to thank the sorcerer for his hospitality and go back home.

I looked around the room that had also been home. A wide bed, a desk, a small vanity with a surprisingly large mirror, and a chest. All the furnishing was of the best quality, but only a few personal trinkets lay around. Past Saeryn had had few belongings she could call her own.

The curtains by the balcony moved, but no gust of wind followed. Instead, Rasheh entered my room uninvited.

Back in my world, I'd allow myself to cause quite a scene. After his deception, he deserved every bit of humiliation that came with being exposed while sneaking into a woman's bedroom, but I expected that screaming would hardly have the desired effect in Malatrius's household. Servants feared Rasheh—it wasn't hard to notice—and given his role, everyone would assume he had a good reason to be in my room. I wouldn't put it past them to even speculate about my possible transgressions that *required* Rasheh entering my bedroom.

With my options limited, I gave him a displeased glare. He stepped forward, but kept far enough back to make me feel safe. It also helped that he didn't have his sabers on him. But all that was just an illusion of safety. I couldn't forget how swiftly he moved and how easily it would be for him to cut the distance between us. If he so wanted, I'd die without making a single sound.

"You have her shape and some of her memories," he said, though his tone didn't carry his usual disdain. Instead, he seemed curious. "Do you really believe that gaining more of them will make you into her?"

"I *am* her." He might not believe it, but I would not allow him alter the truth of who I was.

"Let's put it to the test, then." With the ease of someone who knew his way around the room, he produced five small flasks from the desk's drawer. "Pick your favorite scent."

Another game, of that I was certain, but if I gave him what he wanted, he'd take his victory and leave. I inhaled the scent of each flask one by one, and it didn't take long to know which one appealed to me the most—a fresh, flowery scent that made me think of a dew in a mountain meadow. Yet I wouldn't fall into his trap that easily. Instead, I pointed to another flask, the one that was lighter than others and had a shape that felt familiar in my hand, even though the musky scent, with heavy notes of sandalwood, it contained didn't appeal to me at all.

Rasheh smiled with satisfaction. "This, indeed, was *her* favorite. But not yours. This one is." He picked up the flask I'd pretended to ignore.

I didn't reply. Something, maybe a tic on my face, must have betrayed me when I checked the perfumes, and

Rasheh caught it. A simple test, and I'd failed it, proving that he was right, though not in the way he thought. I likely would never again be the person I used to be.

And maybe... Maybe he was more right than I wanted him to be. Maybe I had never been that person. The thought of being some kind of a demon, a mere copy with a handful of stolen memories, haunted me once more, but I did my best to ignore it, at least for now. To display my fears in front of a man who cherished seeing my torment would allow him yet another tool with which to torture me.

I stood silent, waiting for that scathing comment that would accompany his triumph after my failed test.

Instead, Rasheh took a step closer. Before I could retreat, he closed me in his embrace, and the gentleness of his touch surprised me.

"You should stop trying to be someone you aren't," he whispered into my ear. "She is your past and always will be, but she's dead, and you aren't her."

I could free myself from his grip easy enough. After all, he'd taught me how to do it during our training. But with all the memories that plagued my recent dreams, my body longed for his touch... No, for more than just his touch, and I ignored the voice of reason demanding I move away. Soon enough, his game would be over, with one last blow to ensure my prolonged suffering, but until then, I could close my eyes and pretend, pretend for those few heartbeats that I was his lover.

Rasheh uncorked the flask with one hand, his other arm still holding me tight. "I thought she'd like it, but she never wore it." Holding his finger over the mouth of the container, he doused it with perfume, and the flowery bouquet of a mountain meadow muffled the overwhelming scent of his skin. "It means that I can smell it on your skin without thinking about what's in the past." He brushed his hand against my neck, rubbing the drops into it.

I stood motionless, and remaining indifferent to his touch drained me of strength and resolve.

I shifted in his grip, and he allowed me to turn. The mocking comment, the finale to his game, must have been coming if he wanted to see my face. I hoped to withstand whatever jab he had at the ready and rob him of his satisfaction.

"You're intriguing both in how similar you are and how different you are," he said.

"So I'm not a demon anymore?" I couldn't resist that bit of challenge. The sooner he was done, the better.

He smiled with confidence. "You are. I just didn't know that you always were, no matter in which life." He pulled me closer. "So, New Saeryn, do you want only the memories of a woman who's been dead for months, or would you like to make some for yourself?"

There it was, the stage set for my fall. The moment I said yes, he'd laugh at me. My body, of course, longed to answer for me. I scanned his face for signs of deception, though I knew he was too good for me to find any.

He smiled as if he knew what was going through my head. He leaned closer and buried his face in my hair, his nose tracing the side of my neck. As he inhaled deeply, I heard both satisfaction and desire in the sound.

It was all deception—as I kept telling myself—and I should know better than to fall for it. But I *wanted* it—to taste his lips and melt under his touch, to make one night into something more than a memory I never got to experience myself. If I was willing to pay a high price for the memories that might have belonged to someone else and which I desperately wanted to be my own, I could as well accept paying for a night that would be at least half real. For my own memory to keep.

Hushing doubts, I gave in to his caress.

I WAS SITTING cross-legged on the floor, practicing breathing in a strict rhythm while Malatrius sat on a chair by the prism cube's wall and leafed through a book. He might look preoccupied, but I had no doubt he would pay close attention once I started the incantation.

The spell was not easy on its own, and the breath rhythm it had to match made it more challenging. In the future, it would allow me to skip recitation altogether, making me much faster and more proficient at casting it, but such mastery required practice.

Once I was ready, I recited the spell with due focus.

"You still make the same mistake," Malatrius said once I was done. "*Kho*, not *ko*, in the thirtieth line."

"Both serve the same function in the spell."

As he tutored me, all his previous teachings gradually returned. Yet the thought of casting even simple spells still made my blood rush with excitement. After stepping through a passageway to another world, I already had all the proof I needed that magic was real, but there was a difference between knowing about it and wielding it.

While I recovered the teachings, the memories of me casting any spells seemed to be gone forever, refusing to be brought back to the surface by any of the sorcerer's tricks, so I had no idea how past me felt about magic. All I had was my own rush of excitement and anticipation.

"*Kho*, not *ko*, in the thirtieth line," Malatrius repeated dryly. "No matter what purpose they serve, you'll get the spell right."

"Yes, master," I replied reflexively. No matter what memories I might still be missing, assuming the role of his student came easier than I'd expected.

He smiled. "Other than that, you did well. I'm satisfied with your progress. You seem to have recovered most of my schooling, so we'll be able to move on soon."

"Move on?" I squinted in suspicion. "I'm here to remember..."

Malatrius's sardonic glare stopped me from finishing that sentence.

"I don't see why you should stop just because you died too soon to learn all that I was offering. You have the potential to become a good, if not great, sorceress. Are you going to waste it because you're only here to remember your past?"

Every word of his reprimand stung like a snake bite, and I hung my head, not bothering with an argument that my father could teach me as well. Past Saeryn had chosen Malatrius without hesitation, so no matter how skilled my father was, his knowledge must have paled in comparison to what the Sorcerer from the Desert knew.

"No, master."

"I thought so. As I said, we'll soon be able to work on new spells. But it's enough for today." His voice softened. "Let's have a meal together."

I got up from the floor, my body agile and light from training with Rasheh. My cheeks warmed at the thought of other things I'd done with him—the ones that made my blood rush in a different kind of way—and I fell in behind Malatrius, hoping he didn't see me blush.

Ever since Rasheh visited my room, he behaved differently. If he called me a demon, he said it in a playful manner, and he never mentioned his dead lover or pointed out things I didn't remember anymore. Instead, he gave me all the caring and passion I could dream of.

Malatrius glanced at me over his shoulder. "Rasheh stopped demanding that I banish you. I take it you found a way to befriend him?"

"It seems so," I replied with caution.

With so much deception in the past and the way Rasheh had treated me until recently, I still couldn't be certain about his intentions, and though I enjoyed his company, I was preparing for an ax to fall. Moreover, I wasn't sure how much Malatrius knew about the past relationship between Rasheh and, well, me.

"Good," he replied. "This was beginning to become cumbersome. I'm glad I don't have to make efforts to keep you two apart for the sake of peace in my household."

I arched my eyebrow at that. My own doubts and suspicions had made me wonder whether that the peace he mentioned was only temporary, and they hung like a storm cloud over my happiness. One thing I knew for certain though, was that if things were to fall apart, Rasheh would be the one to blame.

I watched the comb's path in the mirror as I brushed my black locks. It was part of my evening routine, perhaps pointless in Hyrinea, but one I'd decided to keep nevertheless. Sitting in front of the small vanity felt familiar too, so even though I had no memories of it, my past self must have done so countless times. I wished I knew what her thoughts were, but all the memories so far offered only images and echoes of her thoughts and emotions, keeping most of Past Saeryn's mind locked for me. Every now and then, I caught a glimpse of them within a memory, but I couldn't help the feeling that whatever thoughts she had, she was so desperate to keep them secret, it affected my ability to restore them.

Or perhaps thoughts were too fleeting of a thing to be contained within one's mind in a way that would allow one to unearth them. Sometimes, I was ready to resign and admit that I'd never know my past the way I should have. Other times, I discovered so much desperation within that I found myself imagining and speculating what I *might* have thought in the hope of sparking any true memories. It never worked.

Malatrius seemed unconcerned whenever I brought up my inability to restore anything without his guidance. To him, everyday memories seemed unimportant, as if reliving *this* part of my life would suffice. And while he helped restore my memories, I couldn't help wondering whether he was leading me down a path of his choosing. The path that would present the events in the light he wanted me to see them in while obscuring other things—the ones he'd rather keep hidden.

Yet I didn't want to push, because even without her thoughts clear to me, I knew that Past Saeryn had kept secrets. As much as he might not want to reveal some things that had happened, I could as well discover memories I'd rather not share with him. Unfortunately, it meant that I was on my own when it came to finding them.

Deep in my thoughts and focused on my own reflection, as if she could reveal the truth of what had happened to me, I missed the moment Rasheh entered the room. He didn't have the habit of knocking, as if my room were part of his domain. And perhaps it was, given he spent nearly every night in my bed.

He stopped behind me, pressing his muscular body against my back, and watched my reflection. There was something solemn in his expression.

"I have something for you," he said. "A gift."

He presented a silver chain with a small pendant. Onyx, a piece no bigger than a half of my thumb, sat in a silver filigree frame, intricate in its design and unlike any local jewelry I'd seen. As Rasheh leaned forward, putting it on my neck, memories washed over me in a gentle wave, and I knew that the pendant belonged to Past Saeryn. That she'd received it along with his confession of love. No matter what loyalty tests he had for her, and what secrets she'd kept from him, their feelings for each other were genuine.

"It's yours," he whispered as if knowing what I'd just remembered, "and it always has been."

His words hardly made it through the pounding in my ears. I wanted that pendant, and I wanted what it meant. But no matter how much pleasure we gave each other at night, I wasn't *his* Saeryn. It didn't feel right to selfishly take what they'd had for myself. He deserved better than that.

"Rasheh..."

"Shh..." His finger brushed my cheek. "I should have never taken my grief out on you. She didn't die because of you, and she didn't die so that you could be reborn. It was the gods' evil chuckle that took her away from me. I was so angry that I didn't realize the gods also gave me another chance to be with the woman I love."

Unable to find words, I stared at my own reflection. The dark-haired woman in a student's tunic, wearing an onyx pendant, was me, but it could as easily been the previous

Saeryn. It had seemed so natural to fall into the role of Malatrius's servant and student, and even easier to be Rasheh's lover, but I had to stay true to myself. Those lost memories, those secrets and thoughts that defined the other Saeryn, would stand in the way. My thoughts were different because of that gap. The pendant on my neck or Rasheh's words... Nothing would change it.

Pain growing within, I met his gaze in the mirror. He deserved the truth, and I had to stop lying to myself as well.

"You were right. I'm not her, and I never will be."

I shifted. I wanted to get away from his touch and the intimacy my body longed for. It wasn't mine. But when I got up from the stool, he embraced me. The strength of his grip suggested he wouldn't let me go even if I tried to break free.

"She's dead, but you aren't. I should have chosen you over her sooner."

I held my breath. To hear the words I could have only dreamed of hearing seemed less real than having memories of a woman who had my past life. Yet Rasheh's intense gaze and his tight embrace reassured me it wasn't an illusion. He was choosing me for who I was instead of seeing a mere incomplete copy of his dead lover.

I leaned against him, my eyes closed, determined to keep that moment forever, to etch it into my mind so deep that no death nor memory loss could take it away.

THE SOUND of chimes ringing through the mansion woke me up. With my mind still muddled by sleep, I scrambled for clarity. Rasheh, already up, was putting on his clothes, and his rushed motions brought a flash of memory that chased away the sleepiness. There were assassins in the building!

"Stay here," he told me before he dashed outside.

I didn't listen. I was already jumping out of the bed, getting dressed in a similar hurry. A blurred memory I didn't have time to pursue was forcing me to follow him.

My heart thumped with every step, and images of assassins penetrating the mansion disturbed the real, empty corridor. Once or twice, I leaped over a body only to realize it wasn't there, and if not for the sense of urgency, I would have stopped to regain the control over my mind.

Malatrius's chamber was empty, so there was only one place he could be going, one place where he'd be safe from anyone. I took off toward the prism cube library.

I saw the sorcerer soon after, three turns and two corridors later. He wasn't in a rush, as if his life were not at stake, and I cursed under my breath. Someone in his position would not stoop to fleeing, but to me, such pride was careless. We were alone, but my instincts screamed of danger, and I shook my head, trying to focus. It must be a memory that held me tight, disrupting my perception, but I was hesitant to chase it away. If I did, it might never return.

"Master..." I caught up with him.

A wave of relief almost swept me off my feet when I saw no injuries. If anything happened to Malatrius, there would never be a ritual... I groaned when Past Saeryn's fear swarmed my mind, distorting what was real. The ritual had already happened, and even if Malatrius died now, I would always be reborn.

He looked at me. "It's the final one." Sadness infused his words.

"What—"

The light breeze behind me was a warning, but I didn't

have enough time to react. The assassin's dark silhouette seemed to have risen right beside me, and as my body responded in trained fashion, a blade cut through my arm.

I stumbled backward. The wound wasn't deep, but the burning told me what was coming. My lost memories flocked to me like scared birds, leaving no space for doubt. As I looked at Malatrius, I knew I had little time to live. I'd make it as far as the prism cube library, walking away from Rasheh, who was about to rush in... or maybe not. Maybe this time he'd be spared witnessing my death.

But if he did, Malatrius would send him away to chase down the assassins. Then he'd join me in the library. We wouldn't talk much as he'd prepare the ritual, but before I died, I had to tell him one last thing.

Promise me that you'll bring me back here, master. No matter what my father says, I beg you. Bring me back here, to him.

I blinked, standing in the corridor. Once more a memory took over my mind, but this time it blurred the lines between present and past. I held my hand to my bleeding arm, uncertain whether there was still any threat.

"Do you remember now?" Malatrius asked. "Do you understand?"

"Yes," I whispered.

And I did. He hadn't offered my memories back for the memories themselves. He had so that I could remember the reason I'd wanted to go back. So that I would remember Rasheh. Malatrius couldn't have told me I was in love. I had to feel it for myself. His reluctance to share information with me, his avoidance of certain topics, and his insistence I remembered on my own finally made sense. In the end, he hadn't lied to me. He *never* had.

My arm still stung and blood flowed, but the poison-like burn was gone. "The wound?"

"Just another way to make you remember," he replied. "It's not poisoned."

A shift from behind startled me. I'd forgotten all about the assassin! Everything else might have been a memory, but the cut on my arm was very real, so the man who'd dealt me the wound had to be as well. I couldn't understand why he would stand motionless until now, allowing us a conversation instead of striking again. If he was under a spell, he wouldn't be able to move at all...

Then things came together, and I knew who he was before he removed his veil. Seeing Rasheh's pained face brought a wave of guilt. To allow me to get my memory back, he'd gone through the excruciating pain of reliving the moment when his first lover died. Now I understood why when I first eavesdropped on him and Malatrius, he was arguing with the sorcerer, ready to disobey his master. A promise to Past Saeryn or not, it was a cruel thing to demand of Rasheh.

I reached out to comfort him, but he moved past me quickly and got far enough away that I couldn't touch him.

"I did what you asked, master." His cold tone didn't surprise me. I had to admire that, despite what Malatrius had forced him to do, Rasheh stayed loyal and obedient. "Is there anything else she needs to remember?"

"No, that's all," Malatrius replied, and I could swear he was surprised and perhaps even slightly taken aback.

"Very well. If you don't need me anymore, I'll leave now. I'd like to speak with you in the morning." As he bowed and walked away, not once did his eyes search for me.

Words died in my throat, unvoiced, because I understood.

"It was all a lie, wasn't it?" I couldn't help asking anyway, as if there was a chance I was wrong.

Rasheh had never felt anything for *me* and done it all only because Malatrius told him to. I should have guessed, should have *known*, but instead, I'd foolishly allowed myself to fall for an illusion.

"Things didn't go as either of us imagined. When I sent Rasheh away to track down where the assassins came from, I thought I could bring you back within days. I'd tell him an ancient ritual helped you survive, and he would never have to know the truth. Or perhaps that would be the time you decided to reveal your secret to him. But it took me some time to get familiar with the other world and its workings, and even more time to find you. Then I learned you'd lost your memories, but I still hoped you would remember enough before he returned." Malatrius looked down the corridor, even though Rasheh's silhouette had already disappeared around the corner. "I did what I could to fulfill the promise, but I can't change his heart. He only sees what's been taken from him instead of appreciating what he could have back."

I shook my head. "It's fine, master. He's right to say I'm not her, and he has no reason to settle for a lousy replica." I took pride that my voice didn't tremble, even though my body was ready to collapse from a heartache.

"Give him time," Malatrius said with a sudden softness, and I had no doubt he saw through me. "Busy with the assignment I'd given to him on the night of your death, he didn't have a chance to grieve, and those feelings cloud his judgment."

I doubted any amount of time would change Rasheh's

mind about me, but I bowed nonetheless. It wasn't Malatrius's fault, and it wasn't in his power to change it.

"Thank you, master." Hiding behind formalities was the best I could do. "I truly appreciate your efforts. You kept your promise to her."

To *her*, not to me, because he'd never made any promises to me. He'd only said he'd try to help me restore my memories, and that he had done. As much as I might have hoped otherwise, his house wasn't my home, and I was never really a part of it. Those memories and experiences belonged to the other Saeryn, and my own were a mere reflection of them.

Before Malatrius replied, I rushed off. I didn't remember the moment of my own death, but I could imagine it might have felt similar to the pain tearing my heart apart now. I wandered through the corridors, unwilling to go back to a bedroom full of memories and reminders of my foolishness, and with Rasheh's scent still in the air and on the bedsheets. I needed another place where I could go through my torment—so tonight, I'd sleep in the prism cube library, if the gods allowed me an actual respite from my suffering.

Because maybe Rasheh was right, and I was someone else, some other Saeryn and not the one who'd died.

But I loved him all the same.

Chapter 10

Seeking solace in sorcery

Magic became my escape. Learning how to wield it brought the feeling of control that I didn't have over my own feelings, and perhaps even my whole life. It also provided a distraction from the misery of my mind. Focusing on challenges I could overcome and goals I could accomplish let me pretend I didn't remember Rasheh.

I was certain Malatrius had sent him away, under the pretense of some task that needed to be done, and I appreciated that. No matter how much pain I was in, at least I didn't have to dread leaving my room every morning, anticipating walking into Rasheh somewhere in the corridor, or worse, finding him in Malatrius's company.

This also made me realize that while Past Saeryn might have felt at ease in the sorcerer's home, I was but a guest. The thought stung, as if part of me wished I was still her, no matter what kind of dark secrets she might have kept.

It wasn't only about Rasheh. My relationship with Malatrius felt different as well—the binding oath that tied him with my past self and the games they both played affected how they acted around each other and what they said. I, on the other hand, didn't have anything that I was desperate to hide, except maybe how much Rasheh's rejection hurt me, but I suspected it wasn't much of a secret anyway. I didn't have the fear of the sorcerer killing me for disobedience either.

Yet I felt the same respect for him as she did, and I had to appreciate that even though the circumstances had changed, even though *I'd* changed, Malatrius still made an effort to treat me as if I was the same Saeryn who'd arrived at his household as a slave and climbed the ranks of his servants, gaining his trust enough to become his student.

He even allowed me in his private spell chamber, which spoke more than anything to his fondness of the past me. Had he cared any less, I'd be performing challenging spells in the prism cube library, perhaps isolated, but not offering enough focus.

The spell chamber, its walls and floor all in irregular tiles made from black, lustrous stone, not only offered solitude, but blocked out any noises and outside light. Save one candle in the middle, we were sitting in darkness, and I could hardly make out Malatrius's silhouette from the surrounding walls, as he sat at the far end of the chamber. If I wasn't looking for him, I could pretend I was alone in the dark, silence surrounding me.

"Begin," the sorcerer said.

This was the last in a string of hours-long incantations, and I focused my eyes on the candle flames to get rid of all the thoughts plaguing me. Exhaustion mixed with the exhilaration of the magic flowing through my body, but my control neared perfection as I enunciated every word of the spell with precision and at the right time.

When I was done, the expression on Malatrius's face as he moved into the candlelight's reach told me I'd done well.

"Impressive," he said.

His voice carried the pride of a teacher who'd seen his student succeed, and I beamed. In many ways, I preferred his tutelage to my father's. Judging from what little scraps of memories I'd recovered, my father never seemed to push me beyond what was comfortable to me, and he was quick with praise, but his words of approval never preceded more challenges. Malatrius, on the other hand, mercilessly pointed out every slip, demanding perfection in every little spell I performed, but it came with the trust that I was ready for whatever he was challenging me to do.

"I'm satisfied with your progress. Despite your earlier... *rebellious* remarks, you seem to have committed to your studies."

I bowed my head to conceal any feelings that my face might betray, seeing as that commitment was fueled by the raw pain I was trying to escape.

"Thank you, master. I appreciate your praise and your time. But I think... I think that perhaps I should be heading home soon," I said. "It's been weeks, and my father likely worries about me. He doesn't know what I know, so he's distrustful."

Malatrius regarded me with narrowed eyes, weighing his response, and even though I had no reason to be suspicious, under his gaze, I felt uneasy. My father's warnings once more rang in my ears. The Sorcerer from the Desert wasn't a friend to us... Or perhaps only to him, I reminded myself.

He gave me a sour smile. "I think he would trust me even less if he *knew* what happened. I do trust him less than I did when I first killed him. Besides, I've been wondering about your memory loss, and I still don't understand why you have only forgotten about your time here and the arts."

I didn't hide my disappointment. Until he said it, I'd allowed myself to believe that his fondness for me was genuine. I should have expected that all he was looking for was a way to turn me against my father.

He lifted his hand, stopping me from speaking that accusation out loud. "You've trusted me so far—with your life, your death, and your memories. You owe me as little as hearing me out."

Of course he'd use that argument, but he was right. To deny him presenting whatever thoughts he wanted to share would show a lack of gratitude. No matter what his true intentions were, he *had* helped me remember, and in the past, he'd done even more for me. Without his benevolence, I'd still be a slave, or dead without a chance of ever being reborn.

I gave him a short nod, doing my best to conceal my displeasure. And, in the end, he had to know that hearing him out didn't mean I would believe him or agree with what he said.

"Have you ever considered why you were born?" he asked. "Clearly Kithandar doesn't feel anything for your mother, but even without it, he could have obliged her with a child. Yet you're not your mother's precious daughter. Instead, he's kept you close, taught you the arts, and gone as far as revealing the secret of his power to me to ensure you could be reborn. Why?"

I smiled. If that was his only doubt, I'd be happy to put it to rest. "He wanted someone to share the secret with. Even sorcerers get lonely."

"But they also get jealous and protective of their

power." Malatrius arched his eyebrow. "And I found your education in the arts quite... limited."

"I have time, don't I?" I shrugged off his remark, though it echoed Past Saeryn's frustrations. My father made decisions she didn't always agree with, and I sensed her thirst for knowledge and determination, which, so far, I hadn't discovered within myself. "Lifetimes of it."

"This could be the reason," he agreed, but too quickly for me to believe this was an end to it. "Or he doesn't want you to know as much as he does, so you'll never become a threat to him. I have lived long enough to be able to understand the mindset of someone like him. Protective about his secrets and power, but also... indeed, lonely." He smirked. "Watching your mates die off while you keep living or being reborn... I imagine it could be quite taxing."

I remained silent, not willing to give him more arguments he could turn against me.

"Tell me, how many rebirths do you think you'll have to go through to feel lonely as well? All of your lovers dying while you keep coming back?" Malatrius looked me in the eye.

He didn't even have to mention Rasheh for me to imagine how much pain it could cause, but I wouldn't give in to such crude manipulation, and I didn't think it was his goal, so I waited.

"How many forgotten memories before you don't know anymore that you're his daughter?"

I drew a wheezing breath, uncertain whether I even wanted to try containing the anger surging within me. Never, not even with my most daring suspicions, had I thought he'd make such a blunt and bold accusation. "That's..." I searched for the words. No matter how much

Malatrius distrusted my father, he had no right to even *suggest* something so vile, so...

I wasn't allowed to finish my remark *or* my thought. Malatrius lifted his hand and said a word, just one word. I froze, unable to move. My composure shattered upon the touch of his magic, and I couldn't focus on defending myself, even if I could dream of being capable of standing up to him.

"I know the memory-erasing spell too," he said so coldly that I couldn't help wondering whether he was finally showing his true colors. "Within a heartbeat, I could make you forget this moment. I could erase Rasheh from your mind even better than your father did, because I know exactly what I need to remove so that you never feel like you're missing anything. Or"—he leaned forward—"I could ensure you never mention Kithandar or the other world again. You'd be serving me as you did, unaware you had another life."

I listened, unable to break free of his control. He could act on any of his threats without worrying that I'd oppose him, and once he was finished... A cold shiver grazed my spine like a knife's edge. Once he was finished, I wouldn't even know what he'd done.

Yet, instead of doing so, he released me.

"I won't send you back until you're able to defend yourself from it. I might be wrong about Kithandar, but knowing what I'm offering will be of use either way."

I slumped, taking deep breaths to mitigate my recent panic's grip on my body, and I couldn't hold back my challenging tone when I replied, "You don't think you're wrong."

Malatrius nodded. "I simply don't trust Kithandar.

Therefore, I don't want my trust in his daughter to become my undoing."

His remark stung more than I'd expected. "If you trusted me, you'd know I'd never turn on you."

He gave me a dry smile. "Only if you *remember* that you wouldn't. Memories can be erased with some precision if one knows how to do it, which means they can be manipulated. With a bit of work, your father could convince you that you have reasons to come after me. All it takes is leaving the right memories and removing those that would shed a different light on them."

As much as I wanted to trust my father and was ready to defend him, Malatrius had a point. I *was* vulnerable. I didn't believe my lost memories were my father's doing, but the mere existence of a memory-erasing spell meant I was an easy mark for any sorcerer.

"I understand," I said. "How long will it take for you to teach me?"

"However long it takes for you to learn."

This wasn't what I wanted to hear, but Malatrius didn't make promises he couldn't keep. I trusted he wouldn't make it any longer than necessary, so it all depended on how quickly I could absorb the knowledge he offered.

"After that, you'll master the world-crossing ritual," he added. "And then you can go back to the other world whenever you're ready."

"But master..." I protested. Learning how to defend myself from memory-affecting spells was beneficial, while learning how to perform the ritual wasn't. It would take me months to master it, and I didn't need it.

The look Malatrius gave me carried a clear warning that I should choose my words carefully, so I lowered my head in a bow of surrender. The sorcerer had his reasons to make such a decision, so I couldn't win this one. All I could do was learn as fast as my own mind would allow me.

"Yes, master."

His expression softened, sternness replaced with satisfaction. No matter what he said about trusting me, and no matter what personal bond we might share, I was still his student and servant, and it pleased him when I remembered my place.

"Get something to eat and drink, and then bring some more over here. We'll start as soon as you're rested. I hope you'll learn quickly, because I'd rather not have Kithandar knocking at my door and asking questions."

I COLLAPSED on the spell chamber's floor in an unladylike heap, my muscles shivering and skin dripping with sweat.

"It's impossible," I panted as failure set in. "I can't hold it steady enough."

Experiencing the immense power and focus necessary for success, I'd finally understood why my father so readily offered such a ritual as a reward for Malatrius's help. With all that it took to open the passageway, he must have assumed the sorcerer would never be able to cross between the worlds.

"Not yet," Malatrius replied, unmoved by my distress. "But your attempt, even if unsuccessful, proves that one day you will."

I shook my head. "Even if it is so, it's going to take me years."

I wasn't ready to stay in Hyrinea for that long, and it had little to do with my father worrying about me, so that was why I avoided looking at Malatrius. The cunning sorcerer would read too much on my face, because thoughts of Rasheh were still too painful to deal with. I needed distance, and not the physical space that Rasheh had so readily granted me by leaving Malatrius's household, but something more. Something that would separate me from all those memories I'd rather not dwell on... Something like another world and another life.

"Or a great amount of desperation," Malatrius replied with a dry smile, as if, regardless of my efforts, he knew what thoughts lurked in my mind. "If I refused to transport you back, you'd do it sooner than you think."

"I have my doubts, master."

"And perhaps they are what is holding you back." He looked down at me. "Anyone can learn the arts. I could even teach Rasheh a few simple tricks if he desired. But to learn as much as you did in such a short time is something few can do. Despite your father's lack of tutoring you beyond basics, in your time here, you've learned quite a few challenging incantations. More than any of my other students in such a short time."

It was high praise from someone like Malatrius. I also couldn't help being curious, because the way he said it made it sound like he had quite a few students. If three years was a short time span for him, just how old was he? I doubted he would tell me or share the secret of how he remained looking younger than he likely was.

"Whether you believe it or not, you're now capable of traveling between the worlds through other means than dying," Malatrius continued. "And thus, today is the last day of you being my student. You can now consider yourself a sorceress, though you should seek more knowledge in the years to come."

He gave me a nod of respect, as if I were his equal, even if in the smallest of ways.

"As we agreed, I'll open the pathway for you whenever you're ready, but you're welcome to stay a little longer should you want to simply rest. I noticed you seem to enjoy my orchard. Rasheh should be back in a few days, and—"

"I'd like to go tomorrow, master." My response was perhaps too quick for the composed sorceress I was supposed to be, but I didn't care.

He looked at me in thought. "You're running away. You should talk to him before you leave."

My lips twisted into a grimace. "I might as well have a conversation with a wall. His lover is dead, and nothing I say or do will convince Rasheh..."

My voice broke. Convince him of what? That I was a worthy replacement? A copy close enough to the real Saeryn?

I looked away, but I doubted Malatrius missed the tears gathering in my eyes. "She couldn't have known what would happen when she died. She tried to do what she thought was best, but she's gone, and I'm not her."

"But you are," Malatrius said. "The memories you've lost might have changed you, but you are still the Saeryn who stared at me defiantly in her father's castle, taking a risk few would dare take."

"Am I, master?" I asked. "What if memories can be created as well? Placed in the mind of a demon shaped into a dead daughter?"

Malatrius's smile was quite condescending. "I doubt Kithandar is skilled enough to perform such impossible feats, but even if he had more power and knowledge than I believe he has, one would need to know the memories one wanted to plant."

I understood. My father had no way of knowing what happened at Malatrius's household. If I wasn't his true daughter, the one who set out from the castle as the sorcerer's slave and spent three years in his service, I wouldn't have been able to restore any of my memories in Hyrinea. I *was* Saeryn.

I breathed out with relief as doubts faded.

"What you've lost and how you regained it made you into a different person, but that person has grown out of the seeds that you have sown yourself," Malatrius said. "You might not be exactly who you once were, but isn't it true for us all?"

I looked up at him with curiosity. It wasn't the wisdom of his words, but the way he spoke—as if he was still the same man as years or even decades ago. As if he was... timeless in his unchanging ways.

He smiled and shook his head slightly. "You haven't known me long enough to notice," he said and laughed when I looked away, embarrassed at having my thoughts exposed. "But indeed, as time passes, I'm more and more set in my ways. Your presence here was a refreshing challenge."

All of a sudden, he leaned forward, a cunning smile stretching his narrow lips. "And I still think that you're running away and that you should say your farewells."

I openly grimaced at his returning to the topic I was hoping we'd already abandoned. "He doesn't care for *my* goodbyes, and my face reminds him of what he lost. There's no point in tormenting us both."

I expected an argument, perhaps a detached voice of reason or an authoritative demand, but the sorcerer only nodded.

"As you wish. Tomorrow morning, then."

I could read on his face that he wasn't satisfied with my

stubbornness, so I let him see my relief. "Thank you, master."

One more night in a place that haunted me with pain, and I'd be back to my old life, choosing carefully what to remember and how to remember it. After working so hard to restore my memories, it felt like a waste to decide to let some of them go, but at least this time, it would be my choice to do so.

"There is one more thing that you should consider," Malatrius said.

I tensed. Even though I had every reason to trust his promise he'd send me back, I couldn't help but expect another excuse or delay.

"What is it, master?"

"The real reason you sought my help. That is one memory I cannot help you regain."

"But I already remember..."

I didn't finish when I understood what he meant. As much as I'd rather forget, the day I met Rasheh for the first time was clear in my head.

He leaned forward, another cunning smile accompanying the gaze of his narrowed eyes. "And do you remember that you didn't tell me the whole truth back then?"

A gasp escaped. "You *knew*?"

I shouldn't be surprised. He must have watched me closely back then, studied my every word and every expression, first searching for threats and lies, then perhaps out of curiosity.

The image of a golden firebird watching me with its black eyes lingered within the memory of that conversation we had in the prism cube library when I revealed everything to him, but I had nothing more. Out of fear or caution, the past me had avoided even thinking about it, burying it so deep it didn't resurface when I restored that memory.

Malatrius inspected his wrist, the thin scar flashing with magic, as if the echo of the oath that bound us still lingered within. "It was clear that you were trying to save my life that night. I allowed that one secret to stay hidden. I was also convinced that when the right time came, you'd share the truth with me." He sighed and looked me in the eye. "But with your death and lost memories... The key to that one secret may lie hidden in the other world, and I can't help you there."

I pressed my lips into a thin line, sensing a hidden warning about my father once more, but in the end, I had to nod. Fragments of memories weren't enough to give me an answer, but they echoed Malatrius's argument. In the past, I had a reason to risk my life as a slave instead of asking my father to haggle with Malatrius on my behalf.

With my back straight and chin up, I responded, "All the more reason to go back."

Malatrius smiled as if he had no doubt that my words were but another argument for the escape from Hyrinea I longed for. Yet he didn't point it out.

He simply said, "Tomorrow morning," and headed out of the spell chamber, leaving me alone with brand-new concerns and questions.

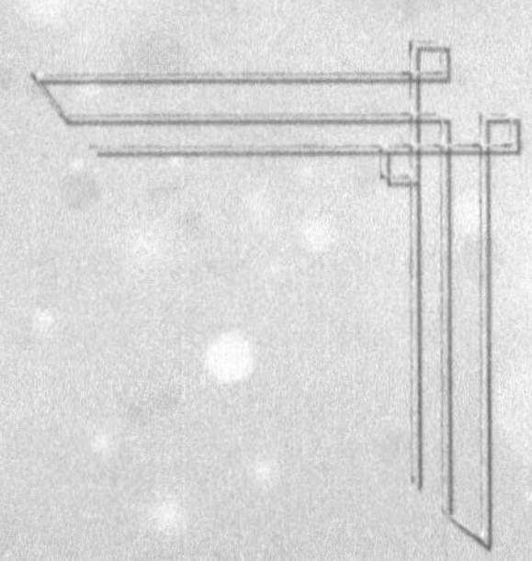

Chapter 11

The other home

The hot air smelled the same. The desert looked different. It wasn't a matter of different light, since I'd seen the desert around Malatrius's household at various times of day, but a different shade of sand and the way it reflected the sun's rays. Even the shape of dunes seemed off in comparison to what I was used to.

The passageway closed behind me, magic dissipating rapidly as the link between the worlds vanished, and there was something final to it, like slamming the door on one's way out. Of course, I *could* still return to Hyrinea, whether via my father's help, my own passageway, or even death, but it wouldn't be the same. Leaving Malatrius's lands felt like leaving a portion of my life behind, and surprisingly, I found myself feeling uneasy about it.

With just one bag, the same with which I'd left the hotel what seemed a lifetime ago, I began a slow ascent of the dune. My feet sank into the sand, slowing me down, but according to Malatrius, I wouldn't have to go far. There was a belt of greenery nearby where I'd find a settlement. Not much of civilization, perhaps, but I had enough of the local currency to arrange some transport to the nearest town. Then I would send a message to my parents and make my travel arrangements.

The thought of going home brought more unease instead of comfort. Perhaps it was because even though I felt like a guest in Malatrius's home, the longer I stayed there, the more it felt like a place I should be—practicing the arts and learning anything the cunning sorcerer was willing to teach me.

Moreover, I was returning home a different person. Previous Saeryn was dead, not because of the poison that had unexpectedly cut her life short, but because of all the memories she'd lost—but the young woman who was struggling with her own mind and had no memories had vanished as well, replaced by a confident sorceress. A fledgling one, but a sorceress nonetheless. Even if my skills were no match for either my father or my teacher, Malatrius had told me before we parted that I had the right to call myself so. One day, perhaps, I'd become a former student he could be proud of.

As I took yet another step up the dune, sinking ankle-deep in sand, a realization made my heart sink as well. I wanted Malatrius to be proud of me more than I cared about my father's praise.

I tensed, struggling to keep going. While I could free my feet of the sand holding them down, my thoughts weren't as easily cleared. If my memories were correct, my father had taught me little of the arts, and he wasn't quick to help me recover that part of my past once I was reborn.

That led to the question of how accurate Malatrius's suspicions were. After all, the past me had kept secrets from her own father and gone to great lengths to gain Malatrius's trust, even though she wouldn't have had to if only she'd allowed her father to strike a deal instead of preparing an elaborate plot to steal the sorcerer's scroll and get his attention.

Perhaps it was better if I didn't mention to my father how much I had learned and what skills I possessed, at least not until I was certain I could trust him.

I paused mid-step and burst out laughing. This must have been what Malatrius really desired: Kithandar's own daughter questioning her father's intentions. After months spent in the desert mansion, it was so easy to forget that I had little reason to mistrust my father.

Yet uncertainty remained—lasting proof that the Sorcerer from the Desert was subtle in his manipulations. Had he been cruder, I'd have had long brushed off any doubts.

Such thoughts inevitably led me to thinking about Rasheh. The sorcerer had managed to change my mind about saying goodbye to him as well. Even though I didn't wait for his return, I'd taken Malatrius's advice—a short letter waited for Rasheh, along with a small locket containing a lock of dark hair. I smiled despite the sadness that lingered whenever I thought of him. He didn't have to know I'd spent the whole evening soaking my own hair in the old Saeryn's favorite perfumes, then washing it several times in scented water. He hadn't gotten to say goodbye to his love, but at least he'd have a keepsake.

And so would I...

The pendant he'd gifted me was tucked in my bag. It might have been a better idea to give it back to him, but I couldn't bring myself to leave it behind. Good memories or bad, it didn't belong to Rasheh. He'd said so himself: it was and always had been mine.

With that bittersweet thought, I searched for some other notion to occupy my mind as I finally crested the dune.

Much closer than I'd thought, lush greens circled a small pond. A few herd animals were grazing at the edge of the desert, and people were going about their day. While I descended toward the settlement, which consisted of half a dozen large tents, I was already plotting my route home. A week sailing down the river, enjoying solitude and adapting back to a more advanced way of living—and behaving the way society expected me to—then a journey across the sea, and on a train through the continent.

And then...

Excitement rushed through my veins. With the past behind me, secure within my memory but without any need to be called upon anymore, I could start planning for the future.

THE CHAUFFEUR OPENED the vehicle's door, and I stood before the five-story family mansion. The crisp autumn morning welcomed me with a breeze foretelling an early winter to come. After the sand and seemingly endless sun, a bit of cold was refreshing, but with my body not used to it anymore, the chill in the air made me want to rush inside the building instead of taking in the mountainous landscape I hadn't seen for so long.

Two meager bags of clothing and the toiletries I'd bought solely for the trip were all the chauffeur unloaded, but he still insisted on carrying them for me as I approached the massive wooden door and knocked.

Back when I was a child, I liked to imagine no humans

nor monsters would be able to open it, and our old servant, Gawen, was the only one capable of such heroic deeds.

And as if straight from my childhood fantasies, he was the one to greet me. His face brightened and his many wrinkles shifted as he smiled. "Miss Saeryn! Welcome back!"

"It's good to see you," I replied with sincerity. "Are my parents in?" I had sent word ahead, but with such a long trip, I hadn't been sure exactly what time or day I would arrive, so even though it was still early, they might have had other plans and left already.

"Waiting eagerly for you." Gawen collected my bags as he let me in. "Milady took your absence quite badly, her humors getting the better of her... several times," he added in a hushed voice. "Even your father didn't seem his usual self, though he tried to reassure your mother that you'd be fine. The lack of letters didn't help either," he added in a scolding tone that suggested he'd shared my parents' concerns.

The mere thought of asking Malatrius to open the passageway between the worlds so that I could send word home almost forced a chuckle out of me, but Gawen wouldn't understand why I was so amused, so I forced a more pensive expression, unsure whether I could fool the man who'd watched me growing up.

"I stayed in a quite remote area."

Whether he believed me or not, he let it go.

"They're in the day room. You should greet them, Miss Saeryn. I'll bring the luggage to your room and tell Lasa to prepare some food. You must be hungry." His eyes skimmed my figure—I was nowhere near famished, but definitely toned after weeks of intensive training.

I sent him a smile of gratitude and hurried deeper into the mansion. The oak walls with paintings I had admired so many times in the past should have offered the comfort of familiar surroundings, but instead they towered around me like a sinister forest of faraway places and ancient people, and the expensive rugs' frills seemed intent on tangling my steps. I scolded myself for conjuring such childish images, but my mind still longed for the sight of the sorcerer's desert home. I hoped that as time passed, I'd rid myself of such sentiments.

I knocked at the day room's door, and as soon as I entered, my mother let out a cry of joy and rose from her chair, dashing toward me. Within heartbeats, she was by my side, hugging me and crying, even though she rarely allowed herself such displays of emotion.

"My dear little girl! You're back! Look at you... all grown up now. Did you have a nice journey? Did you have a good time?" She kept blabbing. "I hope that half-barbaric scholar fed you properly!"

She took a step back to inspect me, and to avoid a too-close scrutiny and more questions, I used an old trick.

"Of course I had a great time, Mother!" I replied with as much exaltation as I could muster. "You should have seen his library! So much knowledge on the lost languages. And the ruins... So many inscriptions to study, so many nooks to explore! I even found one that Professor Atrius had over-looked." With each sentence, the lies became easier, especially as I knew she wouldn't enjoy a scholarly talk for long.

"Now, now." My mother took another step back, my joyous outburst allowing her to regain composure, replacing the concerned mother with the proud and composed noble-woman she was. "You can tell me all about it later. Now you need to eat something. I told Lasa to keep some breakfast warm, but I'm going to check on her. In the meantime, I'm sure your father would like to greet you back home as well."

She threw him a displeased glare, since he was still sitting in his chair, as unmoved as usual. Surely she couldn't have expected my father, of all people, to put on a childish show. Besides, we had things other than greetings to exchange, preferably after she left the room.

"Father," I said as she rushed off.

He didn't move from the table, and I realized he had been studying me while I talked to my mother. "How was your journey?" he asked in vizari.

"Fruitful. I believe I restored all my memories." I chose my words with caution and kept a neutral expression. No matter how much I'd rather not give in to the mistrust that Malatrius had so skillfully sown, wisdom dictated diligence.

"Your vizari certainly got better." He stood up, looking me up and down as I approached. "What of Malatrius's intentions? Did he tell you why he wanted you to return there?"

It didn't escape me that he'd chosen not to inquire about my memories, but it suited me well.

"I believe he saw a chance to shake your composure." With such a long trip home, I'd had plenty of time to put my lie together, but not a single idea sounded plausible enough to pass my father's scrutiny, so I chose to pretend I didn't know anything. "Nothing in my memories suggested he'd made any promises to me. Judging by some of his subtle remarks, he might have been looking for a way to turn me against you. Unless I read him wrong, and he truly felt grateful I'd died saving his life. I wouldn't put it past him to fear I might have come to collect that debt in circumstances not so favorable to him, so he chose to pay it off in an easy and convenient way."

My father cringed at that. "I doubt he felt grateful. A sorcerer like him knows little of gratitude."

I nodded as if agreeing. "Either way, as soon as I thought I'd recovered enough memories, I demanded he send me back. I can live without knowing all the humiliation and torment he put me through for his own enjoyment." I made the lie sound true by letting bitterness echo in my words. It was easy to conjure it at the mere thought of Rasheh. "So what now, Father?"

He offered such a wide and warm smile that I couldn't help doubting Malatrius's claims. At the same time, I couldn't discard them either. Stuck between them, sooner or later I would have to choose which one to side with, because I wasn't fool enough to believe that leaving the Sorcerer from the Desert back in the other world would end the rivalry I might have sparked between them. What was worse, I still didn't know what reasons I'd had to do what I did the way I did it.

"Now you live your life however you want. Pursue studies or find a man that would make your heart skip a beat. Travel. Experience things. You deserve it."

"I thought that since I have my memories back, you could resume teaching me." I made my disappointment clear.

"I will, in due time." He brushed my cheek. "For now, I want you to have some real youth. You've been through so much to complete the ritual. You sacrificed so much. All the money your mother and I have could use a willing spender. Buy some nice things for yourself. Go to parties with friends. Do anything you want, like a young woman of your status should. And later, when you've had enough and feel like you've truly lived, we'll move away from society and make sure you learn all that you need to know."

I swallowed, my thoughts inadvertently dashing back to the desert mansion. I'd *had* a life, and I had experienced more than I could have desired. I'd even already met a man who made my heart skip a beat. I had enough already. But I couldn't tell all of that to my father, unless I wanted to part with secrets I'd rather keep and bare my pain before him.

And even if I chose to do so, he'd already moved away, returning to his chair, as if the matter was settled. He sipped his coffee.

"Just do me one favor, please," he added in a light-hearted tone. "If you decide to marry, do pick someone other than the pompous ignoramus whom your mother is dead-set on matching with you."

I couldn't help but burst out laughing. If there was any value to Philidert, it had to be the amusement his presence brought, though not born of his own attempts at humor. With him around, neither my father nor I would ever lack a reason to joke.

My mother reentered, her face shaded with a hint of jealousy at my unrestricted joy. I never laughed like that around her, and for the first time in years, I found my feelings toward her tainted by regret and pity. I'd always shared secrets with my father, and from him I had learned to treat her in a dismissive manner, so we'd never bonded. And the distance at which her noblewoman's pride seemed to keep everyone didn't help in narrowing the gap, which had only widened with the years passing as I shared more of my father's secrets.

"Lasa has breakfast ready for you," she said. "Come. I'll join you, and you can tell me all about your adventures in those uncivilized lands." Unexpectedly, she took me by the arm, as if the months of my absence had rekindled long-forgotten motherly feelings. "Later we could go for a ride to town and maybe stop by the Asnu-Thigais'? Philidert has been asking for news regularly, but I didn't tell him when you were coming back so that you could surprise him." She winked.

I knew she had the best intentions, but I was tired of her allowing herself to believe so blindly that my society-dictated politeness was something more. At the same time, I couldn't tell her I didn't wish to see Philidert at all, because after having my heart twisted and wrung out, his over-bearing presence would be a tormenting reminder that the man I'd chosen didn't want me. This pain wasn't something either of my parents needed to know.

"Maybe later." I forced a smile. "He can wait a bit longer, and I'd like to get some rest and a nice bath before I show my face in town." I wouldn't be able to avoid him forever, but maybe at least for a couple of days.

As I followed my mother out of the room, I hid a small sigh. Facing old problems wasn't exactly how I'd been planning to start this new stage of my life.

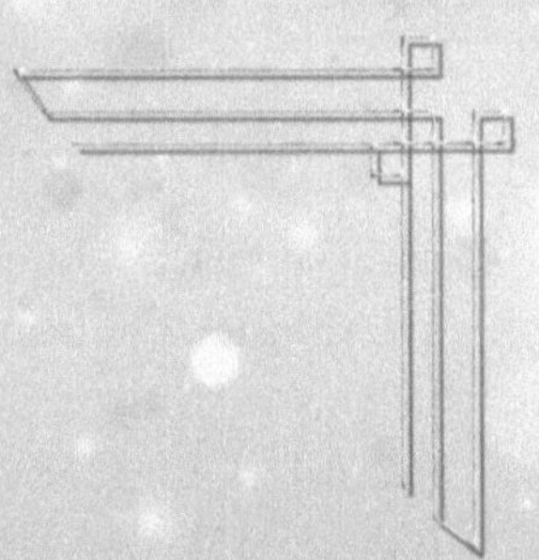

Chapter 12

A person she grew out of

If there was something I hated about summer solstice, it was the endless string of social obligations. Unfortunately, while a family dinner and attending the rites in the temple sufficed for commoners, noble-born were expected to celebrate publicly whether they wanted to or not. Had I been more farsighted, I would have planned to be out of the country pursuing knowledge, which would have been a plausible excuse, since I'd already filled my winter and spring with research and studies.

With every new invitation I couldn't turn down, I regretted not paying closer attention to the passage of time and letting summer celebrations sneak up on me. It was too late to arrange anything else, unless I wanted to fabricate a serious illness—something neither of my parents would approve of. I had to attend.

I sighed, looking through my wardrobe in a spacious hotel suite. Seven evening dresses for seven events, and I wasn't looking forward to any of them.

At least my mother had insisted that this year we join the celebrations in the capital, which meant I had a chance of disappearing into a crowd and perhaps even sneaking away, instead of being stuck in a rather tight group of close neighbors, with Philidert following me everywhere I went like a forlorn puppy. The mere thought of him made me grimace. Of course, I wouldn't be able to avoid him, as the Asnu-Thigai family had arrived in the capital as well, and I was expected to at least exchange greetings with them.

But Philidert likely wouldn't be my only problem. As the sole heir of my family's considerable wealth, with a tragic accident to add excitement to my otherwise mundane life story, I'd likely draw the attention of many other eligible men, and hardly any of the conversations with them would be anything more than the empty courtesies and small talk that society expected, or worse—attempts at charming me into agreeing to marry them.

Resigned, I picked the first outfit and put it on. At least I'd won the battle with my mother, who was insisting on getting me a maid. The idea of someone disrupting what little solitude I had, given the circumstances, made my disagreement adamant enough for her to give up. It was bad enough that my parents occupied the suite across the corridor.

The dress flowed beautifully, a mix of dark sky-blue with black trim and matching tiny beads for decorative accents, but as I looked at myself in the mirror, I missed the simpler outfits Malatrius's servants wore. After months of attending too many social events, catering to my mother's constant nagging to not bury myself in research and not finding any support from my father, I longed for the desert mansion and its work-filled days. The relatively short time I'd spent there seemed to hold more purpose than my whole life back in this world.

Part of me dreamed of returning there, despite the

unpleasant memories. After all, memories faded, or perhaps I could even ask Malatrius to remove the few most painful ones, and I had no doubt that Rasheh would do everything in his power to avoid me, so I wouldn't see him often.

I shook my head. Going back was not possible. It wasn't a matter of being unable to open the passageway, since poison or a blade could transport me back as well. But without the oath binding us and without the reason the old me wanted to end up in Malatrius's household, I didn't have a place there anymore. The daughter of his rival and a fledgling sorceress couldn't remain his servant, stuck performing menial tasks, and Malatrius had already taught me all he wished to share with me, so I wouldn't be his student either. I couldn't even be a mere mistress to his loyal servant, as Rasheh had made it clear he wanted nothing to do with me.

I sighed. Perhaps my father's advice had carried wisdom I didn't yet possess myself. Maybe I should, indeed, pursue an academic career, or at least set out to travel around the continent. New places and new faces could push my thoughts in a different direction and leave the memories of sand behind.

A quiet knock on the door brought me back to reality. When I opened it, there stood a man wearing the hotel's uniform.

"Your parents are waiting, ma'am," was all he said, and then he bowed and left.

I was so lost in my own thoughts, I didn't realize how much time I'd wasted on fruitless pondering, so I rushed through my makeup and hairdo, hoping they were good enough to stand up to my mother's scrutiny. They likely weren't because, wrapped in my longing for simpler ways and the mindset of a humble student and servant, I'd kept away from anything sophisticated. One glance at my jewelry box made me wince. I didn't want to wear any of it. Everyone already knew we were wealthy—why make a blunt demonstration of it?

Then one item caught my eye. Among countless gold and silver masterpieces with intricately cut gems lay a simple necklace with an obsidian stone. Responding to my emotions, my hand shot toward the box, ready to shut it, as if I could also shut off the memories of the man who gave it to me. But as I glanced in the mirror, I changed my mind. With my meager makeup and simple hairdo, a lack of gaudy pieces would contribute to a modest, shy look.

My hands shook slightly as I put it on my neck, but the woman who looked back at me from the silvery reflection wasn't the old Saeryn in her plain tunic, hair let down. It was the woman I was becoming, confident and elegant. I smiled to her, certain that as some memories faded, she'd grow more familiar.

Then, purse in hand, I left the room and made my way down to the lobby as quickly as was acceptable for a noblewoman.

The hotel's corridors resembled an endless labyrinth of doors and turns, and the frustration of traversing such a maze kept me from appreciating the tasteful décor, white and gold ornaments in geometric patterns and trimmed indoor plants. It was a relief when the vast lobby finally came into view.

My parents were sitting in the comfortable chairs of the semi-private waiting area. My father, as usual, wore an evening-black frock and a top hat, expressing elegance and wealth through simplicity and good quality. By his side, my mother resembled an exotic bird, shining from the jewels she wore—multifaceted topazes that matched the gold sequins of her dress, its sleek design undoubtedly following the newest fashion.

She looked me up and down, a grimace of displeasure sneaking into the corners of her lips. "You look like your own impoverished cousin."

"Real wealth doesn't need to show off money," I fired back. Even though my mother's outfit was by no means gaudy, her remark demanded retaliation. The evening was going to be hardly sufferable even without her derogatory comments. "And your dear Philidert would probably love it if I wore even less... of anything."

She drew air with the hiss of disapproval I knew so well. "That's hardly an acceptable remark for a young lady."

She glanced at my father, but I couldn't tell whether she was blaming him for my behavior or seeking support.

With my ire rising, I didn't back away. "It matches the situation, Mother. Sometimes it seems that if you could, you'd be happy to push him into my bed."

My father rose from his seat. "That's enough, both of you." His cold voice made it clear how little he cared about our fight. "Let's go. Being late isn't as fashionable as some claim."

My mother threw me one last glare, full of anger and hurt, but said nothing and joined my father, so I followed them without a word as well. The sooner we got to Prince Sulla-Amahai's palace, the sooner I'd be able to get away from them both.

～

I'D VISITED Prince Sulla-Amahai's palace once or twice in the past, but that was long before I lost three years of memories and restored them, making new ones along the way—so even though I remembered the palace, everything from "before" seemed faded and irrelevant. And because of that, I was allowing myself to take it in as if I were seeing it for the first time.

The vast halls were filled with crowds, gentlemen in frocks and ladies in their best dresses, but the noise remained mild, as if no one dared speak louder than the musicians playing in the background. Every now and then, a glass clinked or someone's laughter rose above the quiet conversations, but those rare occurrences were all that indicated the prince was holding the biggest event in the country and not some small, private get-together.

I skimmed past tasteful furniture and polished marble floors, past flowers and ornaments, and I couldn't help feeling that neither my father nor I belonged to such a spoiled and self-important society. Our place was in Hyrinea, in the lands where magic still thrived and people rightfully respected and feared sorcerers.

That led me to pondering how my father had discovered this world, and why our rebirth alternated between the two of them, though I could speculate it was a safety measure. Should anyone discover his place of rebirth back in Hyrinea, they wouldn't be able to trap my father in an endless cycle of deaths. Reborn in this world, he could return to Hyrinea through a passageway and ambush his unsuspecting opponents.

I sighed. There were so many things I still didn't know, like whether there were more worlds, and how one would go about finding them, or even for how long he had lived so far. And whenever I remembered how my father had brushed off my desire to learn more, I had a hard time keeping my face straight.

"Is everything all right? Do you need rest?" A soft voice pulled me out of my thoughts.

Amalia Shevo-Thusai, a petite brown-haired woman, was looking at me with concern, so I mustered a smile.

"I'm sorry," I replied. "I just drifted off in thought. It's been a while since I attended a ball like this."

She nodded, her expression full of understanding. "We were all shocked to hear about your accident in the mountains. You were never the one to take risks, so it was unbelievable such a thing could happen to you. And the coma, the convalescence... Your father kept us all away, and when you didn't come back from Quathan with your parents, we worried again."

"I'm fine now. A few months away from civilization worked miracles for my health and mind," I said with a warm smile.

I hoped Amalia was still as talkative as she used to be, and I wouldn't have to say much more, but her gossip-hungry face suggested she wanted all the details of my supposed adventures in the "savage lands."

"Are others going to be here as well?" I asked, hoping to steer the conversation away from myself.

"Of course! No one would miss such an event. Morel Halda-Rihai is already mingling with the young ladies."

She indicated one of the niches in which delicate feminine laughter echoed regularly, giving testimony to the handsome nobleman's flirting skills. I could bet that over the years, he'd only perfected ways to keep the ladies' attention.

"Juve and Jivin Olfe-Parnai circle around the prince's exotic guest," Amalia continued. "And I haven't seen Philidert Asnu-Thigai yet, but his family is bound to arrive soon. We can walk over to the entrance hall if you don't want to miss him."

"I'm sure Philidert will find us eventually."

I concealed my real feelings under a smirk, but Amalia still gave me a curious glance.

"I heard that he accompanied your family during the trip to Quathan." Her expression was that of a hound smelling its prey. "There's certain gossip that you and him…"

That remark pushed a grimace onto my lips, and I didn't try to hide it. "I wouldn't be surprised if he spread it myself."

I was quite certain that whatever Philidert felt toward me wasn't love, even if he fooled himself to believe so. My heart ached at the mere thought of Rasheh, but at least the experiences I'd shared with him made me realize how shallow and self-absorbed Philidert's attention toward me was. I was pretty enough and born into a family with both noble name and money to back our high position in society, therefore I had all the qualities to make a good wife for someone of his status. His supposed love or even just affection toward me was nothing but a means to make a future marriage look like something more than a mutual transaction or a way to keep other suitors away.

"So, there's nothing?" Amalia didn't want to let go. "Not even a grain of truth?"

"My mother invited him." I didn't hide the displeasure in my voice. "Better tell me about that exotic guest. Am I missing out on something?" I cared little about whomever the prince invited, but I needed the topic to change before I said too many blunt words about Philidert.

"Oh, definitely!" To my relief, Amalia took the bait. "Handsome but more… primal. There's something savage and wild about him. He makes all other men look docile and weak." Her eyes shone as she spoke. "Nobody knows where he's really from. Supposedly south of Quathan, from one of those kingdoms hidden in the jungles. The prince met him during one of his hunting expeditions."

I wouldn't admit it out loud, but Amalia's words spiked my curiosity. Little was known about the lands south of Quathan, and the jungle kingdoms were largely a myth, with little evidence brought by explorers. Even if there was some truth to their existence, their technical and cultural advancements would likely be insufficient to meet the expectations of the civilized world. To think that the prince would invite someone like that to the biggest celebration of the year... I couldn't help but be curious.

But I had another reason to be interested in that guest. "South of Quathan" was where I'd supposedly visited as well, and I hoped that perhaps Malatrius had decided to revisit my world. It would be like him to make an acquaintance with the prince, if only to grate on my father's nerves. If it was truly him, trouble would follow, but I'd welcome any excuse to keep away from Philidert and social life.

"Now you've got me curious," I said. "Let's have a look."

Amalia chuckled, and her voice, sweet like birds in the summer, drew several longing gazes. I'd be surprised if she didn't marry soon, able to choose from the best eligible bachelors.

"We can have a look, but I don't think Juve and Jivin will let you anywhere near him. They're currently putting all their efforts into making sure the savage warrior, as they call him, notices no women but them."

My hopes sank. If the prince's guest was young enough to attract the sisters' attention, he couldn't be the Sorcerer from the Desert.

"They can't *both* have him," I said as she led me through the crowd.

"Maybe they can." Amalia blushed. "Who knows what those savages like... and how they like it."

That certainly wasn't a remark I'd expect from a refined young lady like Amalia Shevo-Thusai, but most of my memories of her—and my other friends—were nearly four years old. It would be naïve to presume they remained as innocent as we all used to be when we were just entering adulthood, experimenting with many new and exciting... *activities*.

Thinking about it brought a flash of memory, of some pleasurable but inconsequential nights with Morel Halda-Rihai that both he and I had had the wisdom to keep secret from the rest of our friends. Perhaps Amalia had similar secrets.

"Oh, there they are."

Even from a distance I recognized Juve and Jivin—or the Olfe-Parnai Twins, as everyone referred to them—who stole all the attention with their smiles on flawless oval faces surrounded by perfectly groomed golden locks. They wore matching dresses, Juve an azure one with silver accessories, and Jivin silver with azure accents.

But it was the man who stood beside them that made me stop mid-step and gasp. My eyes were clearly deceiving me, and I couldn't decide which was less possible: the prince's guest looking exactly like Rasheh, or Rasheh himself in a world that wasn't his. As he smiled at something Juve said, his moves and the crease of his lips were painfully familiar. He seemed at ease in the twins' company, and his outfit matched what would be considered a Quathani take on continental fashion—exotic, but acceptable in high society.

Then our eyes met and his focus shifted, leaving no

doubt that he wasn't a lookalike. He excused himself, left the sisters, and walked straight toward me.

I stood frozen by the excruciating pain of my own heart, and I could hardly keep my face straight enough to not reveal anything to all the guests around us.

Rasheh stopped before me and bowed. "I was hoping we'd meet here." He spoke the language fluently, and only his slight accent betrayed him.

"Do you know each other?" Amalia looked back and forth between us, though her eyes shot toward Rasheh more often than not.

I couldn't blame her. Even in this outfit, he still had an aura of power and confidence around him, and his shoulder-length hair certainly didn't conform with the continental fashion, which demanded men keep their hair trimmed above their ear line and swept backward rather than let loose.

"Yes, we met when Miss Saeryn was visiting my uncle's lands," Rasheh replied with ease.

I arched an eyebrow at his lie, but I didn't intend to expose it. If Malatrius had sent him to this world, there must be a reason, and such lies were nothing but a way to ensure no one knew the truth about him... or me, for that matter.

"Indeed, we've met." I regained enough control to speak without my voice wavering. "I didn't expect you to travel... so far from home. Do you mind if I take a moment of your time to ask you about your uncle's wellbeing?" With everyone looking, I needed an excuse for a private conversation.

"Of course not!" He flashed a smile and offered his arm. "He's grown quite fond of you and will be happy to hear how you're doing. He'd be *delighted* if you visited again."

The friendliness and warmth with which he spoke could fool anyone into believing that he shared his "uncle's" wish for my return. Anyone but me. Yet if I wanted to avoid questions from the onlookers, I had to play along. I forced myself to hold his arm, and steeled myself for the pain and longing that would accompany such.

As he led me to the balcony, Juve and Jivin approached Amalia, their expressions full of thinly veiled jealousy, and I was certain they would drill my friend to learn all they could about my relationship with the object of their attention.

"Did the master send you? Is everything all right?" I asked in vizari once we got away from the others. The sooner we were done with this conversation, the less I would suffer.

We stopped by the railing. The balcony overlooked the prince's famous gardens, and it made me think back to a similar moment, the one that started it all, when I stood alone at the hotel's terrace and Malatrius approached me.

"I asked him to send me here." He leaned against the marble baluster, but his eyes were on me. "It was a kind gesture. The letter and the locket."

To endure his gaze was too much, so I turned my head toward the garden. "I only passed on what I found in her room."

He huffed. "And that's why the hair by your nape is shorter than the rest?" He leaned closer, and even though I kept my eyes firmly on the greenery below, I could *feel* a smile creeping over his lips. "I could show you exactly where, if the customs of this world didn't restrict me."

I tensed at his teasing tone. He should be happy that the same customs restricted me as well, because otherwise I'd smack him. After all that had happened, after all the pain that I—no, *we both* had to go through, he was back to playing his games.

"Is that why you came? To tell me you knew? You could have saved yourself the journey and just tossed it away."

"I came to ask why you did it. You left before I returned."

I hesitated. My hurt pride demanded that I mock him and push him away, but the question had to be important to him if he'd made a journey into an unfamiliar world just to have it answered.

"She never got to say goodbye to you," I whispered. I talked about Past Saeryn as if she wasn't me, because Rasheh considered us two different people. "She was so certain that she'd be back before you knew, that she never even considered that something could go wrong. She never prepared for such an outcome and left nothing. I thought you might like to have something to remember her by."

The silence that followed forced me to glance at him, but I couldn't read his face.

"That's... generous and thoughtful after all that happened between us," he said.

This must be the closest I would get to not being a demon with his dead lover's face.

"It would have been if you didn't know the truth." I gave him a bitter smile. "What betrayed me this time?"

To my surprise, he shook his head. "Nothing. They were perfect. But she never cut her hair. Besides, she also would have simply given it to me instead of keeping it hidden."

Even though he spoke with confidence, I had a feeling he wasn't sure, at least not until he saw my uneven hair. I should have trimmed it when I returned home, but since it wasn't visible unless someone was looking closely, I'd never bothered. Especially since I couldn't have imagined Rasheh following me to this world, so it didn't matter.

"You have your answer now," I said. "Was it worth such a long journey?"

The arch of his eyebrow, as if he were questioning the true motives of my inquiry, was painfully familiar. "I'm not done here yet."

I tried to figure out the trap he might be setting. If he hadn't come with a message from Malatrius, his reasons must be his own. Unless... Rasheh was a killer, and my father was vulnerable enough in the world in which he didn't expect enemies, or at least not assassins. If his death was public, it would cause a lot of trouble for him if he wanted to return after being reborn.

"What else do you want?" I asked, anger stirring within me.

My brash response had a greater effect than I'd expected. He jerked back as if I'd slapped him, but regained composure quickly enough.

"For now... For now I want to see you smile like you smiled... before I brought you suffering."

I rolled my eyes. After the moment of sincerity we had just shared, I'd expected more than his pretending that he cared about my wellbeing. But if I wanted things to go smoothly, I had to reassure him I'd be fine. And the sooner he ran out of reasons to be around, the sooner he wouldn't be.

With that in mind, I forced a small smile onto my lips.

He scrutinized my performance, but then he nodded. "I guess I shouldn't have hoped for more."

I bit my tongue before asking viciously whether he had any other wishes. No matter how much pain he had caused me, I couldn't really blame him for it. If Malatrius hadn't ordered him to help me relive my memories, he would have never become intimate with me.

A commotion at the balcony's entrance saved me from saying something I would regret later, but one glance at my accidental savior soured my mood instead of improving it. Philidert stood beside Amalia and the twins, waving at me with a big smile, a clear sign that my alone time with Rasheh was ending.

Rasheh glanced at Philidert. "I see your suitor arrived in time to save you. Your suffering will be... altered, I suppose."

I had to appreciate the joke. It seemed that Malatrius had told Rasheh about Philidert, and I was grateful. Things were hard enough without me having to explain my so-called relationship with the annoying nobleman.

"I'd take your malicious remarks over his company any time," I replied before thinking my own words through. "I apologize. That was uncalled for."

Rasheh looked amused as he took a step back and bowed. "But I'll take you up on that promise nevertheless. Let's talk later, without so many curious eyes around... if you would be inclined to keep your balcony door open."

It wasn't even surprising that he knew where I was staying. If he'd managed to arrange our meeting at the biggest social event in the whole of Kvesa, he surely had a way of knowing which hotel my parents had chosen.

"You haven't told me why you're here. What you really want," I said as he headed away from the balcony.

He looked over his shoulder. "Hopefully, to right all the wrongs." He hesitated, and I was certain he wouldn't say anything else, but then he was back to being the confident and daring Rasheh I knew. "And maybe, if that happens, to taste that smile of yours again."

His words made me regret that I'd insisted on knowing.

Part of me, of course, wanted to believe he was telling the truth, but the rest agonized over the prospect of a new, cruel game about to start. And all that in front of my old friends who had no idea what kind of life I'd lived until recently. I stood motionless, focusing my efforts on keeping a neutral expression for others to see while the storm of thoughts ravaged my head.

The sound of Juve's laughter forced me to pay attention to what was going on around me. My friends were approaching, having convinced Rasheh to join instead of leaving.

"You aren't a burden at all," Jivin reassured him. "Our dear Saeryn's friend is always welcome among us, and we'd be delighted if you found us to be worthy company."

Undoubtedly, the twin was using me as an excuse to bring Rasheh closer into our informal circle so that she could spend more time with him. When he bowed in response, offering one of his stunning smiles, I felt a stab of jealousy. It was one thing to lose him to a dead woman, to the woman I once was, and another to a living, beautiful woman and friend.

"How could I refuse such a charming lady?" he replied.

The expression on Juve's face made it clear that I wasn't the only one dealing with jealousy, but at least I knew Rasheh well enough to hope that his behavior was nothing but a game dictated by my society's customs. If he longed for a lover, he wouldn't have to cross between worlds for that, and no matter what I thought of him, I didn't believe he wanted to torment me out of viciousness. Until now, I had been certain that all he wanted was for me to disappear from his life and stop reminding him with my face and voice of what he had lost, and his malicious comments were nothing but a means to an end and a way of dealing with his own pain.

Jivin beamed and grabbed Rasheh by the arm, taking his words as permission to move close to him, but I could hardly pay attention to her, as Philidert was already by my side.

"You look beautiful!" he exclaimed.

To my relief, he didn't try to kiss me on the cheek, though I suspected that was because he wasn't willing to risk being turned down publicly, which would put an end to any gossip about us. After all, for as long as nothing in my behavior contradicted the speculation he was likely spreading himself, people would see us as more intimate than we were.

"So how did you and Saeryn meet?" Juve asked.

Once more, I became an excuse, because I doubted either of the twins was actually interested in the details of our acquaintance, and Juve's question was nothing but a desperate attempt to draw Rasheh's attention away from Jivin.

I expected a lighthearted tale, suitable for the circumstances, but instead, Rasheh became serious. "I was staying on my uncle's lands too. While Miss Saeryn was recovering from her accident and broadening her academic knowledge, I was... recovering as well, from a personal loss." The sadness that clouded his face was genuine, reminding me of what we had both lost along with my memories. If only I had remembered everything, he would have seen *his* Saeryn in me. "Her company... It made the grieving easier." He gave me a nod of gratitude.

I forced a smile at the obvious lie, because my return to Malatrius's homestead had made the grief anything but easier for him. "I'm glad I could help."

As the conversation went on, I found myself missing my

parents' company, even if it meant I'd have to endure my mother's remarks. Philidert stood too close to me, jealousy radiating from his posture, and Rasheh made it difficult for me to keep my face from expressing too much when he, pressed by the twins, told a tear-jerking story of his fiancée dying from a rare disease.

I would have loved to drift off in thought, but since he was telling lies on both our behalf, I had to pay close attention. I'd rather not expose any of our secrets by saying something that contradicted him later. At the same time, I could as well find an excuse to leave early and simply ask Rasheh to fill me in later, if he was going to visit me.

Not that it would happen with so many people around, but I desperately wished for some peace and quiet before facing him again, this time in circumstances where we wouldn't have to play our pretend roles in front of a gossip-hungry audience.

THE PARTY WENT on for too long, and by the time I got back to the hotel, I was ready to collapse on my bed.

The whole evening had been a nightmare of trying to ignore the attention Rasheh was giving the twins, and at the same time keeping track of what was said about the place in which we'd supposedly spent time together. As if that wasn't enough, I'd had to deal with Philidert's jealousy and possessive behavior. He must have sensed there was something between Rasheh and me, even though we kept our distance like acquaintances would, or perhaps Philidert saw the exotic guest as every bit the man he could never be, and his reaction stemmed from instinctual fear of a superior rival.

I sighed. Philidert's reasons didn't matter, just his tiresome behavior. As much as I'd rather avoid attention or scandal, if he continued to be so overbearing, I'd have to put him in his place, preferably in public. But that was a problem for another time.

As I entered my hotel room, the balcony door was closed, and if I left it that way, I would avoid a likely difficult and painful conversation, but I didn't hesitate. No matter what Rasheh intended to say, it was better if we talked.

So I opened the door.

In the corner of the balcony, a dark silhouette leaned against the wall. Rasheh wasn't wearing the exuberant outfit from the party anymore but loose pants and a shirt that reminded me of his desert clothes. Summer in Kvesa was cooler than the usual desert weather, but it was still warm enough for only a layer or two of clothing.

"Thank you," he said.

I stepped aside, letting him in. As much as I'd prefer not to have him in my room, the balcony was hardly private. The last thing I needed was someone spotting us. I already had to deal with the gossip Philidert spread about him and me, so I had no desire to add the stories related to Rasheh.

Silence hung between us, awkward and frustrating. He broke it first.

"I owe you an apology for everything I did. No matter how much I suffered, I had no right to take it out on you. It was childish of me."

"The master made you do it, and I believed what I wanted to see."

I didn't mention that I couldn't understand why the past me—genuinely in love with him, from as much as I could remember—hadn't shared the secret with him. I had revealed it to Malatrius, whom I couldn't even fully trust, but kept it away from Rasheh.

Perhaps I was afraid that the truth would push Rasheh away, that he would treat me differently if I told him. I almost smiled bitterly at the thought that in the end he had treated me—the new me—differently because I chose to *not* tell him.

"So you blame him? Or yourself?"

I curled my fingers into fists, though I doubted it hid their trembling. "I could have been wiser," I said carefully.

"Could you have?" He took a step closer but kept enough distance, as if he only wanted to ensure I wouldn't leave. "A woman with a part of her life lost. A woman who didn't remember who she was. A woman stuck between a powerful sorcerer's game and a foolish man's grief. Could you really have been wiser?"

I sighed. "Why are you here, Rasheh? Haven't you suffered enough? And haven't I? You wanted me gone, yet you've traveled to another world to torment me once more."

"I told you. I want to make amends." He looked me in the eye. "Just because you weren't her didn't mean you weren't deserving of my love."

I huffed. No matter how earnest his words might be, I would be a fool to let my feelings speak. With no good reply, I remained silent.

"Tell me that I should leave," he said. "That you never want to see me again."

"Is that all it will take?"

He smiled. "As long as you're honest about it... like *you* always were."

I had no trouble reading between the lines. "You knew."

He shrugged. "She was the daughter of my master's rival, brought into service against her will. I expected she would keep secrets. She kept them from the day we first met. I just didn't know they weren't a threat to my master, so I kept testing her."

His questioning look made it clear he hoped to learn from me what he hadn't learned from her. But all I could give him was a shake of my head.

"I'm sorry. I don't know. I don't remember. I don't even know why I didn't tell you I'd be reborn after death. But in the end, it doesn't matter. She's gone, and no matter what memories I recover, it's not going to change who I am now," I said with more certainty that I actually felt.

After all, losing my memories had made me into someone else, and so had restoring some of them. There might be secrets that would change how I thought, so I could only cling to the new me I'd become, hoping nothing more would affect me.

"Don't worry about it." Rasheh stepped closer again, and even though he didn't touch me, I caught the scent of his skin. "Tell me something else instead. Do you truly wish me to leave? To be gone?"

Breathing in his scent woke up all the feelings I'd worked so hard to let go. For a heartbeat, I regretted that I hadn't asked Malatrius to remove Rasheh from my memories, but he was my past.

The way he looked at me reassured me that no lie would be good enough, and he didn't deserve one anyway. As he said, I'd always been honest with him.

I swallowed. "No." I let that word sink in before I continued, "But I'm not sure I want you to stay."

"I understand." A shadow passed across his face, quickly replaced by a soft smile. "I'll take my time, then. You deserve... some proper courting, after all."

I chuckled. To imagine Rasheh using flowery words,

kissing my hand, and asking me to dance was amusing, especially when I thought both of the intimacy we had already shared and how direct he was in expressing his feelings and desires.

"Do you even know how to court a noblewoman?" I arched my eyebrow. Hopefully my teasing would lighten the mood enough to ease us both into what we used to have and make me stop doubting his intentions.

"Why do you think it took me so long to arrive here? The master insisted that I knew all the rules of your world and enough of the language to blend in."

"Blend in?" I shook my head. "An exotic guest of one of the most influential men in the country?"

"It fit well enough, and all it took was arranging the right situation, so that the prince would believe I'd saved his life. Would you rather see me carve my way through all those wimpy men, assassinate your father, and take you away in the black of the night?" Without warning, he wrapped his arm around my waist and pulled me closer. "Because it can still be done," he whispered, his breath teasing my ear. His body emanated familiar heat, offering unexpected comfort. "All you have to do is ask."

I eased into his embrace, saying nothing. It seemed so much better to just enjoy his presence without considering the consequences of allowing him so close to me again. My heart insisted he was worth risking any pain, clinging to hope that this once he was earnest, while the reasonable part of me had already considered the implications of Rasheh's arrival in this world. My father would learn about it soon enough, and I would have to deal with Philidert as well.

I pushed all those thoughts away. There would be time

to worry about possible outcomes once I knew where I stood.

"Will you stay for the night?" I asked, ignoring the voice that whispered he could take it as a different kind of invitation.

"Only for a little while," he replied. "I'd rather not risk anyone seeing me here. Unless, of course, you want to create enough gossip to get the twins jealous."

Of course I wanted him to stay much longer, and the traces of desire in his voice suggested he wanted me to say so, but I had to be cautious about how I proceeded. Back in Malatrius's mansion, there was no gossip and judgment, and the sorcerer only cared that we remained loyal to him. In this world though, brash decisions could cause more trouble than they were worth.

"What happened to proper courting?" I teased to hide my hesitation.

He grinned. "Should I carry you to bed now, or should I help you undress first, my lady?"

I should have known that his idea of courting, no matter how tempered by the rules of my world, would still differ from what the society considered proper. I reached for the buttons at the back of my dress, and my fingers met his.

"I still like the idea of taking you away in the middle of the night." His breath teased my nape. He was much closer to me than the task required.

"I would have to call for help if we were to do it the proper way." I couldn't resist.

He huffed his displeasure onto my skin, a teasing touch of his breath making me long for more. "This world takes the joy out of everything, it seems."

All of a sudden, he embraced me, my dress only halfway undone. We stood motionless. I enjoyed his presence and his warmth but found no right words to say. He likely found none either. He could apologize once again or offer reassurances, but only time could heal the wounds, so silence was better, at least for now.

But when I thought of how we could restore what we had, a thought struck me. We might not have enough time for that.

"How long will you be staying in this world?" I asked.

"For however long you want me to."

I scoffed. No matter how romantic such a declaration was, it likely wasn't the truth. "Surely the master—"

"He made no arrangements. So unless you send me back, I'm here to stay, near or far, as you choose."

As his words sank in, I shivered. He couldn't have known it wasn't that easy.

"I can't send you back," I confessed. "The master taught the ritual to me, but I'm not capable of performing it. At least, not yet."

"He did mention it."

He'd willingly come to a world that wasn't his knowing that he might never be able to return home. He'd gone there —here—for me, risking a lifetime in exile if I pushed him away.

Rasheh put a finger on my lips. "Don't worry about it. I'm sure that if you hate my presence here strongly enough, you'll find the power within you."

"And if I don't?"

That familiar, confident smile replaced his gentler expression. "Then perhaps it'll mean that you do want me here." He took a step back. "But that's not something to decide anytime soon, is it?"

Swallowing, I gave a cautious nod. "I appreciate it."

No matter how my body longed for him and how my

feelings betrayed me, I needed time to learn to trust him again. Or, perhaps, for the first time.

He took my hand and placed a kiss on it. He held his lips there longer than my society would consider appropriate, but otherwise he was every bit courteous. His eyes remained on me even when he let go and took a step back.

"Until next time... my lady."

His tone convinced me he was finding amusement and maybe even enjoyment in those very rules he was complaining about, and I smiled as he left my room. Surprisingly and unsurprisingly at the same time, Rasheh's presence beside me felt right, as if it were an important part of who Saeryn the sorceress was.

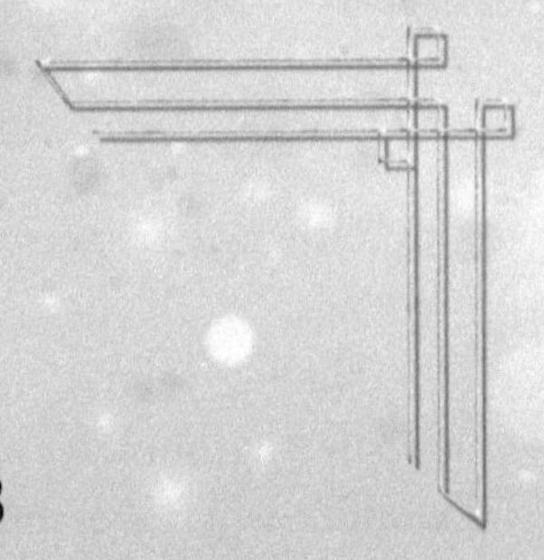

Chapter 13

Worlds collide at the crossroads of the past and the present

Night brought me no rest, and morning greeted me with the same plaguing thoughts. Even a warm bath wasn't enough to ease my mood.

Rasheh's presence in my world, no matter whether I welcomed it or not, posed problems. My father was no fool. He'd recognize a visitor from Hyrinea in Rasheh, and there was only one other sorcerer who knew the world-crossing ritual. Even if Rasheh left the capital immediately, and I joined him later in some other place on the continent or even beyond it, gossip would still circulate, reaching my father's ears. He'd get suspicious, and the last thing I wanted was to make him think I'd kept it secret from him.

Yet revealing the truth to him seemed even worse. I spent a restless night seeking a way to convince him that Rasheh was not a threat but failed to come up with anything persuading. I also, with a hint of shame, had to admit that I couldn't be certain whether Rasheh indeed posed no danger to him. While not a sorcerer himself, Rasheh remained a loyal servant to one, and when it came to making a choice between Malatrius and me—let alone my father—I suspected he'd pick obedience over personal feelings.

Having served the sorcerer myself, I understood his perspective and wasn't bitter about it. It just made me wonder why he wanted to come here, and why Malatrius had accommodated such a grand request. Was there something else at play, or was I searching for plots where there were none? Rasheh claimed to have arrived in this world for me and me alone. I couldn't be certain that his words were *entirely* true, but my heart screamed in favor of his sincerity.

I sighed. First, I had to decide what I wanted for myself, because that choice would guide my actions. If I wanted Rasheh to stay with me, I would have to find a way to secure my father's approval. If I wanted Rasheh gone, I could simply ask my father to send him back. Until my heart settled one way or another, I couldn't solve the matter with cold reasoning alone. Unfortunately, it would take time to make the right choice.

I gave myself a critical look in the mirror. The supposedly confident sorceress stared back at me, but she looked as lost as I felt. I chuckled bitterly. A true woman of power would not be stuck between her father's control and her teacher's influence, and she definitely would not be so indecisive when it came to the matters of her own heart.

Knocking on the door pulled me away from my self-pity. When my father called from the outside, I smoothed my expression and forced a smile.

"Please, come in!" I replied as soon as I ensured my bathrobe was tied and tight. "I'm getting ready for breakfast," I added when he entered.

"It's fine. Your mother woke up just now." He didn't bear any traces of sleep, so he must have been up for quite a while. Though, what business he might have had so early in the morning, I had no idea. "I came to talk to you about her. What you said yesterday... The man I pretend to be can't approve of such behavior."

I nodded in agreement. No matter how strongly I believed that my mother had deserved every word of my response yesterday, I should have known better than to give in to emotions and challenge her in such a way.

"I understand your feelings," he continued, "but I wanted you to experience a normal life before... things change forever." He offered a gentle smile. "Yet that requires you to behave in certain ways and not stretch the boundaries of what the society considers proper, at least not too much."

"Yes, Father. I apologize. I'll be more careful."

There wasn't anything else I could say without sounding defensive, but my short response seemed to satisfy him enough.

"Very well. In return, I'll speak to her about that Asnu-Thigai boy. Of course, if I try to convince her to abandon the idea of you two getting married, she'll only double her efforts. But I'll suggest that she should give you some time, so that you can... think calmly about the idea and get used to it. If she believes that I don't oppose the idea, and you're at least considering it, she might stop pushing." He gave me a wink, as if it were to become another secret we shared.

"Thank you, Father," I replied with genuine gratitude. With that issue at least partly out of the way, it might be easier for me to deal with the turmoil Rasheh had once more brought to my heart and life.

"Though I would suggest you go traveling when the solstice celebrations end. Maybe with the Olfe-Parnai Twins or Shevo-Thusai's daughter," he added. "That way

Philidert won't have an excuse to accompany you if he were foolish enough to follow you like he tried back in Quathan."

I arched an eyebrow at that. We'd never spoken of what happened back then. To me, the parting with Philidert at the hotel seemed insignificant in light of everything that followed, and since my father hadn't mentioned it either, I assumed Philidert had never shared any of it with him.

"I didn't think he'd reveal the humiliation he suffered back then," I said.

My father smirked. "He ran to me as soon as the poison lost its power. He demanded I reveal your whereabouts, so that he could join you, and painted Malatrius as a deceptive charlatan threatening your life and chastity." His smile widened, underlined with cruel satisfaction. "Even though I'm not fond of the sorcerer, I can appreciate his efficiency in dealing with that annoying boy."

"Did Philidert cause you any trouble?" I suspected I knew the answer, but it was better to ask the question than risk the conversation drifting toward Malatrius. Over the past months, I'd spoken about the Sorcerer from the Desert as little as possible, still unsure how much I could trust my father, and I couldn't risk that I'd say something that would make him question where my loyalties lie.

"He wouldn't hear any arguments and threatened to talk to your mother about it..." My father hesitated, then smiled again. "Let's just say I ensured he'll never speak of it again. You needn't worry that he'll ever mention that morning in Quathan."

The way he said it, with confidence but an avoidance of details, stirred my instincts. I could almost hear Malatrius's whispering in my ear, dripping words of doubt. With all the secrets my father and I shared, he rarely was so vague in his responses. After all, I wasn't a delicate flower in need of shielding from the world and its cruelty. Not only had I helped to devise the plan to gain Malatrius's trust, but I'd also witnessed and experienced enough in his service to shatter a weaker mind. If my father withheld the details, it wasn't out of concern... at least not for me. He didn't want me to know, and that awoke my suspicions. I didn't hush them, even though it felt like giving in to Malatrius's suggestions and accusations.

"I'll let you get ready," my father said, and I couldn't help thinking he didn't want us to continue this topic. "Be kind to your mother, and once the celebrations are over, go traveling and enjoy life a bit." He picked up a bottle of my perfume and sniffed its contents, and his brow furrowed as if he were trying to recognize it. "It's too sweet and flowery for you. You should wear something that matches your confidence and future power. Something with sandalwood or musk, perhaps?"

With these words, he left the room.

I stared at the closed door for a long time. I remembered the scents he'd mentioned. They were in almost all the perfumes Past Saeryn owned. Until his remark, I'd believed it was my own self's choice, and that for some unexplained reason, my taste had simply changed after I was reborn. But what if Past Saeryn had also loved lighter and more flowery scents, but wore other perfumes under the influence of my father? What if he'd molded her—molded *me*—in ways I couldn't even imagine?

I shivered at that thought, and suddenly, Malatrius's laughter rang in my ears as clear as if the sorcerer were standing by my side.

I SMILED as the driver opened the door of the vehicle that took me back to the hotel. Even so late in the evening, there were still people around, some exchanging knowing looks, as if they could either guess the reason for my smile or relate to the feeling of joy. Of course, the reality was more complicated than what they saw—a young woman in love—but I hushed those thoughts, looking forward to meeting the man who was likely already waiting on my balcony.

The week of solstice celebrations had turned out more pleasant than I could have imagined. Even Philidert's presence, as imposing as he could make it without breaching etiquette, was more bearable when Rasheh stood nearby, throwing amused glances and sometimes adding brief comments in vizari as if he were talking to himself. Yet, other than that, we kept apart in public, acting as acquaintances would, because even though my heart was already betraying me once again, I wanted to rebuild our fractured bond first. Besides, revealing my relationship with Rasheh meant dealing with my father's possible disapproval, and I wasn't ready for it.

A part of me feared I never would be.

At least Rasheh didn't seem to mind. He took it upon himself to flirt with the twins, never giving one enough attention to make it look like he was more interested in her over the other, and I played the game of pretending as well, treating him like a dear friend with whom I had nothing more in common than several conversations while we both stayed at his "uncle's" mansion.

At nights, back in my hotel room, he made sure I knew he had no interest in either of the twins in many ways that kept surprising me. In the past, both before and after I'd lost my memories, our relationship was one of mutual desire, and even though deeper feelings grew from it, when we spent time together, we'd either trained or made love.

This time, Rasheh kept asking questions, expressing curiosity about everything, from the strange world around him to what my favorite book was. I obliged as much as I could, enjoying his presence and any stories of his own he decided to share. He spoke little of his actual work for the sorcerer but entertained me with tales of fights, adventures, and dangers he'd faced.

Sometimes, I enjoyed the thought of traveling with him, be it across the continent and beyond or back in Hyrinea, but such dreams of freedom were childish. Even if Rasheh was stranded in my world at the moment, he was forever bound to the Sorcerer from the Desert, and I had ties with both my father and Malatrius. Their shadows would be forever cast on whichever path we took.

Already in the hotel's foyer, I fought to keep the ebbing smile on my face. Strangers didn't have to know anything of my emotional struggles. Even if I *didn't* have secrets reaching all the way to another world, I would still prefer to keep any gossip away from my parents' ears.

"Did you enjoy the celebration, madam?" the receptionist asked as she handed the key to me. "You parents returned earlier. So many balls and events must have worn them down."

I gave her an absent-minded nod, trying to appreciate her efforts at making polite conversation. It wasn't her fault that the mention of my parents soured my mood. Lately, my mother had been more bitter, and even though anything could have affected her humors, I had a strong suspicion that Philidert had been whispering in her ear, likely feeling threatened by Rasheh's presence. Each time Rasheh spoke to me or sent me a smile, even an innocent one, Philidert tensed, making remarks that verged on being rude.

As the days passed, his possessiveness had intensified, and he made efforts to stay by my side at all times. I tolerated his behavior only because I wanted to avoid the scandal that would stem from a confrontation, and the summer solstice celebrations were coming to an end anyway. A few more days, and everyone would go back home. I planned to ensure Philidert had no excuse to linger, sharing nothing of my plans for the upcoming weeks, allowing the impression that I would be returning home as well. Before he realized that I'd set out elsewhere, I'd be long gone.

In a way, I knew I would be running away, not only from him but from my father as well. It seemed better to take his advice to travel across the continent, though with Rasheh instead of any of my old friends, and only through letters break the news of my falling in love. I hoped that if my father had time to think and get used to the idea, he would be more open to accepting Rasheh.

It wasn't a good solution, but it was the only one I had for now. As I climbed the steps, I focused on more positive thoughts. The prospect of spending the whole night with Rasheh made my heart pick up its pace, and I nurtured that anticipation. No matter my own concerns, he deserved a smile to greet him.

I turned the key in the lock, but the sounds coming from my parents' room made me pause. Though the hotel's walls were thick enough to allow some privacy, they couldn't keep their raised voices in.

"She's the only child we have!" my mother shouted. "I don't care what absurd plans you might have for her! She has to marry and ensure our lineage thrives. I know she's the apple of your eye, but you have to understand—"

"You're right. I don't care," my father replied with his usual coldness, but his loud voice suggested strong emotions. "I don't care about your family's lineage."

The silence that fell carried no hint to her reaction, but I could easily picture my mother's shocked face. If I searched deep enough, I could find compassion for her. Stuck with a husband with whom she had little in common, distant from him and her own daughter... Perhaps her composed and unmoving demeanor had little to do with her true personality and more with the circumstances and pride that demanded she endure the marriage instead of dissolving it a long time ago.

I was ready to retreat to my room before their argument spoiled my mood, but then my mother spoke again, this time not as loud, so I had to strain to hear.

"I should have known you were a heartless swine ever since two of our sons died," she hissed. "They were both so young, and you didn't care at all. You felt nothing toward them. But when Sae was born, you finally seemed to show some emotions and attachment... I was foolish to believe it. You care so little about her future that you'd let her marry some barbarian from Quathan or another primitive land and let her ruin her life."

I froze. That accusation seemed too close to reality for my mother to have made it up, confirming that Philidert must have been sharing his own insecurities with her.

"What did you say?"

My father's voice made me jerk back defensively. Anger hid under the coldness, and it seemed I would have to tell him about Rasheh sooner than I'd intended... and in less-than-favorable circumstances.

"Exactly what I meant," my mother replied. "There's a man around her, one exactly like that shady professor of yours, Etrus or whatever his name was... Where are you going?"

The door to the room snapped open, and my father stood in front of me, his expression foretelling a storm I couldn't hope to avoid.

"I'm going to talk to my daughter." He didn't even look back at my mother as he replied. Instead, he kept glaring at me with reprimanding coldness.

I swallowed and opened the door to my own room. This was a conversation neither of us wanted anyone witnessing. I hoped Rasheh would have enough wits to stay hidden.

"You owe me an explanation," my father said in vizari as soon as we were alone.

I swallowed. Denying it would be pointless. "He's not a threat," I replied.

My father grimaced, but I could deal with his displeasure as long as I managed to keep his rage away. "Malatrius surely lets you believe so. Whom did he send? And why? Under what pretense?"

"He..." I hesitated. Revealing who Rasheh was would only strengthen my father's suspicions. "He asked Malatrius to send him. It's someone I met in the sorcerer's homestead." I had trouble holding eye contact as my unease grew with the prospect of the confession I was about to make. "He became my lover."

My father's expression shifted, softening a notch. He hadn't expected such a revelation. "A lover? That's... quite careless."

"Things didn't go exactly as we planned," I replied, even though my memories offered only limited insight into what the plan had actually been.

"I can see that," my father remarked with familiar dryness, but his anger seemed to have faded. "Were you going to introduce him to me and your mother at all?"

That wasn't a question I'd seen coming. Instead of scolding me for putting my secret in danger and exposing myself to Malatrius's manipulations, my father seemed at ease with the idea.

When I remained silent, he gave me a crooked smile. "I can see that you weren't planning to. He's Malatrius's servant, isn't he?"

"Yes." There was no point in concealing it anymore.

"And are you certain you aren't being deceived?" he asked.

Hesitation would have its cost, nurturing my father's distrust, but I found no strength to give a confident answer. With the complicated relationship between Rasheh and me, I couldn't afford myself the luxury of certainty. Besides, even if I wanted to trust Rasheh, it didn't mean Malatrius wasn't using him for his own goals.

To my surprise, my father nodded at my silence. "At least you aren't blindly in love. I'll trust your judgment for now. I also trust that if you discover he is a threat or he's been deceiving you, you'll tell me immediately."

It was a clear message: he didn't appreciate I'd kept secrets from him. At the same time, everything about his reaction seemed too mild and too composed, especially in the light of the argument he'd just had with my mother. No matter how much he cared about me, in the past he had been quick to make me suffer the consequences of my foolishness or poor choices.

"I'm not a threat, and I won't become one."

I froze as Rasheh entered the room through the balcony

door. I didn't dare send him a cautioning glance. If he'd chosen to reveal himself, he wouldn't heed my warning anyway.

"I'm Rasheh—"

My father tensed. "I know who you are. Malatrius's assassin."

Rasheh shook his head, his composure enviable. Facing a powerful sorcerer, he showed no fear. "Not here. I didn't come to kill. I came to her."

"So you say." My father grimaced. "I find it hard to believe someone like you would be... *sentimental* enough to abandon your master and allow yourself to be trapped in a foreign world."

"Yet here I am."

"And you know of her... secret."

"My master had no choice but to tell me," Rashed replied. "But I care not of it, nor have I any use for it. It does, though, make any killing attempts pointless, doesn't it?"

I stood motionless, trapped between them and hoping that the lingering silence would lead to an agreement rather than bloodshed. My mind raced, searching for spells that would help me keep them apart should it come to that, but my abilities could match neither my father's power nor Rasheh's speed.

"Very well," my father said. "I'll trust my daughter." He looked to me. "Bring him to breakfast in the morning. People's curiosity is dangerous to real secrets, so we'll give them something else to gossip about. And your mother, I'm sure, will be relieved to meet the young man that got your... attention." He smirked as if he knew Rasheh's behavior would be impeccable.

As he turned to leave, I took a step forward. With the way he'd accepted Rasheh so quickly, he must be in a benevolent mood, so I had to take the chance to ask him a question.

"Father. What Mother said about the past... Is it true *they* died?" I couldn't bring myself to say the words "my brothers."

He hesitated then nodded. "They both died young, and I indeed didn't show much grief. Having lived so many lives, I have a different perspective on relationships, and they didn't seem to have inherited the gift of sorcery, so my attachment was... minor." He sighed. "I regret, though, that they died. If either had survived, it would be much easier to keep you out of your mother's grand plans for marriage. Let's not speak about it again, shall we? Such a topic brings nothing but pain and regrets."

With these words, he left us.

I locked the door behind him, listening to figure out whether he was returning to his room—I wouldn't put it past him to eavesdrop on us—but all I heard was a few steps outside and then the sound of door being opened and closed.

I still led Rasheh away, closer to the balcony.

"He seemed... too friendly." He kept his voice low. "My presence should have stirred his anger and suspicion more than it did." The confidence he'd displayed earlier was gone, replaced by concern and distrust.

"I know." I could find no excuse nor explanation for my father's behavior.

But there was more to worry about than his benevolence toward his rival's servant. The more I thought about the last part of our conversation, the less I could ignore the nagging feeling that my father was deceiving me. Admitting he'd treated his children indifferently was a harsh truth, but it was more likely to win me over than any sweet lies. A nice touch to ensure I trusted his words. Yet sorcery wasn't inherited through blood. Anyone could master it. My father couldn't have known I'd learned about it from Malatrius, so he felt confident in his lie.

That led to the question of what else he'd deceived me about, and what other secrets he'd been hiding. I smiled bitterly. The seed of suspicion, sown by Malatrius months ago, blossomed in full.

Rasheh embraced me. "Maybe we should leave. Even if we won't go back to the master's home, we could go somewhere far away in this world."

His suggestion was tempting, and I'd been already considering it. But with my father already aware of who Rasheh was, the feeling of freedom and safety would be false.

"No," I said. "If we are to be safe, truly safe, I need to figure out what he's hiding."

"You speak like a true sorceress. Master trained you well." His arms closed tighter around me. "I'll help you."

I remained silent. As much as I wanted to deny his claim, I was indeed a sorceress who'd grown up nurturing secrets and devising plans, and the time I'd spent with Malatrius, joining in his games and schemes, only honed those skills.

Stirred by my father's words, my mind conjured flashes of images in that familiar teasing manner that left me with nothing but questions, and I knew Malatrius was right. Some of my lost memories were likely tied to this world, and if I wanted to truly understand everything that had happened, I had to get them back somehow.

Everything else had to wait.

~

THE HOTEL'S restaurant was a vast space filled with tables, indoor plants, and people. It carried the posh atmosphere of the establishment that hosted it, and even though its décor was as tasteful as everywhere else in the building, I couldn't help but feel smothered. The walls, supposedly distant, seemed to be creeping up, and the ceiling, high and adorned with many a chandelier, felt like it was about to crush me. I missed the open-terrace dining I'd experienced back in Quathan, or better yet, eating without decorum or etiquette while sitting on the floor of the prism cube library.

I took a deep breath. The hotel was no different than any other in Kvesa's capital, save maybe some smaller and cheaper places. I simply allowed my mood to dictate how I perceived it. Sitting in the scorching sun back in Quathan would offer no more comfort to my unease than I could get here.

I was already seated, sipping coffee, when my parents arrived at the restaurant.

My father held my mother's arm with courtesy, and nothing in their behavior told of the argument they'd had the previous night. Not even a frown spoiled my mother's forehead, as it had in the past when similar arguments happened. In truth, she seemed a little *too* joyful and pleased, as if my father had made efforts beyond his usual routines to ensure her good mood or—a thought dawned on me—as if the argument had never happened.

In the past, I would have idly pondered the peculiarity of such a situation, but armed with the knowledge Malatrius had shared with me, I *had* to suspect that my father had erased her memory. Perhaps it wasn't the first time, either. I couldn't help remembering what he'd said about Philidert, too, when the poor fool tried to prevent me from leaving with the sorcerer back in Quathan.

Let's just say I ensured he'll never speak of it again. You needn't worry that he'll ever mention that morning in Quathan.

I'd paid too little attention to it back then, but with my mother's unusual behavior, I had to revisit his words. Unfortunately, with my parents already at the table, I couldn't afford myself the time to ponder the possibilities. Instead, I put a warm smile on my face.

"Mother, Father, I hope you don't mind having company during the meal," I said once they were seated.

My mother brightened. "Of course not," she said before my father could reply. "Young Philidert is always welcome to join us."

"Actually, I had someone else in mind," I replied. "He should arrive shortly."

"So we finally get to meet your mysterious suitor?" my father asked teasingly, as if he hadn't seen Rasheh the previous night.

My mother shot me a surprised and somewhat disappointed glare.

"I invited Rasheh Atrius to join us." The surname he'd chosen for himself still amused me, as it both aligned with Malatrius's false persona in this world and spoke of his ties to the sorcerer. "We made acquaintance during my stay in Professor Atrius's lands, and since he's joined the solstice celebrations as Prince Sulla-Amahai's guest, I thought it would be a good opportunity to introduce him to you."

"I hope he's at least somewhat educated, since you say the prince invited him," she replied, her displeasure poorly concealed. "Though I suppose that if you're the only other person he knows in Kvesa, it makes sense that he seeks your company, and it was courteous to invite him. Maybe we should make sure he's introduced to some other families as well, so he doesn't feel lost in the capital."

I was certain that my mother cared little for Rasheh's acquaintance with anyone in high society—simply, such introductions meant he'd be away from me, fulfilling his social obligations to others.

"He's made acquaintance with some of my friends already," I replied. "Oh, there he is."

Rasheh approached with confidence. He wore a Quathani-like outfit, wide pants and a loose tunic, which I was sure would spark my mother's disapproval despite its fine make. Yet to insist he wear a jacket and trousers and groom his too-long hair with oils would make him look like a caged predator. He'd stand out more trying to fit in a culture he knew little of and cared about even less.

"Madam, sir." He bowed to them, and then smiled to me as he kissed my hand. "My dear."

My mother almost choked on her tea, but my father smirked, looking somewhat pleased, as if he'd expected bold behavior and Rasheh hadn't disappointed him.

I held my own expression in check and made formal introductions.

"My daughter says you met during her trip to the lands south of Quathan," my mother said while Rasheh sat down. "Are you a scholar as well?"

He shook his head. "Much to my uncle's silent disappointment, I didn't take to academics. I speak a bit of the ancient languages, since many of the local tribes use modern variants of them, but I'm not, by any stretch, a scholar. I'd boldly say that I consider myself a warrior."

He spoke without hesitation, as if he was sharing his own experiences and not a perfectly tailored lie. That alone told me how much Malatrius must have insisted on Rasheh learning before leaving him alone in this world. The sorcerer had not only obliged the request for sending one of his most valued servants here, but also cared enough to ensure Rasheh could survive here on his own. I hadn't asked him about it, but I wouldn't be surprised if they'd arrived in this world shortly after I returned to it.

My mother brightened. "Oh, you served in an army? Are you an officer?"

He gave her a smile as if he didn't mind her barrage of questions. "One could say so if my uncle considered his men an army. The lands Professor Atrius owns don't have a consolidated government nor any ruling royalty, but I do lead others when we have to deal with unscrupulous men or local tribe leaders."

Disappointment lingered in my mother's expression. She must have been hoping that Rasheh held a position that would be deemed at least appropriate if not desirable in the civilized world. Instead, he'd made it clear he was no one in the eyes of nobility.

If he wasn't the man he was, but indeed just a stranger from distant lands, I could picture how his life would go when the interest in him, an exotic and savage guest, dimmed. Lost in a country that wasn't his, without wealth to support him, he'd fade into obscurity, entertaining nobles of lower and lower status, each ball or gathering of less signifi-cance than the previous one.

But Rasheh wasn't just anyone, and I couldn't picture him falling low. As resourceful and confident as he was, he'd find a wealthy patron with enough enemies to keep his blades busy. After all, no matter which world you were in, there were always more than enough people to kill and not enough people willing to do the deed.

I smiled at that thought, but it was time to stop my mother's questions before she spoiled the meal. "So, how did you and Prince Sulla-Amahai meet? He wasn't around when I was visiting." I hoped that the mention of the prince would remind her that no matter how little she thought of Rasheh, at the moment he had the favor of one of the most powerful and influential men in the country.

Rasheh spun a story skillfully enough to keep his audience's attention, but I hardly paid attention to it. The hunting accident he was describing in an entertaining way surely didn't happen exactly as he said, and his meeting with the prince was not one of chance. If I were to make a guess, Rasheh and Malatrius had arranged the very event from which Rasheh had saved the prince, so that the grateful nobleman would then invite him to travel all the way back to Kvesa.

My father likely thought the same, but he listened with the polite interest expected of a man of his position, smiling and nodding when appropriate.

"And thus, I ended up in a faraway country as the prince's guest at the solstice celebrations," Rasheh concluded.

"Have you made any plans for when the festivities end?" my father asked.

I could swear Rasheh narrowed his eyes ever so slightly, and I couldn't blame him. I sensed a trap coming as well.

"I've made no arrangements yet," he replied.

"Then perhaps you would be interested in seeing a bit of Kvesa's countryside? Our lands stretch near a snow-covered mountain range, and there are plenty of forests and wilderness to explore and hunt in. Our home is big enough to provide our guests with comfort and privacy, and I'm sure my daughter would be delighted if you accepted."

I tensed, and Rasheh shifted in his seat. Such an invitation went beyond my father's benevolent tolerance from the previous night. I glanced at my mother, but etiquette would forbid her from expressing disapproval openly. She sat silent, her face inscrutable.

"That's a generous offer," Rasheh replied, unease lingering in his posture, as if instead of accepting, he was considering making good on his remarks of stealing me away.

My father gave him a wide smile. "It's decided, then. We leave the day after tomorrow. You're welcome to join us for the travel. If not, feel free to arrive at a later date."

At that, Rasheh could only give a polite bow of his head. "I'd be honored to accept."

The waiter brought a large platter of sandwiches, each a miniature piece of art: crispy bread topped with cold meats, cheeses, and a selection of vegetables. A variety of seasonal and candied fruit accompanied the platter, as well as condiments both savory and sweet.

"How do you find Kvesa so far?" my mother asked among the clinking of the plates and cutlery. "It's quite different from your homeland, isn't it?"

While Rasheh obliged my mother with the small talk she expected, I turned my attention to my other parent.

My father leaned over to me. "You needn't worry," he whispered in vizari. "All I want is to be certain that his claims are true. I don't want him to hurt you."

In any other circumstance, I might have taken his reassurances and let my doubts die. But he was not a typical father, nor was I a typical daughter. With our deaths not being permanent, Rasheh posed no real threat to us, and if he broke my heart... Not that my father knew it had already happened once, but he could assume that I would make use of the arts to make Rasheh's life miserable and short in return.

So whatever my father had in mind when he invited Rasheh, it wasn't my wellbeing.

Chapter 14

An oddly shaped piece

My mother stood by our day room's terrace door, looking outside where Rasheh was practicing his routine in the first morning light.

We'd arrived the previous night, and to my surprise, he got a room in the same wing mine was in, though far enough away to be considered appropriate. Of course, he still made it to my bedroom, unwilling to be separated for the night, and only thanks to his presence did I enjoy a peaceful slumber rather than a restless night filled with questions and concerns.

Yet, when he left before dawn, he didn't mention he'd intended to train.

His body shifted in the flowing motions I knew so well, undisturbed by the presence of the comfortable wicker chairs and low tables arranged at the terrace. His sabers cut through the morning mist with each well-balanced step.

I held off a sigh, conjuring all the things my mother was going to say about his lack of concern for etiquette, but even if he had forgone his training routine, I doubted anything could change her mind about him. And as much as I wanted things to go smoothly during our stay, I wouldn't ask him to give it up, especially not in a place he must consider hostile —my family home. If nothing else, the familiar training and the feeling of being as prepared as possible would perhaps ease his tension.

I approached the door with caution and found no disapproval on my mother's face.

"I can see the qualities that appealed to you," she said, her eyes still on Rasheh. "A man who rises with the sun to perfect his skills is noteworthy."

"Yet you don't approve of him," I replied quietly.

A tired and sad smile curled her lips. "I'm trying to protect you from the very mistake I made. Your father was the same. A stranger and an outsider, alluring in the mystery that surrounded him. A sole heir to a vast fortune living alone in a remote area... I fell for it. I thought that his cold personality stemmed from loneliness, and I believed I could change him. I told myself that if I could bring a bit of warmth to his life, he'd open up." She shook her head as if chasing away foolish thoughts. "Philidert... might be lacking in many aspects, but he's a safe bet. Someone to give you a good marriage and good home. But I understand if your heart demands otherwise. All I ask is that you do not rush things. If need be, it's better to be alone than shackled by a bond that brings you torment, and you can afford the choice. You don't have to marry."

With the tangible pain in her voice, all I could do was nod. She likely didn't remember how she herself had insisted I had to marry to preserve our bloodline—a memory lost like, possibly, many others, and I saw a different image of her. The way my father treated her was cruel at times, and I'd had a hand in her suffering too. Being his sole focus,

I enjoyed his attention and care, and never bothered trying to bond with her.

Rasheh finished his training and approached the terrace door. "Madam, Saeryn." He offered us a bow. "I hope I didn't disturb your sleep with my whims."

He held both sabers, now sheathed, in one hand, and beads of sweat marked his warm-hued skin. Against the backdrop of snow-covered mountains and misty evergreen forests, he looked even more out of place.

My mother gave him a polite nod. "You don't have to worry. I'm happy to know that you feel at ease in our home." She looked at me. "I think you both should get ready for breakfast. Your father will rise soon as well, and it would be nice to eat together."

We exchanged more pleasantries, and I offered Rasheh my arm. We made it through the room before my mother spoke again.

"Mr. Atrius—"

"Please, call me Rasheh," he said.

"Take good care of my daughter, Rasheh," she said with a softness that surprised me.

When she left through another door, Rasheh looked at me puzzled, but all I had for him was a shrug. I hoped that her change of heart was genuine. At the same time, it reminded me that, unlike her, my father had to have ulterior motives, and the sooner I uncovered what he intended, the better.

Malatrius had said some of my remaining lost memories might be tied to this world, and that meant they had to be connected to my home. After breakfast, I would insist on showing Rasheh around, and we would use it as an excuse to search for anything that could stir my mind into recalling more images from my past. Without Malatrius, it would be harder, but with what I'd learned about how he helped to restore my memories, I could be lucky enough to find the right triggers.

Rasheh stopped by my room's door, his eyebrow arched. "Is it proper for me to enter?" he asked with feigned innocence, as if he hadn't invited himself in the previous night.

Chuckling, I pushed him in. "I'm only going to pick up some clothes. We're going to your room. I missed training with you. I won't miss bathing with you." With all the uncertainty, I wasn't about to give up any opportunity to simply enjoy his company.

"You could join me tomorrow morning. I'll see how much of your training you've forgotten... again," he said.

I became serious. "I prefer that my father doesn't know about it."

Rasheh nodded. My response must have reminded him that my father was a formidable opponent, and the less he knew, the more advantage we could have. I tried to push that thought away—that I would have to confront him—but it lingered, unwanted and unsettling.

While I rifled through my wardrobe in search of lingerie and an appropriate outfit, he inspected my room with a curiosity that couldn't have been sated earlier, without daylight.

"That looks like a hairpin from the steppes," he said.

I looked over my shoulder. He was standing by my jewelry box, holding out a long golden hairpin adorned with a fiery peacock. Rubies sparkled at the ends of the bird's gold wings, and tiny obsidian pieces shone in place of its eyes. I could swear I'd never seen that piece of jewelry before. Kvesa's fashion had never favored hairpins, and it couldn't be a souvenir from my travels—I usually brought books back. It also seemed unlikely that one of my mother's pieces had somehow made it to my room, and it was hardly her style anyway.

With a sudden realization, I rushed toward Rasheh so fast that he took an instinctive step back, and as soon as I took the hairpin in my hand, memories swarmed me.

SHE'D BEEN to the other world before, but never during those visits had she met anyone but the few of her father's servants who knew better than to divulge any of their master's secrets, including the ones connected to his daughter, so this time it was different.

The woman standing on the balcony was not only an outsider. She was a sorceress as well.

Saeryn stood in the entrance to the balcony, just shy of stepping out, and kept glancing at the woman as if magic could manifest in the guest's mature face and full body, but Sahatiavari looked entirely mundane, save the colorful, flowing outfit she wore. Bold yellows, oranges, and reds mixed with toned browns and a bit of odd steel blue, and on everyone else, such a combination could look gaudy or distasteful, but Sahatiavari wore those colors confidently.

She could be the woman Saeryn aspired to become in the future.

"So *you're* Kithandar's offspring," the sorceress said, her voice just loud enough to reach all the way to the entrance.

Saeryn lifted her chin up. They were alone, with her father yet to arrive, and she regretted letting curiosity get the better of her. She should have waited to be properly introduced, with her father's pride and confidence as her protection.

"What is it, child? You don't speak vizari?"

She tensed, painfully aware that it would reveal that she understood the question. Perhaps the insult was meant to stir a reaction, because at fifteen years old and already learning the arts from her father, Saeryn didn't deserve to be called a child. At the same time, falling for the simple trap justified the sorceress looking down at Saeryn.

With a choice between a retreat and response, Saeryn stepped onto the balcony and approached Sahatiavari. "I do."

The woman glanced at her, mild surprise on her beautiful face. Two thick braids of her brown hair rested on her chest, reaching all the way down to her waist and making her look almost amiable.

"Now that's new. Some courage and independence," she remarked, this time without any jest.

"New?" Saeryn couldn't help asking.

The sorceress gave her a calculating look, as if she were still deciding whether Saeryn was worth talking to. "I've seen his offspring before. Always quiet and obedient. Never taking a step without his approval. You're... different." Another inquisitive gaze. "Or perhaps you aren't, and you'll be gone soon enough, as they all are, in time replaced by yet another one."

Saeryn swallowed, putting all of her willpower into controlling her body's reaction. Until now, she'd believed herself the only child and thus her father's favorite. All the love and caring she received contributed to that conviction. To learn in such a blunt way that she was nothing special shook her very being, but it was still mild in comparison with the suggestion that she might be *disposable*.

Thoughts ran through her head without order and logic, and she gritted her teeth in a futile attempt to keep her lips from trembling.

Perhaps all of this was only meant to shake her composure, to test her. Perhaps, her own father had orchestrated it. Yet something in Sahatiavari's voice rang true, that trace of bitterness when she spoke…

Saeryn kept her curiosity at bay. To react or inquire meant the risk of failing an unknown examination by either or both of them.

"You aren't really my father's friend, are you?" she asked instead.

A sorceress like Sahatiavari would not fall for such a crude accusation, but the question would suffice to steer the topic in another direction. One that would not have Saeryn's pride shattered to pieces in front of a stranger.

"Kithandar has no friends," the woman replied, and then an unexpected smile softened her face. "But if you survive long enough, maybe I could become *your* friend."

Though Sahatiavari never admitted anything openly, Saeryn knew the sorceress had to have a reason to make such an offer: an old grudge or plain jealousy toward someone more powerful than she was. Even if the offer itself sounded genuine, as far as Saeryn could tell, it might simply align with whatever goal the sorceress had in mind.

"There you are."

Saeryn twitched at her father's voice coming from the entrance. "Father," she said subserviently, taking a step back as if it could erase her blatant disobedience.

"I see you've met my daughter," he said to Sahatiavari.

Even though he didn't even look at Saeryn, the tone of his voice foretold punishment to come, and she tensed. She should have known better than to approach the sorceress on her own.

"Hardly," Sahatiavari replied. "She kept spying on me from afar, so I called her over. Yet this poor thing wouldn't answer a single question. Are her mental capabilities challenged?"

Kithandar smiled with satisfaction, and as he glanced at Saeryn, his expression softened. "She simply knows how to behave in the presence of conniving sorceresses who like to play games, my dear. It would be unwise to let you fill her ears with deception and scathing remarks."

"I wouldn't risk your displeasure for mere fleeting enjoyment," Sahatiavari replied. "Besides, I prefer to play games with someone of your cunning instead of wasting time on a child." She threw Saeryn a patronizing glance. "I'll wait till she's grown. I do hope you'll train her well enough to be worth my time."

Kithandar burst out laughing. "Always the same, my dear." He offered her his arm. "Come. Let's see to our games, then."

There were things Saeryn didn't understand. Why Sahatiavari teased and played with her father even though she'd alluded that they weren't friends. Or why her father, though married, looked at the sorceress with a carnal hunger in his eyes. But one thing she understood well: on a whim, or for reasons known only to herself, Sahatiavari had saved Saeryn from her father's anger.

During the week Sahatiavari stayed in the castle, Saeryn was torn between avoiding the sorceress and seeking her out. The unexpected aid the woman had offered in shielding Saeryn from her father's anger suggested that she was indeed an ally, and her words had been at least partly true. But to try talking to the sorceress again meant risking her father's anger for possibly no gain.

As Saeryn thought of what Sahatiavari had said, it made sense. Her father claimed to have lived for many lifetimes... Her mother couldn't have been his first love, and marriage often meant children. Questions swarmed Saeryn's head, but she would have to accept them as forever unanswered, unless she was willing to reveal to her father the truth about her encounter with Sahatiavari.

Part of her wanted to indeed confess everything and beg her father's forgiveness, but the sorceress had lied to protect her, and if Saeryn disappointed that trust, that could mean retaliation. No matter how little time she'd spent in this world, becoming an enemy of a sorceress was a fool's decision.

So, as days passed, Saeryn allowed the opportunities to pass as well. If she dawdled long enough, this would all soon be in the past with Sahatiavari's departure from the castle. Until then, she could still ponder and pretend she was trying to make a choice.

In the end, it was the sorceress who sought her out.

No knock on the door announced her arrival. Sahatiavari walked into Saeryn's room with the confidence of someone who was exactly where she wanted to be and had every right to be there.

"Don't worry," she said. "Your father won't disturb us for a while." She inspected the room, taking in the gray walls, simple bed, and other meager furnishings.

Hardly anything therein bore Saeryn's personal mark, so it wouldn't give the sorceress any clues or openings, and perhaps even mislead her about how Kithandar treated his daughter. Sahatiavari couldn't know that Saeryn didn't spend much time in the castle or this world at all, so she'd likely draw the wrong conclusions. And that could protect Saeryn from being hurt too deeply.

Still, she regarded her unexpected guest with caution. The reassurance that her father would not disturb them meant little. For all she knew, he was aware of this visit and had chosen to keep away.

"Are you setting me up to fail?" This wouldn't be the first time she'd fallen victim to a game—part of a sorceress's training as her father claimed.

Sahatiavari shook her head. "Until you make your play, I care little for you."

"You want me to take the risks you won't take."

"No, child." The sorceress smiled, and a whole ocean of bitterness and sadness shone in her eyes. "I'm simply not desperate enough to act, but you... One day you might be. I'm sure you could use a friend then."

"I don't need friends." Saeryn might be young and not well versed in the games of sorcerers, but she'd experienced enough to know that unlikely and overeager friends often turned into traitors.

To Saeryn's surprise, Sahatiavari smiled. "Good. I wouldn't trust myself either. A man like your father is ready to deceive his own blood if he considers it beneficial to his goals, and you have no reason to think I'm any different." She removed a golden hairpin from her hair, one of a pair. A ruby-encrusted bird glared at Saeryn with its obsidian eyes. "Here's my offer for you, then. A one-time spell to contact me. One request that I'll do my best to fulfill. One day you might be desperate enough to risk trusting me. Until then..." The sorceress offered a shrewd smile. "I suggest you make sure that your father doesn't know you stole my hairpin."

It would be wise to refuse the gift and the game that likely accompanied it, but Saeryn accepted. If she wanted to be a sorceress, running away from deception was not enough. She had to join the game and emerge victorious at the end of it, no matter where it led.

"You're more cunning than the others," Sahatiavari said. "I'm sure we'll speak again."

Without any goodbye, she headed for the door.

Saeryn clutched the golden hairpin. "Do you think... Do you think there's anyone who can truly stand up to my father?" She had no illusions about her own capabilities, and it seemed that Sahatiavari was unwilling or unable as well.

The question made the sorceress stop. Her expression changed as she looked back, and for a heartbeat Saeryn thought the reply would consist of a single, hope-crushing word.

"The Sorcerer from the Desert could," Sahatiavari replied, "if he cared enough about any of us to bother."

Her expression made it clear that the man powerful enough to go against Kithandar was disinterested in other sorcerers' matters—a solution that might as well not exist at all. But Saeryn nodded nevertheless. If he was out there, it meant hope. All she had to do was learn and plan, and until then, ensure her father was as pleased with her as possible.

She smiled. Even if it took her years, she'd find a way.

Chapter 15

The unraveling

I was still clutching the hairpin when the memories released me. Back in the past, even the untrained adolescent would-be sorceress could sense the power of a spell woven into it, but now it remained silent—an object of vanity and nothing more. Even if the spell itself wouldn't be able to reach across worlds, its magic should still linger within. It didn't.

I must have spent it *and* Sahatiavari's favor already.

I tightened my fingers on the hairpin once more, encouraged by the clarity of the last memory. Contrary to those I'd restored earlier, this one felt vivid and close, as if it was truly mine instead of a faint echo.

Yet nothing more came.

Rasheh stood nearby. Having seen me stuck in my returning memories, he must have recognized what was happening, because he spoke only when I met his eyes.

"Have you remembered anything important?"

"I don't know," I replied honestly. "This piece... It doesn't fit with anything else." I knew there was more to it, and that there had to be a connection, but until my mind revealed more, this memory was like a mismatched puzzle piece.

He approached and touched my arm. "Then maybe it's of no consequence."

Neither of us believed it, but I appreciated the attempt at comforting me. With hesitation, I put the hairpin away. There would be time later to search for answers. Now we had to get ready for breakfast, because the fewer reasons my father had to be suspicious, the better.

A knock made us both jump. "Miss Saeryn?" Gawen said through the door.

Rasheh scanned the room in search for a place to hide, but I shook my head. Gawen would never enter any room unless invited.

"What is it?" I called out.

"Your father would like you to join him in the library."

A sudden chill ran down my spine, my limbs freezing in fear, and it took all my willpower to reply in a neutral tone, "Thank you. Tell him I'll be there shortly."

On Rasheh's face I could read my own thoughts—my father was about to make his move.

Without a word, he picked up his sabers, and I knew better than to persuade him to stay. I checked my appearance in the mirror, took a long and deep breath as if it could help, and headed for the door.

Rasheh pulled me away from it and held me tight, then kissed me passionately.

"If you die, you'll be reborn," he whispered. "And if you forget once more, I'll make you remember over and over again, as many times as I have to."

I wanted to tell him it was probably just a conversation, but my own instincts screamed a warning. I forced myself to relax in his arms, burying my face in his chest. I didn't have to fear death, and if I could restore my memories once, I could do it again.

"I will be reborn, but you won't," I said. "If need be, leave me and run."

He didn't reply, and I doubted I could force a promise out of him, so as soon as he let me go, I was out the door.

I made my way through the mansion slowly, taking time to regain my composure. I couldn't allow my father to suspect that I knew about his duplicity. I heard no footsteps behind me. Even in a house he wasn't familiar with, Rasheh still knew how to make his passage soundless and unnoticed.

Soon enough, I made it to the library. It was a room that challenged all others in the house with its size, save maybe for the ballroom my parents hardly used. Tall shelves covered all the walls, filled with books, and as a child, I loved to explore the leather-bound tomes, deciphering their titles. The library neighbored my father's study, and he often stepped out to join me. Together we read, weaved stories, and talked about sorcery, sharing secrets in a language I thought no one else knew.

I used those memories to bring a warm smile to my face right before I entered.

"You wanted to see me, Father?" I asked as soon as I stepped in.

He was leaning over the large table in the middle, studying a sketched plan or rough blueprint, but at my question, he nodded and indicated for me to close the door.

"I'll need you to keep Rasheh occupied for several days," he said. "Do whatever you must. Take him on a hunting trip or plan Philidert's murder... I don't care, as long as he doesn't notice my absence."

"Father?" As I kept glancing at the paper in front of

him, the rough lines looked more and more familiar. I knew the layout of that building. *"Father?!"*

He gave me an apologetic smile. "This has to be done. I have to retrieve the prism cube, or you'll forever be reborn in our enemy's nest, and he won't let me take it without a fight. With Rasheh here, it's the best opportunity we'll have." He pointed at the plan. "Show me where he nested the cube."

"Why don't you just open a passage to it?" I asked to buy time. My heart and mind raced as if they were both competing to get to the finish line, and I had a strong feeling it was the line marking the end of my composure.

"It's straining, and I'd need to rest before I confront him, because I doubt I would be able to sneak away unnoticed, and I wouldn't have enough time and strength to open another passage so soon," he replied. "I know of a place nearby where I can safely enter Hyrinea and prepare."

"What about Rasheh? Even if he doesn't notice your absence, he might want to go back at some point or ask questions."

The smile he gave might have been intended as reassuring, but the cold stare of his eyes was calculating. "There's no need to be concerned. Once all is done, I'll ensure that all he thinks about is how much he loves you."

It must have been the closest he'd ever come to admitting he manipulated memories. I took a step back. I couldn't even think of Rasheh not remembering all that we'd been through... I'd rather see him leave me forever than forget.

"Don't be foolish, Saeryn. It's the only way."

In the past, as the memory I restored with Sahatiavari's hairpin suggested, I'd chosen compliance. It must have kept me safe, allowing me to forge a plan that I still didn't fully understand. Instinct demanded I fall into those old habits, preserving myself no matter what. But at some point, I had to choose to make my stand, even if it meant putting everything at stake, otherwise I'd never break the shackles of obedience.

I shook my head. "No."

An ugly grimace crept over my father's face. I knew it well, that expression of disappointment and displeasure that foretold grave consequences. I steeled myself for his response.

He lifted his hand, and a quiet chant reached my ears. I knew that rhythm. I knew that spell. And what was most important, I knew how to resist it. Days of arduous practice had trained my body and mind to react in an instant.

And then a memory flooded my thoughts.

She was gasping for air and moving frantically. The dark space looked unfamiliar, but she didn't care when she remembered what had happened moments before. She struggled to get to her feet, but her own body disobeyed her will.

Strong arms wrapped her in an embrace. "Shh... You're reborn and safe. Everything's going to be fine now."

She knew that voice. Her father's confidence and reassurance brought little comfort to the turmoil of her mind, but at least he could help her make things right. "Father, you have to send me back. Please. I have to go back."

"Shh." His arms closed tighter around her. "It's all in the past now."

"No, you don't understand!" Her shout echoed off the walls around her as she fought his overbearing embrace. She was... in a cave? No, it didn't matter. All that mattered was... "I have to go! I have to tell—"

"Shh."

He whispered something else, an incantation, perhaps. Its rhythm was familiar, so she must have heard that spell before... The world-crossing ritual—that had to be it! But before she could fish out the relevant memory from the depths of her mind, the spell was finished, and all her memories of sorcery faded one by one.

She forgot all that had happened.

I'd forgotten all that had happened.

My heart beat unsteadily at the realization of what my father had done. I'd had every reason to suspect him already, but to experience the memory in all its horror shook me deeper than I was prepared for.

I didn't have the luxury of pondering it. Magic flowed around me, commanded by my father's will, and if I didn't do anything, soon I would forget again.

A dark figure flashed past me. Rasheh attacked unexpectedly—neither of us had noticed him sneaking into the library—and made it all the way to my father, his saber poised to strike.

My father didn't dodge.

One word, one word only, and a blast of magic threw Rasheh back, forcing one of his sabers out of his hand and flinging him into the air. He landed heavily on the bookshelves at the far end of the room. I froze at the realization that one more word could send Rasheh to his death.

"Keep out of it," my father said coldly. "For the sake of my daughter, I'd prefer not to kill you."

To my relief, Rasheh was already regaining his balance, battered but not beaten. The tight grip on his remaining saber made it clear that he wouldn't heed that warning. It also left no doubt that he would not heed my advice and run while he still could.

My father eyed us both. We might be nothing to him, but he couldn't fight us both at the same time...

My heart skipped a beat. He didn't *have* to. All he

needed was to kill Rasheh first, even if it cost him his own life. When he returned, I would be helpless and alone. I could try to protect Rasheh, but in the end, it would mean little. My father could dispose of me and deal with Rasheh once I was gone.

With no other choice, I stepped in between them. If I died, I would be reborn at Malatrius's home, and I had to hope my father would rather avoid that.

"Father, please!"

I found no mercy nor compassion in his eyes. "Don't turn on me, Sae, after all that we've done together. Don't throw away your birthright."

"There has to be another way." I doubted there was, but tying my father up in conversation could buy me time to act. Or for Rasheh to realize that he had to run. Without him, I could die and warn Malatrius.

My father gave me an ugly smile. "Do you really think the Sorcerer from the Desert will forgive you for all the lies you've fed him?"

Such a remark must have been calculated to cause a rift between me and Rasheh. I gave my father a defiant stare, because I was quite certain that by now, Malatrius knew all the secrets I'd kept and lies I'd told. And even if not, I still preferred to take my chances with him.

"Move," Rasheh whispered.

When I didn't, he circled the room, exposing himself to attack.

My father focused on him. "Put your weapon down and I'll spare you both."

I narrowed my eyes. Such an offer was not only too good to be true but also against my father's vengeful nature. He tolerated very little disobedience, and standing openly against him meant that I deserved all the punishment. If he wanted to teach me a lesson, killing Rasheh would be one I'd never forget. On the other hand, letting my lover live meant my father would have the means to control me for as long as I cared about Rasheh.

With my father's attention on Rasheh, I took my chance and whispered the first words of a spell. Even if it failed, I had to *try* to give Rasheh a fighting chance.

"My daughter, you know better than that," my father remarked without even looking at me. "You've already crossed too many lines."

I got the message. It was one thing to disobey him, and another to go so openly against him and his wishes.

I smiled bitterly when the conversation with Sahatiavari flashed once more in my head. I became desperate—exactly like she said I would. And perhaps I'd also become exactly what his other children had, and I would end up like them too. After all, neither Rasheh nor I were the one sorcerer who could best my father.

A simple spell tossed Rasheh through the air again, the thump that accompanied his landing was louder this time, followed by some books falling to the floor. I sought comfort in the thought that I didn't hear any bones cracking.

My father was on me already. His confident strides made me stumble backward, and I realized too late it was a mistake. Trying to retreat while so unfocused, I could not dream of resisting the power of his spell, especially as it wasn't the one I'd trained so hard to deflect.

It crushed every defense I scrambled for, and my resistance wouldn't last much longer, as the paralyzing spell claimed my limbs. The awareness of looming failure must have shown on my face, because my father smiled with satisfaction.

He'd won. In the end, he always won.

Then his smile faded, replaced by shock. He stood oddly motionless, with his eyes wide and the tip of a saber sticking out of his chest. His mouth moved as if he were about to say something, but instead he collapsed, and so did his spell around me.

Behind him, my mother stood with her hands tight around the saber's handle.

"I couldn't let him hurt you. I couldn't let him hurt you," she kept whispering while she stared at the corpse.

Rasheh made it to my side, his moves not as smooth as usual, but at least he could walk. He wrapped his free arm around me in a gesture that was both comforting and protective, while with the other he still brandished a saber as if, even in death, my father could pose a threat.

The body darkened, and a distant memory surfaced, telling me what would happen. Without surprise, I watched the body fall apart into specks of dark ash, bit by bit, carried into the air by the magic emanating from within. Similar to sparks carried by a fire's flames, the ash rose only to vanish before it reached the high ceiling.

My mother stood motionless, her eyes wide, but her lips stopped quivering. "He's going to return, isn't he?" she asked me.

The process she witnessed must have reminded her of something she'd seen already, and that made me wonder whether she'd ever tried to kill my father before. The killing must have unlocked a memory that breached a dam, and other forgotten ones came surging forth. It had never dawned on me that, having spent almost thirty years of her life by my father's side, my mother was his victim as much as I, perhaps even more, because he cared nothing for her.

I wanted to ask her questions or perhaps offer some comfort, but we had no time. It took less than a day to be reborn in another world. I had no idea whether my father would decide to lose another day to return here through death, open a pathway to this world, or go after Malatrius before we had a chance to warn him—but we had no time, no matter which choice he made.

I gave her a solemn nod and took a deep breath as I formed a crude plan. "Mother... you have to go. He didn't see you, so if you act as if you spent the morning away from here, he'll have no reason to suspect you."

As cruel as it was, for now she would have to deal with her rediscovered memories on her own.

She hesitated, looking back and forth between Rasheh and me. "Can you even fight a monster like him?"

I bit my tongue before revealing that I could be considered the same kind of monster. The time for explanations and secrets would come later, if we all survived... and remembered it.

"We know someone who can." I hoped she would take it as reassurance that I intended for someone else to handle the matter. It seemed better if she didn't worry. Even if she wasn't aware I couldn't die, she knew, if just instinctively, that I could be broken and left memory-less at the mercy of my father, her husband. "Go now, and if I'm not back soon, tell everyone I'm accompanying my father on some academic travel."

A knock on the door made us all jump.

"Mr. Philidert Asnu-Thigai has arrived," Gawen announced through the door.

It had never occurred to me before, but I couldn't help wondering whether Gawen's insistence on not entering any rooms unless explicitly invited was actually something my father had imposed on him. Both the library and his office contained secrets he likely didn't want anyone to glimpse, and I wouldn't be surprised if he'd severely punished anyone for interrupting him or witnessing something they shouldn't. It would be like him to terrorize his own servants, and it would explain why Gawen erred on the safe side, choosing not to enter *any* room.

Yet, this once, I felt grateful. Even with my father's corpse gone, we presented an odd sight, with both my mother and Rasheh holding unsheathed sabers.

My mother straightened her back and smoothed her expression. When she took a step toward us, nothing in her movement suggested that she had just killed her own husband and discovered memories that likely contradicted reason.

She handed the saber back to Rasheh, offering a warm smile along with it. "Perhaps I was wrong about you," she said. Apparently, a man who rushed to my side with no regard for his own safety was someone worthy of me in her eyes.

She left, carefully closing the door behind her, but I could hear her voice in the corridor.

"Philidert, dear, it's good to see you! My husband and daughter locked themselves in the library, so maybe you would accompany me on my way to town? I have to pick up a few things, and I'd simply *hate* to be driven so far all alone."

I didn't bother straining to hear Philidert's response. I was certain he wouldn't refuse my mother, and remark about my father and I being busy in the library was a clear message that we wouldn't allow anyone to bother us. Eager to please my mother, Philidert would take her away for the whole morning, and it would remove any suspicion of her involvement should I fail to find a way to stop my father.

But I *had* to find a way.

With strengthening resolve, I looked at Rasheh. "I have to die too. It's the fastest way to warn the master."

"I'm not letting you go alone. Either we go together or not at all."

I grimaced. Part of me argued that a man like him should know better than to be sentimental in a situation like this, while the other part pointed out that nothing else displayed his true feelings better. He was choosing to stay by my side instead of warning his master of grave danger. Or perhaps he thought I needed his help more.

He smiled as if he knew what I was thinking about. "Open the way between the worlds, Sae, and we will go together."

I could point out that I wasn't powerful enough, that trying to perform the ritual was a waste of precious time, but so was arguing with him. And attempting to kill myself while he did everything to prevent it seemed equally unproductive. The only way to convince him was proving that I was incapable of opening the passage... or succeeding. Malatrius believed I was ready.

I looked him in the eye, cold composure replacing all other feelings. "Pull the curtains closed and light a single candle."

He obeyed without hesitation, as if at this very moment I wasn't his lover. And he might be right. I was a sorceress. I knew the passageway ritual.

And with all gods as my witnesses, I was desperate enough to complete it.

∾

DESPITE OFFERING the world-traversing ritual as compensation for Malatrius's help, my father hadn't wanted him to actually travel between worlds. I'd understood why when I learned the ritual myself. Such complex sorcery demanded immense focus and impeccable skill, both of which Malatrius possessed, but it also required a clear image of the other side in one's mind. The Sorcerer from the Desert had never been to my world then, so my father had assumed that any attempt at opening the way would fail. He didn't know that Malatrius would bet on our world having deserts. The golden sands in Hyrinea might be different than the dunes of Quathan, but they provided an image clear enough to allow the way to open. The rest was just Malatrius's power and skill.

That simple oversight by my father had led to all the other events.

I, on the other hand, had had no trouble choosing the place to open the passage. Past Saeryn might have known the prism cube library better than I did, but collectively, our memories were more than enough to keep a strong link— and in the end, returning to Hyrinea turned out to be easier than trying to reach my own world under Malatrius's tutelage. And when I thought about it, that made sense. I had many fond memories of my home, but they were scattered across many rooms and family lands, so none could compare to the emotions, good and bad, the prism cube library evoked.

And thus, two days ago, much to Rasheh's open satisfaction, I'd collapsed on the prism cube library's floor, exhausted from having performed a ritual I'd claimed to be incapable of completing.

The memory of the strain still resurfaced whenever bouts of weakness took over my body, and if I had a choice, I'd be spending a week or two in bed, performing no more challenging a task than reading a scroll or munching on candied fruit. Such frivolous whims! My father was coming, and I had a role to play in his defeat.

I shivered at that thought. Malatrius had a plan, but then, he didn't share the details with me.

"You know what you need to know," he said. "Everything else would be an unnecessary risk to the plan should anything go wrong. I don't want this to become the only attempt we have."

I swallowed, trying to find comfort in the thought that if I failed... if *we* failed, there could be another way, another try, but only if my father didn't learn the details of what had been planned.

Not that it made my task—and the wait—any easier. Malatrius was ready, having cleared the way into his household and ordered guards and servants to keep away from this wing at night, but *I* didn't feel all that prepared. Especially since I was still recuperating from the grand ritual that had earned me no more than a nod of approval upon arrival, as if all the Sorcerer from the Desert had to say about my feat was "I told you so."

I smiled. In a way, it was still praise, and something I would have appreciated if I weren't so exhausted and anxious. For the second night in a row since we'd arrived in Hyrinea, I was guarding the entrance to the prism cube library, even though Malatrius was elsewhere, and serving as bait in his plan. My presence by the cube's entrance would convince my father that the sorcerer was inside. To what end, I knew not, and despite my willingness to trust Malatrius's plan, I couldn't help my unease.

Perhaps it was for the better that he hadn't shared details with me. The anxiety I felt was genuine, and it would make it easier to deceive my father.

The sound of cautious footsteps put me on alert.

Rasheh made soundless movement seem effortless, and he wouldn't risk revealing his presence with such careless noise. Servants and guards had been told to keep away, and none were foolish enough to draw Malatrius's anger by venturing nearby.

When the silhouette of a man shifted the dark in the corridor, I lit the nearby oil lamp with a quick spell and unsheathed my saber.

My father stumbled, blinking at the sudden light, but as his eyes adjusted, he smiled bitterly.

"I can't say I'm surprised to see you here. Disappointed, yes, but not surprised. Tell me, did you find enough resolve to do it yourself, or did you have to ask your lover to kill you?"

I wasn't going to tell him that I knew the ritual. "Does it matter?" I pointed the saber's tip toward him. "I can't let you through."

"And let's suppose that you won't. Let's suppose that you'll stop me, doing my enemy's bidding," he said. "What will you achieve? A week's respite, at best, before I come again, and again, and again."

I didn't reply immediately, as if the true meaning of his words was sinking in, and made my blade hand waver enough to look convincing. Then I steadied it, pretending I'd regained my resolve.

"Malatrius knows how to stop you. All I have to do is keep you away from here long enough for him to finish his ritual."

His eyes narrowed. He knew me well enough to read truth in my posture and voice. What he didn't know was that it was a perfectly tailored truth. I could only guess the thoughts going through his head, but he had to be considering multiple possibilities. Malatrius was not some overambitious sorcerer with more flair than skill. He was powerful and knew of many secrets—and one could be just what he needed to defeat my father.

"You truly believe it. And maybe it is true..." He smiled. "If so, then you'll be next."

The thought had already crossed my mind, especially with Malatrius's secrecy about the plan. Perhaps he was reluctant to share the details because, if I knew them, I'd be able to avoid the fate the sorcerer had in mind for me.

I let my father read those feelings on my face. Malatrius had made it clear I had to play for time in any way possible, and showing doubt would keep us talking. "I'd rather be dead than without my memories," I replied, hoping I showed enough hesitation to give my father the impression of my fading conviction and trust in Malatrius.

He looked at me with satisfaction. "What if I let you keep your memories? I'll also spare Rasheh's life, though his memories... They'll have to be removed, and you know it."

I grimaced. "Like you removed mine?"

"With you, I was... unprepared. Three years of waiting, and the way you returned to me, desperate and begging me to send you back, forced my hand," he said, almost sadly.

I had no pity for him. I wouldn't be surprised if he'd planned to erase my memories all along, perhaps in a more controlled manner, but still getting rid of anything he considered unappealing or threatening.

I swallowed, looking him in the eye. "Why did you let me restore them?"

He sighed. "This spell... It's complex and has its risks. I overdid it and almost destroyed who you were. With every day that passed, you were becoming more and more undone, and your mind was struggling to make sense of everything. In a way, Malatrius's offer was the gods' gift.

He'd help you remember, you'd never know why you had forgotten to begin with, and I could start over," he admitted without any shame.

I glared at him. "The least you could do is lie about it so that your offer would sound more real."

"It wasn't a lie when I said I'd let you keep them this time," he replied. "You are not what I groomed you to become, but still worth more than any of my other children. And I have time. I can wait till you come to me asking to relieve you of that burden. When your lover dies of old age... or perhaps sooner, by accident or from sickness." He looked me in the eye. "One day this pain will be too much to bear, and you'll come to me. Until then, I'll let you keep all of your memories."

"I..."

My hesitation was entirely real, though it wasn't because he'd convinced me. If our conversation was anything more than me trying to keep him out of the prism cube library, this would be the moment when I agreed to help him, or defied him for the last time, but I had no idea how much longer Malatrius needed.

"Sae, my daughter. It's time to decide whether you will throw your lot in with a man who is using you against me and cares little for you, or if you'll stand by your blood."

I desperately hoped that the sorcerer was nearly done with whatever he was preparing, because these few heart-beats of hesitation spanned all the time I had left.

"Very well," I said, trying to get a few more moments of conversation. I took a step to the side, lowering my saber and revealing the dark entrance to the library. "I'll help you."

My father smiled with the satisfaction of someone who'd won yet again, and who had expected to win. "No. You'll die and join Rasheh in the other world. Tell him whatever lies are necessary to keep him unaware of what happened, and I'll join you both once I'm done here."

He reached out, a spell already on his lips, and my body reacted with the training Rasheh had put it through. I ducked and slashed at my father. The blade drew a thin line of blood, not enough to kill or seriously wound, and I breathed out with relief. If one of us had to die, better me than him.

Fury twisted my father's face. I had betrayed him for the last time, that was certain.

He lunged forward, magic enveloping him like a menacing cloak.

A shadow hit him from the side, throwing him off balance. It took me a moment to recognize Rasheh as the black-clad figure.

My father desperately clawed at me as he stumbled to the side and into the library. His fingers closed on my tunic, and he pulled me toward him. I dug my feet in, though the stone floor did little to prevent me from sliding, and I was too light to counter his weight.

Rasheh swung his saber. The blade swooshed in front of my face, too close for comfort. My father's scream tore through the library's silence, echoing within as pieces of my tunic fell to the ground along with his fingers.

He lunged at us, ignoring his wounded hand, rage and magic in his eyes, but little control. Rasheh kicked him square in the chest, sending him back into the library. Then he quickly picked up and threw the severed fingers inside and pulled me away from the entrance.

A quiet rumble rose, echoing through the corridor, and the library's door shut. Its walls flowed in a familiar way, shivering and shrinking. A rainbow glowed from it, perceptible even in the oil lamp's weak light. With a final rumble and hiss of magic, the vast room that used to be a library was reduced to a piece of a gray rock even a child could pick up and carry.

And my father was inside.

Rasheh took the saber out of my hand and sheathed it along with his other blade. He didn't say anything, just embraced me, and we stood motionless in the empty room, letting relief wash over us until the sound of steady footsteps announced Malatrius's approach. He walked with the confidence of a man who knew he had no reason to rush.

"Kithandar the Undying is no more," he said, eying the grey stone on the floor. "Trapped between life and death until the cube is opened again."

I tensed and freed myself from Rasheh's arms, taking a step back—as if it would make a difference, since between Rasheh and Malatrius, I neither had a way to run nor the ability to survive any confrontation to come.

"And when I die, I join him," I said through my tight throat. Perhaps my father was right after all, and the Sorcerer from the Desert cared little beyond using me to achieve his goals.

Rasheh reached out to me, but I shook my head. He was still Malatrius's servant, and I had to know the truth first. At best, if the sorcerer chose to spare me, I had one lifetime, and that made me question all that I'd gone through.

Malatrius's lips curved, but the smile didn't reach his eyes. "In the letter he left me in the library's secret compartment, your father was very adamant that the rebirth ritual was to be performed within the cube, which made me believe he was planning to retrieve it later. I thought it would serve me ill if I followed his advice, and I performed it elsewhere. Thus, you will be reborn here, in my home, but in a place of my choosing. One that will allow me to see what you have become before I decide whether I should set you free."

I shivered but couldn't blame him for taking precautions. I was, after all, my father's daughter, and I couldn't be killed either.

"I suppose that's fair." I eyed the cube with weariness. "Can we be certain my father isn't dead in there?" To go through all the hassle and discover he was waiting for me in the other world or was already making his way back...

Malatrius nodded. "The scrolls I consulted all agreed that when the cube is in its dormant state, its contents are suspended in time. A candle won't burn out, and food won't spoil within," he said. "But to be certain, I had a slave enter the library with a simple task, copying a scroll. After reducing the cube to its dormant state, I nested it once more. The servant came out alive, though not quite... sane. The scroll had not been copied, and nothing in the library had changed, which suggests he had no freedom of movement within."

I exhaled slowly. If Malatrius was certain, I could be as well. He'd not risk my father freeing himself and stirring trouble.

"When I first agreed to take care of Kithandar, I didn't think that the solution to defeating him would be so simple and that he himself would deliver a perfect prison for me to use."

His remark made me wary again. "What do you mean, 'take care of Kithandar'?"

"As much as it might make me sound like a common mercenary, I made an agreement to get rid of your father." He looked at me with no remorse nor apology. "And though I do admit I might have grown fond of you during your stay here, you don't think I would have let my enemy's daughter live if I hadn't hoped to use her against her undying father, do you?"

He kept watching me as if hoping my reaction could tell him something, but I was too busy realizing that Malatrius had known all along that my father couldn't be killed, even before I revealed it to him along with my plea for the rebirth ritual—and even before he first set foot in my father's castle. While we'd prepared an elaborate plan, the Sorcerer from the Desert had used it to his own ends.

"I was told you might have precious insights into his secrets," Malatrius continued, "and though you knew much less than I hoped for, in the end, you proved your worth, so I have to give a nod to the person who insisted I keep you alive."

The way our first meeting in the castle played out now made more sense—why he'd so quickly agreed to spare my life and enter a binding oath, and later, why he allowed me to climb the ranks in his household. All the while I was desperate to gain his trust, he was working to gain mine.

The realization that I'd been played and used was less bitter than I might have anticipated. After all, I was always meant to be a pawn, either in my father's grand plans or in Malatrius's scheme. But there seemed to be another player moving pieces on the board as well, and their insistence on keeping me alive could mean I was about to be passed into yet another pair of manipulative hands. My lips moved, ready to form the important question: who?

I never posed it. As the fiery wings of a black-eyed golden bird beat within a resurfacing memory, I already knew the answer:

"Sahatiavari."

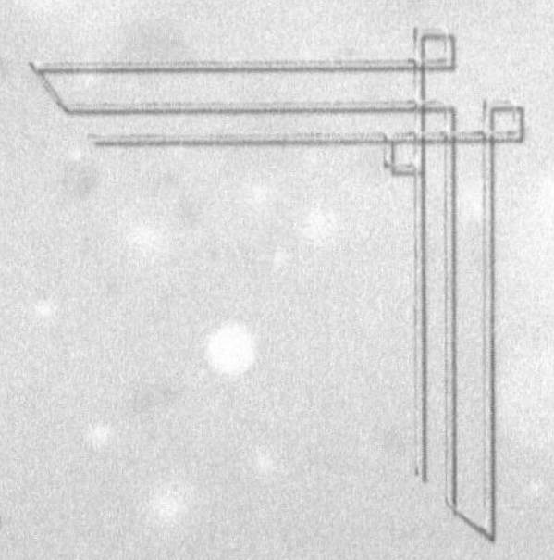

Chapter 16

The sorceress and the sorcerer

She chose to do it deep in the night, long after her father had retired. Her own room seemed too dangerous for what she intended, so she carefully made her way through the castle corridors with a small lantern as her only companion. The servants were all asleep, and the guards patrolled the battlements, so the way was safe enough, but Saeryn didn't stop flinching at even the slightest sound until she reached the tower in the far wing of the castle.

She'd discovered it during one of her explorations of her father's grounds, and back then it had hardly any excitement to offer—a winding stairway leading to a few forgotten rooms filled with old furniture and dust. But it also had an attic with a creaking floor and wobbly ladder. Anyone who wanted to climb up would have to make noise, so Saeryn could be certain she was alone.

As soon as she made it to the top, the old wood punctuating her every step up with a quiet complaint, she headed for the far corner of the attic, shielded by piled bags and crates. They smelled of hay, reminding her of the pallet she had downstairs, so simple in comparison to the soft and comfortable bed she'd left in another world. She chased those thoughts away, recognizing them for what they were—her own mind's distractions aimed at easing her growing anxiety, which would lead down the winding, self-sabotaging road of doubt and hesitation. She had little time, and she needed to focus.

She would not back out, and she'd see her plan through.

With that in mind, she pulled out the golden hairpin. Its magic was as strong as years before, when Sahatiavari gave it to her, and since then Saeryn had done her best to guard the treasure, keeping it away from her father's attention. She clutched it in her hand. To activate an already-woven spell was child's play, so all that remained was to wait.

In the darkness disturbed only by the small flame, thoughts came unwanted, bringing tension and fear. Sahatiavari might have lied back then, or she simply had already forgotten a promise made to a girl she cared little about. And even if she was willing to keep her word after all this time, the nature of Saeryn's request could send the sorceress reeling.

Magic intensified around her. As Saeryn focused on the golden bird's black eyes, her body felt light, and an image formed in her mind, as if she were traveling across the sky on its fiery wings, but her back against the cold stone of the tower wall reminded her that it was only an illusion.

Then the magic settled, and another image appeared before her eyes, foreign and unusual. She almost lifted her hand to see if she could reach far into the distance, but she feared it would disturb the spell, so she watched motionless.

Sahatiavari sat up, loose sheets covering her body and a

grimace of displeasure marking her otherwise still-beautiful face. Despite the years that had passed, the sorceress looked exactly the same. She didn't seem to have aged even a day.

Sahatiavari stared off, until her mind's eye, guided by the magic across the distance that separated them, settled on Saeryn, and her grimace vanished.

"Leave," she said, with a short glare toward someone outside of Saeryn's view. "Now." There was no anger in her voice, only the power and authority of someone you obeyed immediately. Then she focused her attention on Saeryn. "I hope you aren't wasting my time, girl."

Saeryn ignored the insult. Having aged a few years and gained a lot of experience, she understood now that she'd be a "girl" to the sorceress until she showed her worth.

"It depends on how far you're willing to go," she replied. "I'm in need of a friend and desperate enough to trust you, but what I have to ask of you... it's not a small favor."

"I'm listening."

To ask for reassurances of trust or secrecy would be naïve, as there were none to give, and Saeryn couldn't help asking herself once more whether she'd indeed grown desperate enough to trust a stranger with whom she'd shared two noncommittal conversations. For all she knew, Sahatiavari would do what she'd said—listen—and then promptly report it all back to Saeryn's father.

But without the sorceress's help, the carefully woven plan was bound to fail, and Saeryn would never free herself of her father's influence. A shiver shook her at the thought of how overbearing he was becoming, and how hard it was to keep her head down all the time. If she wanted her freedom, she had to take the risk.

Sahatiavari waited in silence, her expression neutral.

Saeryn took a deep breath, and as she started to speak, it felt like walking off a cliff straight into an unknown abyss. "If you're willing to be my friend and lend me a hand, convince the Sorcerer from the Desert to go after my father. Not to kill him once, but to stop him for good. A request from a scorned and abandoned lover who's not strong enough to get revenge herself should be convincing enough."

The sorceress grimaced again, her disappointment showing. "I suppose he'd believe it, and I could make such a request, even for the price he's likely to ask. But that's a foolish plan. If Malatrius goes after Kithandar, you'll die along with your father."

Saeryn smiled. "Not if you tell him I know Kithandar's secret. That I know how he cheats death."

Sahatiavari's eyes widened, and a spark flashed within. "I hope you truly do know it. But even then, it will serve you ill when Malatrius goes after your knowledge."

The sorceress didn't have to say more. Saeryn had no trouble imagining all the methods the Sorcerer from the Desert could use to extract such knowledge from her, and none of them were pleasant. Yet no grand plan was free of gambles, and if she wanted to win her ultimate reward, she had to take the ultimate risk.

"If you can convince him I'm more valuable alive than dead, I'll worry about the rest," she said.

Even if Sahatiavari was a true friend, she would not learn about the rebirth ritual that would be a part of the bargain her father would strike with the Sorcerer from the Desert, and that alone should make things easier for her. Besides, deceiving her own father, though tricky at times, had become Saeryn's second nature over the years, and watching her every step was a skill she had honed by now. And just like she knew Kithandar's routines and reactions to choose the right responses, she'd learn the Sorcerer from the Desert's ways too, even if one slip could end her.

"So is there more to your plan you'll share with me?" Sahatiavari asked.

"There is." Now that she'd taken the first step, Saeryn could reveal more. If Sahatiavari betrayed her, it wouldn't matter how much she knew. Saeryn's punishment would be severe either way. "I'll trade the details for another favor, if you're willing. Nothing as grand as my first one, though."

The sorceress burst out laughing. "Bold. I like it. Perhaps a day comes when I won't call you a child anymore." She moved about as if making herself more comfortable. "Tell me your plan and what else you'd have me do. The spell will hold for as long as you need it."

She had till dawn, then.

The dusty wooden floor and cold stones offered little comfort, but Saeryn still made an effort to stretch her limbs, tense from the anticipation. Having gambled everything on one hand, trusting that Sahatiavari would keep her promise of help, she could share most of what she'd planned and ensure that the sorceress knew the intricacies of the scheme, so that she could make sure Malatrius was prepared for a theft to happen—and whom to blame for it.

And then, once all was said and settled, in the morning Saeryn would go to her father to share the last piece of their plan to draw the attention of the Sorcerer from the Desert: they would steal a scroll or another precious item from him.

～

I HADN'T BEEN PLAYED. I was the one playing.

I'd pitted my father and Malatrius against each other in a desperate attempt to gain independence. The truth sank in, along with the realization that this perhaps was the one memory I didn't wish to restore, especially not in front of the Sorcerer from the Desert himself, after Sahatiavari's name slipped from my lips, revealing how much I knew.

He was still standing nearby, but now he watched me with the smile of a predator who had finally found its prey.

"Sorceress." In that one word, he managed to encompass it all, the distance that had pushed us apart the moment I revealed my role in the whole scheme, the nod toward my cunning, and the distrust that perhaps had always been there.

And I'd be lying if I said it didn't hurt.

I gave him a cautious, slow nod. No words could change what I'd done.

Rasheh was looking back and forth between us, bewildered. He couldn't understand why the atmosphere in the room had suddenly changed, foretelling a confrontation, one in which he would have to choose a side.

"Tell me, did Sahatiavari know? Or have you manipulated her as well?" There was no warmth in Malatrius's voice.

I hesitated. Part of me wanted to protect the sorceress from whatever consequences she'd have to suffer because of her part in it all, but lying to Malatrius in a moment like this seemed the worst possible choice.

"I asked her for help," I said. "Her reasons for aiding me are her own."

He kept watching me, and my breathing hastened, fear growing within me as I remembered that Malatrius was as generous to those loyal to him as he was unforgiving to those who betrayed him. By my own deeds, even if I hadn't remembered them until this very moment, I'd lost all hope of appeasing him. After all, it wasn't every day that the Sorcerer from the Desert learned that he had been played—and not even by his equal, to add insult to injury. I was certain the price I'd pay would be more than fitting for his power and position.

Resigned to my fate, I relaxed somewhat.

"I'm surprised you haven't planned for this moment," Malatrius said with a snide smile. "All that scheming, and in the end, you're at my mercy."

"I didn't plan for many things," I replied somberly, looking at Rasheh with regret. He was the victim of Past Saeryn's plots too, because she should have known better than to allow herself to fall in love.

At least I could hope that Malatrius showed mercy to him and sent him away before delivering my punishment.

The sorcerer considered my reply. "I suppose I haven't either." His emerald eyes locked on me. "You'll do well enough out there, sorceress. Though I'd suggest that in future you should be more careful whom you decide to use in your schemes."

It took me a moment to understand what he was saying. "You're letting me go."

His smile carried enough warmth to reassure me that he meant it. "I still have some fondness of you left, and a risky scheme like that does deserve a reward. It's been a long time since anyone had enough courage to play such a dangerous game with me—and nearly won, despite so many unknowns and setbacks." He gave me a nod like a teacher praising a promising student. "Besides, I'm quite curious what kind of woman you'll become in a few lifetimes. Kithandar... He was a much more decent sorcerer several centuries ago."

The way he said it made it clear he'd witnessed my

father's rise to power, and that alone made me realize why the Sorcerer from the Desert was feared and respected by all—and more importantly, why they stayed out of his way. Having lived so long, Malatrius was far more powerful than anyone could even imagine. My father had been a fool if he thought he could win against him, but then again, like father, like daughter—I'd taken a chance with Malatrius as well.

"I sincerely hope that you'll make choices which lead you down a different path than his, but if I'm wrong..." He shrugged. "You'll be back here soon enough, and I'll correct my mistake."

"I understand."

The message in his words was clear: if I crossed him again, or otherwise proved unworthy of his benevolence, I would suffer.

I looked around. It seemed that all had been said and done, and I had no reason to linger. My plan had worked, but the victory over my father felt less satisfactory than the past me had hoped. The price I'd had to pay for winning my freedom was losing the trust of the best teacher I could have dreamed of and the company of the man I loved.

Malatrius's expression softened, as if he knew what I was thinking. "Your deception will neither be forgiven nor forgotten," he said, but with no cruelty, "and it will be a while before I welcome you again to my household, but I see no reason why you can't take a day or two of rest before you depart. You would be wise, though, not to wander into those places in which a guest wouldn't be welcome." He glanced at Rasheh. "I take it you will want to accompany her when she leaves?"

I held my breath, waiting for the answer.

Rasheh bowed without a word.

Malatrius huffed in amusement, as if they'd just shared an unspoken joke. "I can do without you for a while, but remember to be back when the time for the spell comes. I won't teach it to anyone. Besides, I could always use news on how our new sorceress is doing."

I had no idea what kind of a spell would require Rasheh's presence, and I wasn't surprised Malatrius had decided to be vague about it. I didn't deserve to learn any of his secrets... at least not for a long time, until I'd proven myself worthy of his trust again. Even if he was letting me go, he'd still watch my steps closely, and when Rasheh returned to him, he'd likely give the sorcerer a detailed account of all my deeds. Still, knowing that he was allowing his most loyal servant to accompany me, despite his mistrust, gave me hope that one day, perhaps, I'd indeed be welcomed back.

I looked at the prism cube, still on the floor, quiet and unassuming, as if it didn't contain countless scripts on sorcery and one of the most dangerous sorcerers to ever live. "It's a shame that the library was lost."

Malatrius looked at me incredulously. "Do you really think so little of me?" he asked. "I had it all moved shortly after you arrived. I saw no reason to waste the vast knowledge your father had gathered throughout the centuries. The prism cube is nothing more than a prison now, and I'm sure I'll find a place to keep it... undisturbed. Kithandar could use a millennium or two of solitude." He waved at me. "But you should go and rest, so that you leave before I decide you should join him. And do not get my master assassin killed on your journeys. It's hard to find servants worth the hassle of the longevity spell."

As if on cue, Rasheh approached and pulled me away. I didn't try to resist. Malatrius's remark was a clear reminder that I wasn't truly back in his good graces, and his benevolence had its limits. I wasn't willing to test them.

"Longevity spell?" I whispered to Rasheh as we walked away.

He gave me a wide smile. "You didn't think it took a mere few years to become a master assassin, did you?"

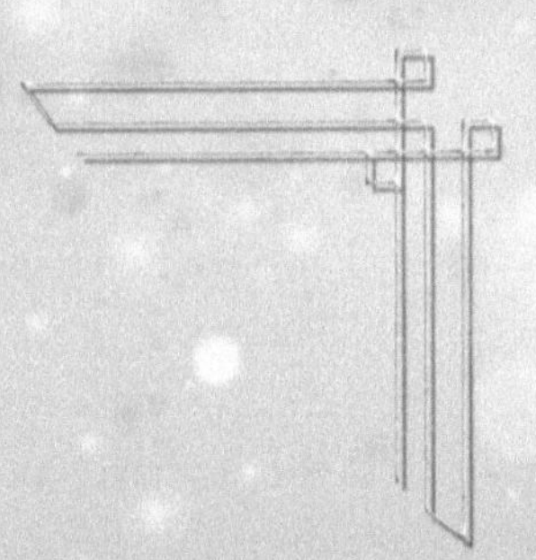

Epilogue - The stars on the horizon

The luxury liner made its way through the waves carrying us toward the continent. I could have tried to open the way directly home, but instead, I'd asked Malatrius to send us back to Quathan. I needed time to piece all the lies together, ensuring no one suspected anything. As much as my father had shared secrets of magic with me, he hadn't prepared me for navigating the deceptions that came with hiding our nature and double lives from the people of this world, so I was on my own, and I'd chosen the long journey home to come up with a convincing story.

I stepped up on deck, empty this time of night, enjoying the breeze and clear, starry sky as I made my way to the stern. In my hands rested a small gray cube, and it made me think back to the first time I carried it with me, down the mountain path leading away from my father's castle. So much had happened since then, some of it likely still lost within my memories, but for the first time in what seemed like forever, I felt whole.

I approached the railing.

"Master won't be happy that you stole it." Rasheh moved silently to my side.

I should have known I wouldn't be able to sneak out of our cabin without him noticing.

"Do you think that if he didn't want me to *take* it, he would have left it sitting on the floor of an empty room for three long days?" I asked.

"If he wanted you to have it, he would have given it to you," Rasheh pointed out.

I shrugged. "Perhaps. Are you going to stop me?"

He became serious, and I had no doubt that I had the servant of the Sorcerer from the Desert in front of me, not my caring lover. "Why did you steal it? Do you not trust him to keep it safe?"

I hesitated, searching for the right words. Before we left Hyrinea, I'd made a promise to Rasheh—no matter what happened, I would not lie to him. I might have been vaguer on keeping secrets, but with the matter of the prism cube about to be resolved, one way or another, this would change too. We'd worked too hard to trust each other to risk that trust for anything.

"I'm sure he can, but... I think nobody should know where it is. Not him, and not I," I said. "It should be in a place where no one can ever find it, in a world that has no sorcerers who would know how to open it." I looked Rasheh in the eye. "The possession of the cube makes neither of us more powerful, but it's a risk for both of us. For all that he did, Kithandar the Undying should disappear forever."

During the three days we'd stayed in Malatrius's household, the sorcerer had obliged me with answers, and I learned the sad plight of my father's previous children, whom he'd groomed to be perfect companions and loyal servants—and whom he killed mercilessly when they turned out to be disappointments, including the one born of his union with Sahatiavari, so I finally understood why the sorceress had been so eager to come to my aid. She might have seen in me a daughter she had long ago lost.

I didn't object when Rasheh took the cube from me. He turned it as he looked it over... and then tossed it into the sea.

"I'm certain that if the master wishes to do so, he'll be able to retrieve it, and for now, I ensured it's out of your hands, sorceress," he said with a hint of playfulness.

I arched an eyebrow. "Are you my beloved or the sorcerer's spy?" I teased, because his excuse would make Malatrius laugh.

Besides, I believed in what I'd told him. If Malatrius had wanted to keep the cube away from me, he wouldn't have left it out in the open. More likely, he'd allowed the theft to see what I would do with it, and Rasheh's presence ensured "a correction of any mistakes," as Malatrius had once put it.

"Both," Rasheh replied without a trace of shame. "But now that my duty is out of the way, I'd rather focus on something else. Are you going to stay in this world?"

"For a little while."

I had to talk to my mother and set up everything so that Saeryn Arlothi-Mara didn't disappear without a trace in case I ever needed to use that name again. My father had kept his persona and estate intact, and every other generation, a member of Arlothi-Mara would emerge from the family's seclusion, joining society. I intended to keep it that way. Just because this world hadn't discovered magic—or perhaps forgotten it long ago—that didn't mean I should disregard it.

"Then we could go traveling, here or back in Hyrinea," I added, making it sound like a choice.

Sometimes Rasheh still acted like a loyal servant rather than a companion, as if I were yet another sorceress he was serving. And though I understood his deep ties with Malatrius and the obedience he owed to the sorcerer, it had nothing to do with us. When he was with me, we would be equals.

"Hyrinea," he said without hesitation.

I burst out laughing. "Admit it, you hate being here."

All teasing aside, I agreed with him. I knew enough about my own world, even if I hadn't traveled to every nook and cranny of it, and Hyrinea was a place of the unknown, of wonder. For a moment, I pondered whether my mother would like the other world, but I discarded the notion of taking her along. Zefinia Alrothi-Mara was every bit the proud noblewoman, used to the luxuries and respect due to someone of her social position. Perhaps later, when I reclaimed my father's castle as my own or found another place to settle, I could convince her to visit—but something told me that my mother would rather forget everything that had happened than add to her already disturbing memories. After all that she'd been through, she deserved a quiet and happy life.

"A sorceress needs a library, and you'll find no scrolls here," Rasheh said. "You've been tutored by the Sorcerer from the Desert himself, so you have a name to live up to. The skills and knowledge of common town tricksters won't do."

I smiled back at him. "Hyrinea, then."

I rested my hand on his shoulder, and he took it as an invitation to embrace me. I looked toward the horizon, dotted with stars above and their blurred reflections below.

It looked like everything I'd imagined freedom would be.

Thank you for reading

Thank you for reading! If you enjoyed the book, please consider leaving a review.

Sign up to learn about other upcoming books:
authorjm.com
and receive your complimentary copy of Scourges, Spells, and Serenades – a collection of fantasy short stories.

And if you haven't yet, check out Joanna's two complete series: epic fantasy Pacts Arcane and Otherwise starting with By the Pact, and contemporary fantasy Shadows of Eireland starting with Humanborn.

About the Author

Joanna might be a bit too cautious to do anything even remotely daring or dangerous herself, so she writes about daring adventures and dangerous magic instead. Yet, she found enough courage to abandon her life in Poland and move to Ireland, and then some years later, she abandoned her life in Ireland to move over to the US. She's determined to settle there, once she finally chooses which state to reside in.

When she's not writing or thinking about writing, she plays video games or makes amateur art. She lives the happy life of a recluse, surrounded by her husband, a stuffed red monkey, and a small collection of books she insisted on hauling across two continents.

You can find the full list of her publications and more about
her at:

http://authorjm.com

and connect with her via social media:

facebook.com/AuthorJMac

instagram.com/authorjmac

indiepocalypse.social/@AuthorJMac

bsky.app/profile/authorjmac.bsky.social

threads.net/@authorjmac

x.com/AuthorJMac

goodreads.com/authorjmac

bookbub.com/authors/joanna-maciejewska